The Ballad of Samuel Hewitt

THE BALLAD OF

SAMUEL HEWITT

NICK TOOKE

The Porcupine's Quill

1   2   3   ·   21   20   19

Published by The Porcupine's Quill, 68 Main Street, PO Box 160,
Erin, Ontario NOB 1TO. http://porcupinesquill.ca

Readied for the press by Stephanie Small.

Represented in Canada by Canadian Manda.
Trade orders are available from University of Toronto Press.

Library and Archives Canada Cataloguing in Publication

Title: The ballad of Samuel Hewitt / Nick Tooke.
Other titles: Samuel Hewitt
Names: Tooke, Nick, 1970– author.
Identifiers: Canadiana 20190204532 | ISBN 9780889844278 (softcover)
Classification: LCC PS8639.O65 B34 2019 | DDC C813/.6—dc23

We acknowledge the support of the Ontario Arts Council and the Canada Council for
the Arts for our publishing program. The financial support of the Government of
Canada through the Canada Book Fund is also gratefully acknowledged.

For Norman

———————

CHAPTER ONE

Ashcroft, British Columbia. June 1934

Always the same dream …

The boy drags his feet up a spiral staircase, sore afraid. The stone steps are narrow and the walls are wet. If he brushes up against the masonry a foul-smelling liquid bleeds between the joints, sticky to the touch and black as pitch. He knows by now what he will find at the top, but turning around is not an option. Water behind him rises like upwelling ink, lapping at his ankles whenever he stops.

At the top of the stairs a heavy wooden door hinged with iron stands ajar. The boy is breathing heavily now and his breath plumes before him in the cold. He pushes open the door to find a raven as big as a man crucified on the opposite wall. It lifts its head wearily as he enters. 'Water,' says the raven. 'Please.'

He woke up with the sheets twisted round his legs and torso like a shroud. In a panic he unravelled himself from the covers and kicked them onto the floor. He lay there gasping in the dark. After a while, when his fear subsided, he sat up and looked at the clock. It was four in the morning. He pulled on his jeans and his plaid shirt, crossed to the door and opened it and stepped into the hallway. The faintest glimmer of light up the stairwell told him his father was still downstairs, or had forgotten once again to snuff the candles.

Samuel descended the stairs in his bare feet and entered the kitchen. He found his father still at work, bent double over the dented refectory table, quietly talking to himself. Beside his left elbow stood a stack of used envelopes two-foot square. The meagre light of one tallow candle—and his impoverished eyesight—required him to lean within four inches of each postage stamp so as not to rip the image of King George. Between his knees a tea chest into which he dropped spent envelopes. At his right hand a shallow pan of water. And arranged like mosaics along every available surface—the kitchen counters, the range, on top of the icebox, even the floor behind and beside the table where he worked—spread great, uneven sheets of blotting paper drying the recycled stamps.

Samuel crossed quietly to the table, stepped over the bench opposite and sat down. His father had braided his beard and gathered back his hair with a greasy leather thong. To Samuel he looked like a man lost at sea.

Tallow smoke rose into the cool, dark room. The shadow that his father cast onto the grimy wall was twice his normal size, angular and thin, like a mantis. 'I had that dream again,' said Samuel.

'"We are such stuff as dreams are made on,"' said his father. He gestured at the stack of envelopes. 'Help a man out there, won't you?' he said.

Samuel lifted an envelope off the pile, carefully tore out the stamp and pitched it into the water, then reached across the table for another. 'I saw one of the cheques they sent you,' he said. 'From Toronto. A dollar fifty, Dad. For a week's work. Minus the postage to send them.'

For the first time his father looked up. He peered at his son over the rims of his glasses. He blinked in an exaggerated manner, then tossed the stamp he'd been holding into the pan. 'A dollar fifty's a dollar fifty,' he said.

'You should go to bed.' Samuel reached and stopped his hands.

His father shuddered. He looked up. 'When I come asking you when I should or shouldn't go to bed, you'll know you're old enough to tell me,' he said.

Samuel released him and his father sat back. He let out one long breath. 'Besides,' he muttered, 'I don't sleep. I dream.' He pushed his glasses up the bridge of his nose and carefully surveyed his handiwork: the pan brimming with stamps, the great sheets of blotting paper. He appeared to be counting. 'Okay.' He nodded. 'Okay. Until tomorrow.'

Samuel collected the brass candlestick and stood. 'It is tomorrow,' he said.

He had been a soldier, Robert Hewitt, one of the few in his regiment who came back from France. Before the war he'd wanted to act, but when he got de-mobbed he studied instead and became a schoolmaster, the kind of schoolmaster who could recite whole passages of Shakespeare, Milton and Homer by heart. He would soliloquize at length in front of the classroom, much to the delight of his students. He could cook a meal fit for a king, play the fiddle like a Gypsy and dance like the devil himself. Much to the delight of his wife.

Poor Caroline. When they were newlyweds, moving out of the city had seemed like such an adventure. 'Come to Ashcroft, British Columbia' proclaimed the pamphlet, 'the sunniest place in Canada.' Caroline came from money and it thrilled her to turn her back on it. They were hard up, to be sure, even more so when Samuel was born, but Caroline had her garden. Her husband had his job. They needed so little, it seemed.

Then in 1929 the economy collapsed. Black Tuesday, October 29: 'World Markets Nosedive to New Depths' read the headlines. 'Wall Street in a Panic', 'Wall Street Lays an Egg'.

Bennett's legislators closed the school in Ashcroft shortly after, leaving Samuel's father at loose ends. Obsolescence withered Robert. He grew ever more remote and laconic. He began to speak in riddles, contradictions. Answered questions with questions of his own. In the end he would not speak at all.

He broke his silence only when his wife punished her son for some new stubbornness or other. He became eloquent, then, in Samuel's defence. Caroline sometimes chastised Samuel just to hear her husband speak.

Samuel never saw it coming. She had stormed out before, his mom, but had always returned. Looking back, Samuel tried in vain to discern when the fracture first appeared. They'd always yelled, and always laughed, for as long as he could remember, and if you're raised in a tempest, what do you know from normal? Samuel had heard the epithets proclaimed around town: Bohemian. Eccentric. Disturbed. Disgraceful. He'd heard them all, whispered behind white-gloved hands in the pews of the Presbyterian church.

The bench seat scraped across the floor as Samuel's father rose. Stiff from his labour, his father steadied himself on the tabletop before stepping over the bench. Performing a kind of *pas de cheval* through the acres of stamps, he made his way toward the kitchen door with astonishing agility, as if in his body there lingered still some memory of his former grace.

Samuel led his father up the stairs to his bedroom at the end of the hall. Robert sat on the edge of the bed and took off his glasses, folding them before placing them on the night table. He lay down in his clothes, his lips moving soundlessly.

'Do you want me to read to you?' Samuel asked.

'Sure.' His father lay his head on his pillow.

'Shakespeare?'

'Why not. A sonnet.'

Samuel placed the candle on the nightstand and sat. 'One sixteen, then, your favourite.' Samuel knew that sonnet by heart because he believed in its truth. 'Let me not to the marriage of true minds admit impediments,' he began. 'Love is not love which alters when it alteration finds, or bends with the remover to remove….'

After Samuel had finished the poem, his father rolled away to face the wall. His chest rose and fell steadily and his mouth stopped moving. Samuel leaned and kissed his father on the forehead, then blew the candle out. Sitting there on the edge of the bed, he asked the darkness how it happened that what a man loved most could also ruin him.

Samuel went looking for work in the morning and returned empty-handed. He'd been out every day since Christmas and worked three weeks at the most, digging irrigation ditches for William Cornwall, and he knew even that had been charity. Cornwall had enough able bodies on his payroll already, each with a family to feed.

They didn't use the front entrance, Samuel and his dad. Likely because it was through that door that Caroline had left some months ago though they'd never acknowledged it. They never mentioned her at all, as if uttering her name might jinx her imminent return. So when he rounded the side of the farmhouse on his way to the back door, Samuel couldn't make sense of the moving truck he saw parked before the porch. The body was painted a fire-engine red with its owner's name stencilled in white onto the driver's-side door. MacGilivary had nailed wooden rails into the box to raise the sides and Samuel watched him and another man rope together the last of his mother's inheritance. Before sliding home the bolt on the tailgate and climbing into the cab, the two men glanced at Samuel and exchanged a few words under their breath.

Mr MacGilivary was a man Samuel's father knew, whose son he'd taught at school. After MacGilivary started the engine, he wound down the window and reached to shake Samuel's hand as men are wont to do with boys at their father's funeral, with boys who too soon become men. Then he shifted the truck into gear and drove away.

Samuel watched the truck lurch and wobble down the track and through the gates until, with a grinding din of shifting gears, the truck disappeared over the hill. Then he ventured inside. He reached to hang his jacket on the peg behind the door but it was gone. Carrying his jacket, he walked slowly down the hallway, his footfall echoing in the empty corridor.

He found his father staring out the parlour window, blinking and expressionless, gripping an ivory-coloured piece of paper in one hand, a golden ornamental apple in the other. He made no move to acknowledge that his son was even there. Pallid rectangles dotted the walls wherever picture frames had hung, and stacks of his dad's books leaned sideways or lay fanned across the floor. When Samuel asked him what had happened, his father simply pointed to the mantelpiece. His mother, it seemed, had left a letter for him sealed inside the same Bohemian stationery.

Samuel knelt and righted the books into tidy stacks. Only then, when he had restored some kind of order, did he cross the rug-less floor and approach the mantelpiece. His mother hadn't bothered with the broken tall-case clock. His letter leaned against the yellowing glass.

He picked up the envelope and studied the looping shape of his name. As if in those cursive, unbroken characters he might divine his mother's mind. She hadn't taken everything, just anything of value. Most of the furniture, all the Wedgewood and the Spode. Of the golden apple his father carried, and its two siblings left on a shelf, Samuel knew nothing, and had never thought to ask. They had simply always been there, forgotten and gathering dust among the snapshots of his parents' wedding day.

He stared at the letter for a long time. His father didn't move a muscle. At length, Samuel decided that whatever the letter might reveal he did not want to acknowledge. He simply tucked the unread letter behind the clock, turned and walked out of the house.

Later that afternoon, he saw his mother one last time. He was sitting on the front stoop while his father slept and she rode right up to the gate on a black Arabian stallion. In the evening sun the tack and brand-new saddle shone like bronze. She stayed far enough away that he couldn't see her expression, but he knew what she wanted. The stallion skittered and danced in the roadside dust. His mother called out his name and raised a hand but he did not wave back, and after a while she rode on.

Toward sundown he saddled Ignatius and rode up into the hills above the house where the grass gave way to rabbitbrush and black sage and deep within the clefts of toppled scree, like ancient burial chambers, a few last rattlesnakes guarded their nests. Three-quarters of the way up the valley, before the path switchbacked up the steeper slopes, a massive chunk of granite jutted from the benchlands like a fractured tooth. It was a monolith of terminal moraine left over from the last ice age and a place to which he always repaired when he sought perspective. More and more often since his mother had left. This evening with some urgency now it seemed she'd left for good.

Samuel climbed down off the horse and looped the reins around a sage bush. He scrabbled up the side of the rock, its smooth grey surface still warm from the sun. From his vantage point the valley and everything in it contracted, became manageable. The cattle no bigger than ants. Railway tracks either side of the river like faded scars. And the Thompson itself, deafening in the narrows where the water seethed and roiled, thin as a ribbon at that distance, and soundless.

He sat and took off his hat, and looking down for the last time upon his father's eighteen acres of ungrazed bunchgrass, at the little wooden house with its four windows and a door, like a child's drawing, he thought that it was not hard to see how a man like his father irritated Daniel Beckinsale. The rich man's cattle grazed right up to his fence—and through it whenever they could—on three sides. To the north, toward the river, ran prairie so overgrazed it was a dustbowl, unfit for anything but the slag of a copper mine Beckinsale had recently unearthed. They were islanded, in other words, by land so bent to the man's industry that their eighteen fallow acres were an insult.

But choosing not to lease his land to ranchers or raise cattle himself had been one of Robert Hewitt's first decisions, and he never changed his mind, not when he lost his livelihood, nor after his wife's dowry was spent. He loved the look of bunchgrass, the wind smoothing its surface like an unseen hand. To stand waist deep among it then and watch the meadow sway like a single organism, like the sea. *Your breath*, he would say to his son, *the invisible air, is what you have in common with the grass. Listen to the rustling of the stalks, they are talking. Everything wants to be heard.*

And indeed, Samuel's very first memory was of lying in the meadow, on a tartan blanket his mother had spread, watching a dragonfly hover and dart above the grass canopy like a blue thread loosed from the sky. Inspired by the sound of the wind in the grass, his mother would sing ballads—mournful stories of loss and betrayal and of doomed enterprises, she told him—that her Irish nanny, Afric, had once sung to her.

Samuel watched the river devour the sun and the land fade to grey. Drawn out of their hollows by the dusk and a sky full of flies, bats clicked and whistled through the blue air. Beside him, the horse cropped noisily at the scattered wheatgrass. He stood and brushed the dust from the seat of his jeans and put his hat back on. All of his father's sympathies ran to the innocent, the undisturbed. The underdog. That his father had been vanquished by the opposite was an outrage in his son's eyes, and a perfidy not easily forgiven.

He rode back in the growing dark. The gelding knew the trail so well Samuel could have slept in the saddle. And he might have, if a coyote hadn't crossed his path. It stopped in the trail and stared at him with one forefoot raised, a slack rabbit dangling from its jaws. The coyote's tail was long and stringy and one torn ear twitched. It stared at him for no more than two, maybe three, seconds, but in that brief and baleful challenge, in the last of the day's light, the whole of its history was contained. The gelding shook its head and shied sideways. Then the coyote was gone.

CHAPTER TWO

'So that's it, huh?' said Charleyboy.

'Yep.'

They were sitting above the Thompson on a low cliff, at sundown. Charleyboy's eye was so badly bruised he couldn't open it.

'You told your dad?'

'I've told him I'll send him some money.'

'So he knows.'

'Charleyboy,' said Samuel, 'I don't know what he knows. Just when I think he's gone silent altogether, he surprises me.'

'Well, there's your answer.'

'What's the question?'

'What you can do to help him. You can help him by helping yourself.'

Above the din of the river they heard a door slam, a woman crying. It had to be coming from Charleyboy's house, for there was no other house nearby.

Charleyboy stared straight ahead and threw the rock he'd been clutching as far as he could into the river.

'He ever hit her?' said Samuel.

'Once. That I know of.'

'What'd you do?'

Charleyboy shrugged. 'Told him he ever did it again I'd kill him.'

'Your sisters?'

Charleyboy turned to Samuel, eyebrows raised. 'He ever touched either of them he'd be dead already. I'm glad they got married, even if they are too young. They got out,' he said.

'You don't have to come, Charleyboy. You've got a reason to stay.'

'Don't worry about it,' said Charleyboy.

'Your family needs you.'

'It's none of your goddamned business is it? What my family needs. Look at me.' Charleyboy jabbed his finger at his black eye. 'He had her by both arms and was shaking her, so I stepped in. After he gave me this he went out onto the porch and my mom started yelling at *me*,' he said, 'telling me to leave them alone.'

Charleyboy shook his head and let out one long breath. He fell back on the sand and laced his fingers behind his head. 'I asked her how she could love someone who did that to her. She said that love wasn't what I thought it was.'

Samuel fell back on the sand beside Charleyboy. He arranged his hands the same way.

'I see your mom around the stables,' said Charleyboy after a while. 'Spends a lot of time with that crazy stallion. She always asks after you.' He rolled his head toward Samuel. 'Pressed me all about Annabeth.'

'What'd you tell her?'

'Told her you broke that girl's heart.'

'You lied.'

'Sure. Your mom don't need to know everything.'

Samuel stacked the heel of one boot atop the toe of the other, as if to measure out the heavens. 'I can't believe Annabeth's going to marry that Cornwall kid,' he said.

'I can. His dad owns how many head of cattle?'

'I've loved that girl since the third grade, Charleyboy. We made a promise.'

'Right. When you were how old?'

'That doesn't make it less real.'

'They're not worth it, Sam,' said Charleyboy. 'None of them are.'

'Yeah,' Samuel said after a while. 'Yeah, they are.'

Ignatius ambled into view, proceeding methodically from one patch of bunchgrass to the next.

'Silas told me Beckinsale paid north of a thousand dollars for that stallion,' said Charleyboy. 'Not even to race or breed him. It's all for show.'

'For my mom.'

'Did you know there's a picture of your mom riding that stallion, a painting, up at the house? Silas told me. He said in the picture she's wearing a hat with an ostrich feather sticking out. And riding sidesaddle.'

'Sidesaddle? Well, that settles it.'

'She came from money, right? Your mom?'

'So?'

'Old habits die hard.'

'That doesn't exonerate Beckinsale.'

'Doesn't what?'

'Beckinsale still has a lot to answer for,' said Samuel. He sat up and picked a branch out of the sand and snapped it and threw both halves over the edge of the cliff. 'He insulted my dad to his face once,' he said. 'Down at Johnny's. In front of a dozen people. Told my dad he wasn't man enough to satisfy a woman like my mom.'

Charleyboy nodded, but didn't press. His uncle had been there that day and had told him all about it. How Sam's dad had just smiled, paid for his merchandise and quietly guided his son out the door.

'So? Don't let him get the better of you,' Charleyboy said. 'Beckinsale thinks he can do whatever he wants. Hasn't paid me in eight weeks. I was just getting ahead. That next paycheque was my way out.' He nodded his head at the house. For the time being the screaming had stopped. 'We got to do something, Sam. We got to hit him where it hurts.'

Samuel stood in one swift motion and looked over the edge of the cliff. The river ran like pewter in the moonlight. 'I'm way ahead of you,' he said.

'What have you got in mind?'

'We're going to steal that stallion.'

Charleyboy sat up. He looked at Samuel like he was crazy. 'We're gonna steal your mom's horse,' he said. 'You can't do that. Beckinsale'll kill you.'

Samuel turned. 'He's got to catch us first.'

'You never stole anything in your life,' said Charleyboy.

'We'll sell it and split the money.'

'Sell it to who?'

'Padraig Coltrane.'

Charleyboy buried his head in his hands. He looked up at Samuel through the web of his fingers. 'You're insane.'

'Beckinsale hates him. That'll hit him where it hurts.'

'Coltrane's a cold-blooded killer.'

Samuel picked up his hat and squared it firmly on his head.

'You're not kidding, are you?' said Charleyboy. 'Aw, what the hell.' Charleyboy stood up and brushed sand from the seat of his jeans. He turned to look at his house, at the junk in the yard, the screen door hanging loose from one hinge. He shook his head. 'Lucky for you I got nothing to lose.'

The rain fell so heavy that night it hit like hail. It flattened the bunchgrass and bounced off the dust until the path that wound up to their small pinewood house ran like a river. Water gushed out of the downspouts in columns, the eavestroughs overflowed and rain splashed off the windowsill onto the bedroom floor, coining dark watermarks on the bare wooden boards. The storm lasted ten minutes at the most, then just as suddenly it ceased. The sky cleared. Samuel's father turned from the window, tightrope-walked the length of a single floorboard, avoiding the cracks, climbed back into his bed and rolled toward the wall.

Samuel snuffed the candle. He was halfway to the door when his father spoke. 'You've got to learn when to quit,' he said.

In the new dark of the room Samuel couldn't quite see him. 'What's that, Dad?'

'When to let go.' His father spoke with some urgency, as if anxious not to falter or forget. He sat up. 'When you were eight I took you fishing in Farwell Canyon, on the Chilcotin River. You never really liked to fish but I thought it would be good for you, you know, for us. Father and son. There were steelhead in there as long as your leg. I sent out my fly and handed you the rod and told you to hang on tight if you snagged one. You were up to your waist in the water. When I went ashore to get you tackled up, you hooked into one that knocked you off your feet. I saw it rise and knew that line wasn't strong enough. Wasn't strong enough,' he repeated, and paused to catch his breath. 'But you wouldn't let go. You got back to your feet and when that fish threatened to take the spool clean off the reel you followed it downriver. You were up to your chest by then and when I got to within arm's reach you slipped. Next thing I knew you were caught in the rapids, somehow holding that rod out of the water, trying to reel the damn thing in. I knew what was coming round the bend, so I dove in after you and lucky for us there were some Indians dipping in the narrows, tethered to the riverbank with these long hempen ropes. They grabbed you by the collar of your shirt and me they reached for with a net I just about managed to hang on to. They hauled us out. Saved our lives,' his father said. 'Saved our lives.'

Through the open window, an oblong pool of starlight fell across the wooden floor and halfway up the bed. Samuel could see the outline of his father's legs and feet under the covers but his face remained in darkness.

'I looked over,' his father continued, near exhaustion, 'and you were coughing up your lungs on the riverbank, but still holding on to that rod, still fighting that fish. One of the Indians cussed you and cut the line and you were about ready to fight him over it. About ready to fight,' he said, 'and you with no real propensity for fishing. Do you remember?'

'I remember,' said Samuel.

'You've got to learn when to quit.'

'You never quit anything.'

'And look where that's gotten me.' His father leaned forward and reached for the drawer in the nightstand. He opened it and groped inside. 'Here,' he said. He handed Samuel a disc on a silver chain. 'To remember the lesson.'

'Who is it?'

'Jude.'

'I thought you and churches didn't mix,' said Samuel.

'A prophet should never be judged by his followers. Here, take it.'

'You'll get her back, Dad. She can't stay with that shit-heel forever.'

'Watch your language.'

'We'll get her back.' Samuel took the chain, trying not to cry.

'Go on,' said his father. 'Go on, now.'

Half an hour later Samuel walked out of the house with his saddlebags packed. The heady scent of wet sagebrush clung like resin to his clothes and skin. When he reached the barn he slipped inside and felt for the electric light. Ignatius nickered in the dark. The single bulb above the hayloft hummed and sputtered when he hit the switch and burned bright for no more than a few seconds before it flickered again and died. Samuel threw open the doors, led Ignatius from his stall and began to saddle him in the barn bay. The shine on the leather and the steel bit glowed a muted blue in the moonlight.

The dog had followed him down from the house and lingered hopefully in the open doorway. 'Not this time, Spud,' said Samuel. He buckled the cinch-strap round the gelding's belly, waited for the horse to exhale, then tightened it. 'You couldn't keep up. Besides, God knows where we'll end up. Maybe somewhere they eat Jack Russell terriers,' he said, tucking the loose end behind the buckle. The dog wagged his tail when Samuel spoke.

Samuel checked the saddlebags one more time as the dog looked on. There were oats for the horse in one pouch and a blanket and some tinned beans and cheese in the other. A sharp knife, a clean shirt. Some beef jerky. He buckled the saddlebags shut. 'You look after the old man,' he said, without turning around.

He passed the reins over the horse's head, slid his foot into the stirrup and stood up into the saddle. The doorway framed the rising moon and the rim of the valley, the dog in silhouette beside the jamb. 'Stay here, Spud,' he said.

The dog would not look at him. After a while he sat down. 'Good boy,' said Samuel. He clucked the horse forward and rode out.

Samuel passed beneath his father's bedroom window and did not stop. Did not glance up to see his father standing there, folded into shadow. The rain had not yet soaked into the clay, and in that second sky Robert Hewitt watched the moon in pools of standing water roil and disband beneath the horse's hooves. He saw the grey, weathered house engulfed in stars, and his own image windowed away like a jailed penitent.

It was quiet in the valley. After Samuel had rounded the corner, Robert heard the gate click open and shut and the slow drag and clop of the horse's shoes on the wet tarmac, diminishing down the road into town. When all was silent again he sat down on the floor, back to the window, eyes closed. '"Be not afeard,"' he began. '"the isle is full of noises, sounds and sweet airs.... Sometimes a thousand twangling instruments will hum about mine ears,"' he continued, a passable thespian. His eyes blinked open. '"and sometime ... voices."'

Charleyboy swung onto Ignatius first and shimmied back behind the cantle to make room for Samuel. They wound down the dirt road off the reserve and crossed the bridge and rode west through town toward the river flats. Charleyboy whistled a tune he'd once heard in a Gary Cooper movie. Where the road forked south up the valley side, the way was freshly paved and Samuel eased the gelding onto the shoulder to ride more quietly in the sand. Crickets clinging to the stems of damp rabbitbrush scattered before them in the silver light like thrown seed. It was quiet on the prairie and they did not speak. They heard only the sound of the horse's breath and the pounding of their own hearts.

At length the post-and-wire fence gave way to milled wood painted white. High up on the hill they could see Beckinsale's mansion. The driveway was a quarter mile long and lined with cherry trees. They rode beneath the driveway arch and cut between the trees, then dismounted and walked over the closely mown grass using the horse for cover.

'You ever seen grass like this?' Charleyboy drawled. 'I've never seen grass like this. No, sir. Looks like a billiard table.' He leaned and brushed it with his fingertips.

There were trees on that lawn planted sixty years ago by Beckinsale's father, a remittance man obsessively driven to recreate the estate denied him by the laws of primogeniture. Cedar of Lebanon, copper beech. A lime that had not survived the dry heat. The trees rose tall and foreboding into the clear, starry sky like watchful giants.

Within sight of the stable doors the two boys tethered the gelding to the limb of an ash and stood looking up at the house.

'Two just men bent on revenge,' said Charleyboy in a low voice. 'Not knowing where the road will lead them.'

'Are you going to keep this up?' said Samuel.

'Am I making you nervous?'

A second-storey light switched on.

'No,' said Samuel, 'but that does.'

'That'll be one of the servants,' said Charleyboy dismissively. 'You watch. The light will go out in a minute.' He took off his boots and knocked the mud off them.

Less than a minute later the light went out.

'Taking a piss, probably.'

'You're not acting much like a horse thief,' said Samuel.

'What does a horse thief act like?' said Charleyboy. He put his boots back on and grinned. 'You ready?' he said.

The gateway to the stable yard boasted two decorative wrought-iron panels, each nine feet across, fastened to the grey stone masonry by four enormous hinges. When the gates were closed, as now, the two halves of an arabesque atop each mounting crown slotted seamlessly together, reuniting within their circumference the scrollwork letters 'D' and 'B' for Daniel Beckinsale. By the light of the stars they could see enough to watch their footing on the crossbars—which meant anyone awake by chance and glancing down into the yard could see them.

Charleyboy had been a stable hand for six months. He knew enough of the comings and goings to reassure Samuel that Silas would have been dead to the world by eleven as always, snoring deeply, with a bottle of whiskey on the floor beside his cot. You could set your watch by him, Charleyboy said.

But still. Silas was a violent man, and big. He'd cuffed Charleyboy so hard one time for not locking the stalls Charleyboy had heard nothing but bells for two days.

Besides, getting caught in the yard after dark was one thing. Being snatched for horse theft was another.

They straddled the crown of the gate and quietly climbed down the inside, dropping the last three or four feet. They crouched when they hit the ground and waited. The only light in the yard was a single lamp shining outside the scullery door, and they were well outside its lightfall. Charleyboy groped along the stone wall for the key. Silas hung it from a spike driven into the mortar. After this night he would hide it somewhere else.

Charleyboy unlocked the gates and left them ajar. He hung the key back on its spike and motioned for Samuel to follow. Beckinsale's kitchens and servants' quarters backed onto one side of the square, and a few outbuildings made another. The stone walls and gate formed the south side, and then the stable to their right with its high, iron-hinged doors on the north end, facing the house. They entered the stable bay through a low door about halfway along the side of the barn. Samuel turned and latched the door and they stood listening in the dark. One or two of the horses came forward in their stalls to nicker at them.

'Where does he sleep?' whispered Samuel.

'Down there,' said Charleyboy, nodding through the tack room to the bunkhouse at the end.

'You're sure he's passed out?'

'You don't see him, do you?'

'I don't see much of anything,' said Samuel.

Charleyboy led Samuel down the bay toward the tack room. It was dark save for a few thin slats of light from the yard lamp outlining the tall stable doors. He stopped and clucked into a stall. 'This is Beckinsale's favourite,' whispered Charleyboy. 'She's a good horse.' A big chestnut mare thrust her head over the half-door and nuzzled the back of his hand. 'She wouldn't give us any trouble.'

Then in the dark behind them came the crack of breaking wood, followed by a clattering and a high whinny.

'What the hell is that?' said Samuel.

'That's your horse,' said Charleyboy. 'He's already wrecked one stall.'

'He's going to wake everybody up.'

The stallion stamped the concrete floor.

'Yep,' said Charleyboy. 'We gotta be quick.'

When Samuel reached the stallion's stall the horse kicked again at the boards and splintered another. Samuel searched over the Dutch door. He could make out no outline, just the breath of the horse and a heat and a shifting in the darkness.

Charleyboy stood warily beside him, stealing glances at Silas's door.

The stallion hove up on its front feet and jackslammed the door this time, driving both boys backwards.

'Jesus,' whispered Samuel.

'We could take another horse,' said Charleyboy. 'Hell, we could take two.'

'No,' said Samuel. 'It's got to be this one.'

Charleyboy stole away and came back out of the tack room carrying a lamp, a hackamore, a blanket, a saddle and a length of catch rope. He handed Samuel the blanket and rope, hung the off-stirrup from the horn of the saddle and swung it onto the crossbar of the Dutch door. He lit the lamp and hung it from a nail driven into the jamb. 'All right, then,' he said, 'we got to get a saddle on this crazy bastard.'

Charleyboy quickly built a loop with the catch rope.

'You want to hold the rope?' said Samuel.

'You bet.'

The stallion slammed the boards at the back of the stall.

'Sweet Jesus,' said Samuel.

'I don't think he's going to help you,' said Charleyboy. He dug into the pocket of his jeans and pulled out a handful of cubes. 'Sugar,' said Charleyboy. 'Makes him purr like a kitty cat.' Charleyboy balanced two cubes on the flat of his palm and reached into the stall.

The horse quit snorting and came over. His long Andalusian head emerged into the lamp light like an African mask. He flared his nostrils once, then peeled back his pink lips and lifted the sugar off Charleyboy's hand as if blowing the boy a kiss.

'Always did want to ride this horse,' said Charleyboy. He patted the stallion's neck. 'Nobody's managed it yet. For too long. Do you know what his name is?'

'I don't really care, Charleyboy.'

'Phaeton.'

'Phaeton? Well, that be a lesson to you.'

Charleyboy offered Phaeton more sugar and while he was eating it, Charleyboy slipped the rope around the horse's neck and pulled it snug. He carefully opened the splintered door, took up the slack and stood off to one side. 'Okay,' he said, 'get in here with that saddle, Sam.'

Samuel stepped into the stall. The stallion shied sideways yanking Charleyboy with him. 'Put your arm around his neck,' said Charleyboy.

The horse stood seventeen hands high and weighed upwards of 1,400 pounds. 'I can barely reach his neck,' Samuel said.

The stallion shied again, knocking Samuel off his feet.

'Hurry it up,' urged Charleyboy.

Samuel rose from the floor and jumped and hugged the stallion round the neck. The stallion tried to shake him off but Samuel hung on. His feet were not touching the ground. 'Give him more sugar,' said Samuel.

'I don't have any more sugar. Ear him down,' said Charleyboy.

'What?'

'Bite his ear.'

'You bite his ear.'

'I'm holding the rope,' said Charleyboy.

The stallion shot out one hind foot and then threw himself sideways, dragging Samuel with him into the darkness. There was another loud thud as Phaeton, or perhaps Samuel, struck the boards. When the horse twisted out again into the light Samuel was still holding his neck.

'Bite it!' urged Charleyboy.

Samuel lost his grip on the stallion's neck and fell. When he tried to stand he stumbled sideways and fell over. He'd lost one boot and his shirt was untucked, twisted and ringed with sweat. 'You try it,' he said.

'Wow. Some kinda horse thief,' said Charleyboy.

'I'll hold the rope,' said Samuel.

'You'll want to get your boot first there, cowboy.'

Samuel searched the chaff for his boot and found it flattened among a pile of dried dung. When he'd dusted off his boot and pulled it on he limped to the door and snatched the catch rope out of Charleyboy's hand.

Charleyboy grinned. He vaulted the door and hazed the horse into a corner and, when the horse tried to muscle past him, Charleyboy seized him in a side headlock and bit his ear. The stallion shrieked and thrashed his head, but Charleyboy only growled and bore down harder, like a bull terrier, until the stallion's knees buckled at last and he knelt in the chaff with his head twisted sideways, breathing heavily, and pinning Charleyboy flat on his back.

'How does it taste?' Samel asked.

Charleyboy spat and wiped his mouth on his shoulder. 'Don't let that rope go slack,' he said. 'And get that damn blanket and saddle on him.'

Samuel handed off the rope and took the blanket from the door and settled it on the stallion's back and lifted and rocked the saddle into place. The stallion didn't move a muscle. He slipped the hackamore over the horse's ears and muzzle. He encouraged the horse to its feet and tightened the strap. 'All right,' he said.

The stallion snorted and blew.

'Easy, boy,' said Samuel.

'We're not done yet.'

The other horses in their stalls began to whinny and stamp as the boys led the stallion down the barn bay. They were almost at the doors when the stallion jerked the rope out of Samuel's grip, burning his hands. Phaeton reared onto his hind legs and pawed the air and pranced and stared.

'Does that hurt?' said Charleyboy. He caught the end of the trailing rope and handed it back, but before Samuel could get a grip on it the stallion twisted away and went hammering down the bay toward the bunkhouse. He slammed up against the tack room door, turned and shrieked.

A light came on in the bunkhouse. Silas pushed open the door and came stumbling out through the tack room in his shorts. 'What in God's name is going on out here?' he yelled.

The horse reared again onto his hindquarters and came pounding down the bay. The stirrups were kicking out and one of them must have caught on a board because there was another crack of breaking wood.

'Last chance,' said Charleyboy.

Phaeton dove past them and slammed into the barn doors. The stallion's mouth was open and his eyes bulged like eggs. By now the other horses were shrieking, too, as if the barn were afire. Silas came limping toward them holding the lamp up. 'Is that you, Charleyboy?'

'Grab the rope, Sam.'

'Who's that with you?'

Samuel caught the end of the trailing rope and walked the horse down the length of the barn. He held on to the hackamore as the horse tossed its head.

'Don't let go of that goddamned horse,' yelled Silas.

Charleyboy threw open the barn doors and Samuel led the horse into the yard. The dust in the barn rose like smoke in the light of the yard lamp. Silas was almost upon them. 'When are you going to ride him?' said Samuel.

'Soon as I get beyond that gate.'

All kinds of lights were on in the house now. Silas turned and hobbled back down the barn bay.

'There he goes,' said Charleyboy.

'Where's he going?'

'To get his gun.'

The stallion was high-stepping and shaking his head. It took two of them, one on each side of the hackamore, to lead him through the yard.

'He's gonna bolt, Charleyboy.'

'I damn well hope so.'

'Wait for me at the bridgehead.'

'You sure?'

'Yeah, I'm sure.' Samuel opened the gate and hurried the horse through. Out of habit he turned and shut the gate. The panels came together with a soft clang.

'What the hell are you doing?'

'Closing the gate.'

'Grab ahold of that rope, man.'

They heard yelling in the yard. Charleyboy put one foot in the stirrup and swung his leg over. The stallion snorted and shook his mane before leaping sideways, swinging his tail.

'Whoa,' said Charleyboy. 'Take off the rope, Sam.'

Samuel lifted the catch rope over the stallion's head.

'Heeyaa,' said Charleyboy. He dug his heels into the horse's ribs. The horse went nowhere. 'Heeyaa,' he said again.

It wasn't until Samuel slapped the stallion on his flank that he bolted, almost toppling Charleyboy off the back of the saddle. Charleyboy pounded down the driveway and out through the main gates before turning and galloping down the road holding onto his hat.

It was light enough now nobody could miss them. Samuel limped over the lawn to where he'd tethered Ignatius and untied the reins. He was about to climb into the saddle when he heard shouting. He turned to see Silas running through the stable gate wearing nothing but his shorts and boots and hauling to his shoulder a Winchester .22 calibre rimfire rifle.

CHAPTER THREE

The first rifle shot splintered the branch above Samuel's head and rained slivers of wood onto his hat. The report echoed through the valley like a crack of thunder. Samuel ducked and glanced back to see Silas levering the spent shell from the chamber. He spurred the gelding to a gallop and sawed off the saddle to hide along the horse's neck and he was lucky Silas fumbled the shell; he was through the main gates and onto the road when the second shot splintered a cherry tree a good twenty feet behind.

He galloped down the blacktop into town, down Railway Avenue, past the Central Hotel, the CPR terminus and Wing Chong Tai Convenience and Feed with its single bulb burning inside the window. He hauled on the reins when he came to the bridgehead, both he and the horse breathing heavily. Beneath him the Thompson River roared, drowning out all other sound, and so it was only by chance that he spied, steering onto the bridge at the opposite end, a black Model T that could not seem to keep a straight line. It was too late to hide, so he stood his horse before the fire hall trying to think up an excuse.

It was the town mayor returning from his mistress and another night of drink. When the mayor reached the fire hall, Samuel waved as nonchalantly as he could. Leaning for support over the steering wheel, the mayor nodded in a solemn, comically dignified manner and, evidently still in first gear, turned and whirred up Bancroft Avenue.

Samuel whistled into the stand of cottonwoods beside the fire hall.

'Is it clear?' Charleyboy rode the stallion out of the trees, the horse glossy and black as polished ebony.

'I got shot at,' said Samuel.

'They get you?'

'No.'

'The horse?'

'Horse is fine.'

The stallion stamped in the dust and tossed its mane and chewed at the rope hackamore. 'Whoa,' said Charleyboy. He grinned, then his face straightened. He sat up in the saddle the better to see over Samuel's shoulder.

Samuel spun around so quickly his foot came out of the stirrup and he nearly toppled off Ignatius's back. But it was only the mayor parked and leaning out of the driver's-side door to vomit.

Charleyboy rode the stallion into the road. The horse tossed his head and stamped on the bridgeboards, raising columns of sand from the cracks. 'Let's go,' said Charleyboy.

Samuel slotted his foot into the stirrup and reined Ignatius around, digging his heels into the gelding's belly. Charleyboy followed. He leaned into a jockey stance and soon overtook Samuel, his shirttails flapping out behind, and together they fled over the bridge out of Ashcroft up onto the broad Chilcotin trails.

Charleyboy reached the top of the hill well ahead and he grinned as Samuel galloped over the last rise. Samuel halted his horse, his heart pounding. The road out of town was two miles long and very steep and the stallion was mollified at last. Charleyboy leaned and patted the stallion's neck. He grinned and whispered something Samuel couldn't catch.

They caught their breath and gazed down upon the town they'd grown up in, no more than a mile or so below them but a whole world away. The southern rim of the valley lit up like a seam of ore expanding downwards, and they could make out the switchbacks and the bridge and Railway Avenue, still in shadow, but with no riders yet.

Charleyboy nudged up the brim of his hat and crossed his hands before him on the pommel. 'How much you think we'll get for him?' he said.

'I don't know, Charleyboy. We need to keep moving.'

They reined the horses around and cantered side by side. The gelding eyed the stallion with misgiving.

'What if nobody's buying?' said Charleyboy.

'Don't even think about it.'

'About what?'

'About keeping him.'

Charleyboy pressed down the corners of his mouth. He gazed fondly at the horse's black mane.

'We didn't get the papers, did we,' said Samuel.

'No, we didn't.'

'Then we won't get half what he's worth.'

The stallion's new shoes clattered loudly on the blacktop.

'She named him Phaeton,' said Charleyboy, 'because Beckinsale rode him first and got tossed. Couldn't handle him.' The stallion snorted and shook its ears. 'Easy, Phaeton,' said Charleyboy.

Samuel turned in the saddle to look back. 'There's no one following us.'

'You sound disappointed,' said Charleyboy.

They rode another half mile before Samuel slowed and reined off down an unmarked trail.

'You've heard that story about Coltrane, haven't you?' said Charleyboy. 'He was second in command to … somebody. I forget his name.' Charleyboy thought for a while. 'O'Neill,' he said.

The trail they followed snaked over a rocky plateau of big sagebrush and bunchgrass before dropping off the shoulder of a cliff into switchbacks.

'Coltrane challenged O'Neill and O'Neill had him beaten up,' Charleyboy continued. 'Tarred and feathered him, so the story goes. Coltrane was supposed to leave town but he didn't. He crawled under a porch somewhere and when he'd recovered he found O'Neill in the whorehouse. Kicked down the door, threw the whore into the corridor and broke the man in half. And I mean literally,' said Charleyboy. 'Stuffed his balls into his mouth. The cop who found O'Neill said he'd uncoiled some.'

'It's just a story, Charleyboy.'

'Bit his own balls off,' said Charleyboy. 'Coroner couldn't decide if he'd died of a broken back or if he'd choked to death,' he concluded. 'And this is the man you want to deal with.'

Samuel halted Ignatius at the first bend.

'Where are we going anyway?'

'Getting off the main road,' said Samuel.

Beneath them, on the floor of a gorge cut at right angles to the Thompson, the Bonaparte flowed due south and collided with the bigger river in a maelstrom of white water. From where they sat their horses, high above the twinkling river, the valley was a study in chiaroscuro. The sandstone had collapsed in ridges down the canyon walls like pleats in a bolt of gathered cloth. The sunward slopes were ablaze and the shadows they cast so black as to hide every salient feature.

'I know where we're going,' said Charleyboy.

'It's pretty, isn't it?'

'You told me she died.'

'She did,' said Samuel, 'last summer.'

The trail had not been used since then. Antelope brush had begun to reclaim the wheel ruts. Twice they lost sight of the path and had to backtrack.

They pushed on in silence until they reached the valley floor and rode south beside the river. At length they came upon a dilapidated oasis of unpruned apple trees and apricots, some raised beds of desiccated vegetables. Beanpoles made of willow cane and bound with torn cloth leaned sideways or had fallen altogether into tangled frames like devil catchers. Some apricots on the higher branches were ripe already, and the boys balanced on their saddles to pick them and sat feasting with their hands full of golden fruit like thieves in a forbidden orchard.

Charleyboy spat out a stone and savoured the other half of an apricot. 'They say she killed her husband,' he said, his mouth full.

Samuel eyeballed the ridge above for riders. 'She didn't kill her husband. She never had one.'

'What about that French guy? The one they found floating down the river?'

'They were never married.' Samuel ate.

'But they lived together.'

'Sometimes.'

'Well?' said Charleyboy.

'She didn't kill anybody.'

'Why didn't he marry her?'

'He asked. She turned him down.'

The grass was long and newly wet in the orchard and the horses tore huge mouthfuls.

'How come you knew her so well?' said Charleyboy.

'She was my nanny. For a spell.'

'Why?'

Samuel shrugged. He scanned the trailhead again. 'I don't know. I think my mom thought every good family should have one.'

'She was French.'

'Yeah.'

'And a witch.'

Samuel ate his last apricot and wiped his hands on his jeans. 'She didn't give a damn what anybody thought,' he said. 'I think that's why my mom liked her so much. At first, anyway. I stopped coming after a while.'

'I'm not surprised,' said Charleyboy.

Samuel thought he saw someone up on the switchbacks. He stiffened and reined Ignatius to one side. Charleyboy spun in the saddle to follow Samuel's gaze.

'You see anyone?' said Charleyboy.

'No. But we need to keep moving.'

They rode out of the orchard toward a small, one-room log cabin and stopped before the porch, their shadows bizarrely thin and elongated, buckling at the broad set of wooden steps and reaching almost to the door. The logs were chinked with mud and weather-beaten, but dovetailed snugly at the corners and true. It was newly roofed, had endured since the days of the voyageurs and would likely endure another hundred years.

Charleyboy reined in the stallion and appraised the whole spread with fresh eyes. He could hear the river where it narrowed and fell. Scintillas of diamond water flickered in between the cottonwoods. He smelled apples when he closed his eyes. 'I know there are fish in that river,' he said.

'Yep. Sockeye in a few more weeks. So many you can walk across their backs in the shallows.'

'Damn,' said Charleyboy.

Samuel clucked Ignatius forward.

'Who owns it now?'

'We do.' Samuel shrugged. 'Eloise left it to my dad.'

'You're joking.' Charleyboy nudged the stallion forward and fell in line behind Ignatius. 'This is paradise, Sam.'

'Yep.'

'It's all I've ever wanted,' said Charleyboy. 'Besides riding in the circus.'

'Well. Who knows,' conceded Samuel. 'When the dust settles.'

'And we're out of the revenge business.'

'Uh-huh.'

'And done horse thieving.' Charleyboy turned and took one last look. 'We're not coming back, are we?'

They rode on. The river narrowed and spread like an hourglass. The bank was soft and white with new cotton and the horses made hardly a sound. After a while, Charleyboy cleared his throat and sat tall. 'Two fine friends,' he announced, with a flourish of his arm, 'ride off into the great unknown, with nothing but the shirts on their backs, the wits they were born with ...'

'And a thousand dollars' worth of horseflesh,' said Samuel.

'And a very expensive horse.' Charleyboy laughed.

They drove their horses into the Bonaparte at a slow and shallow turn. Where the river was deepest the water reached almost to the stirrups and they lifted their knees to keep their boots dry and watched the water part and braid to cither side of the horses' thighs. Shoals of trout scattered and hid under the rocky ledges. Samuel and Charleyboy rode up the opposite bank through a grove of enormous cottonwoods and turned to look back at the river.

Phaeton shook his head and stamped, as anxious as Samuel to be gone, and it was all his rider could do to keep him under control. The stallion backed into a cottonwood and bolted and Charleyboy had to rein him hard. At length he brought the horse to a standstill a small distance downriver. He'd lost his hat in the ruckus and he grinned back at Samuel. 'What are you waiting for?' he yelled. 'And pick up my hat.'

Where the two rivers met, the swifter, slate-green waters of the Thompson ripped through the floor of a gorge, buckling the Bonaparte sideways and sweeping it west. The boys sat their horses on a gravel fan beside the confluence and studied the canyon for a likely route upriver. They thought to ride east, and quickly, along the upper edge of steep cliffs, but once they climbed they found the valley side collapsed in pleats of scree all the way to the sheer face and feared the horses would find little purchase. One wrong step and horse and rider would tumble forty feet or more into the Thompson. The canyon ran thus for some four or five miles before opening into a broader desert corridor of scattered ponderosa pine and prickly pear.

'That's farther away than it looks, isn't it?' said Charleyboy.

The river was so loud he had to raise his voice. Charleyboy peered over the edge of the cliff. The stallion shifted and stamped, dispatching handfuls of gravel over the edge. 'Precipitous,' he said.

'What?'

'Pre-ci-pitous,' said Charleyboy, louder this time.

'You've been reading those books my dad gave you,' said Samuel.

They dismounted and scrabbled up the incline to higher ground. Gravel and rocks dislodged by their progress went clattering down the slope over the cliff and disappeared into the rapids without a sound. At length they reached a trail of sorts along a narrow bench a quarter mile above the roiling waters, but at every turn they found the bench collapsed or buried by a slide and they had no recourse but to climb and lead the horses once again and the day was growing very hot.

At noon they stopped altogether to lie down in the shade. They found shelter at the base of a solitary hoodoo and turned the horses loose to graze upon the spare, dry grass. Charleyboy had agreed to keep first watch. He lay with his boots crossed at the ankles and his hands behind his head. 'I'm not sleeping,' he said. 'Just resting.'

Samuel collapsed and took a long drink from his canteen. When he was done he wiped his mouth with the back of his hand and screwed the cap on before laying the canteen aside. 'What do you reckon Beckinsale's doing right now?' he asked. He leaned back against the sandstone pillar and looked up at the sky. 'You know he's told Chief Macintyre. And the mayor.'

Swallows nesting in crevices high up on the hoodoo wheeled and tilted under the sun. They could hear the chorus of their young calling for them. Samuel reached for the canteen. 'He's probably called the army on your ass,' he said. He took another drink and passed the canteen to Charleyboy.

Charleyboy raised his head long enough to drink and hand back the canteen and then lay down again. 'It's gonna take an army,' he said.

Samuel watched the swallows. Flies had been circling and one of them landed on Charleyboy's nose. 'Hey, Sam,' said Charleyboy, brushing away the fly, 'tell me again about the fish in that river.'

'You're a glutton for punishment.'

'Tell me anyway.'

'All right,' said Samuel. 'There are cutthroat trout year round. Big, fat ones with black spots. You saw them yourself. And then late September,' he went on, 'the sockeye come to spawn. So red and so many, the river's like a brick road. You can reach in and grab them by the tail.' Samuel took another pull from the canteen. 'I used to do that. With Eloise.'

'The witch?'

'Yeah.' Samuel shook his head ruefully. 'The witch. Bunch of your people used to come down, too. It was they who showed Eloise how to smoke them. Right there on the riverbank. Most of them didn't speak English, let alone French. Older folks, Eloise's age. They'd speak to her in Salish and we'd answer in French and they'd invite us to their fire, to smoke the fish. We'd take home a hundred between us and never make a dent. The sockeye just kept coming.'

Samuel nudged Charleyboy in the ribs with the canteen, but his words had been a lullaby. Charleyboy was fast asleep.

The tale of how Samuel and Charleyboy became brothers was local legend. In lieu of a hockey league in Ashcroft, or a baseball diamond, fistfights between whites and Indians passed for spectator sport. The men would fight outside the Central—the one tavern in town—and the boys would prove themselves in the lot behind Wing Chong Tai Convenience and Feed, where a roughshod ring had been fashioned out of packing crates. Johnny Lam, the owner's son, conducted brisk business selling soda pop and taking bets.

On any given Saturday the 'redskins' would descend in numbers from the reservation like the heathens of old to square off against the usurping settlers. Among the youngsters, Charleyboy had a reputation. He was tall and rangy, like his father, with muscled shoulders and a thick, flat chest, a pugilist's big-boned wrists. Samuel was no match for him. Charleyboy was nearly two years older, so their paths rarely crossed, and it was only because of Sally Driver that they fought at all.

Sally fancied Samuel and hated Annabeth. Out of spite Sally told Charleyboy that Annabeth liked him, so Charleyboy made a pass at Annabeth while Samuel was inside Wing Chong Tai buying soda. Samuel stepped out onto the verandah with two Cokes to witness the end of the exchange—Annabeth slapping Charleyboy in the face. Charleyboy looked genuinely astonished.

Half the youth in town loitered on the boards between the uprights of the awning that afternoon, like birds on a wire, laughing and clinking their pop bottles. They became silent as the trouble unfolded. Charleyboy searched the crowd for Sally Driver, who was nowhere to be found. Samuel handed the two Cokes to Josh Hartford and asked Charleyboy what the hell he thought he was doing. Charleyboy told Samuel to mind his own business, and that was that.

Within minutes a crowd of fifty had assembled. Brown and white gathered on opposite sides of the ring. Girls huddled together in twos and threes under the tin verandah of the loading dock, out of the searing afternoon sun, and on cue Johnny Lam appeared through the screen door at the back of the shop, impresario to the proceedings. Within his jurisdiction, Marquis of Queensbury rules were observed, minus the referee and the brand-new gloves. No blows below the belt. No wrestling. No fighting on the ground. If a man went down, the other fighter retreated to his corner. The fight was over when a man didn't, or couldn't, stand back up.

Annabeth pleaded with Samuel. Samuel's buddies pleaded as well. There was only one way this fight was going to end, but Samuel wouldn't back down. The odds were four to one against him before he stepped into the ring.

Josh Hartford laced up Samuel's gloves. The leather was stiff with the dried sweat of previous fighters. 'Catch him quick,' said Josh, threading the laces through the eyelets. 'Use the element of surprise.'

Samuel nodded. He cocked his head over Josh's shoulder to study his opponent. Charleyboy did the same.

'And Sam,' said Josh, securing the laces with a double knot, 'there's no shame in staying down.'

Samuel and Charleyboy advanced from their respective corners. Charleyboy stood four inches taller and he jabbed casually from the outside, gauging the distance. More experienced than Samuel, he made sure to keep the sun behind him, causing Samuel to squint. One of Charleyboy's jabs caught Samuel sharply in the nose, drawing first blood. Samuel jabbed back, came up short, danced sideways to alter the angle and landed a jab of his own. Then another. Charleyboy smiled. He stepped in, hands high, jabbed and followed with a straight right. Samuel's head snapped back. Charleyboy followed with another right. Samuel ducked and countered with a left hook to the body but he didn't catch Charleyboy flush. His glove grazed off his opponent's ribs. Charleyboy smiled again. He feinted. Samuel flinched. He feinted again. Samuel kept his guard high, but with his longer range Charleyboy landed a blow to Samuel's solar plexus that winded him. Samuel went down on one knee.

The crowd had become very loud. The brown boys called for blood and the white boys yelled advice. *Get inside, Sam. Go for the body.*

Samuel caught his breath and stood. He shook it off and stalked around the perimeter of the ring. Charleyboy stood dead centre, watching him, spinning slowly on his heel. Then Samuel danced back in, his hands high. When Charleyboy committed to a right, Samuel ducked underneath it and caught Charleyboy this time with a solid blow to the ribs that jerked him sideways. Charleyboy wasn't smiling now. But Samuel's advantage was short-lived. Charleyboy jabbed to open Samuel's guard, then followed with a right cross to Samuel's ear that nearly dropped him.

Samuel saw nothing but purple and green. The crowd was going crazy now, but Samuel heard the screaming as if from a distance, beyond the ringing in his ears. He steadied himself. He danced sideways, but Charleyboy anticipated and landed another cross that sent Samuel to the ground.

Stay down, Sam, he heard someone say. *It's not your fault, Sam,* urged another. *He's much bigger than you.*

But Samuel didn't stay down. The blow had drained the strength from his shoulders and he couldn't hold his hands as high. Samuel put his head down and barreled forward. He landed a blow to the body and he felt Charleyboy flinch, then an uppercut that landed square on Charleyboy's chin. Charleyboy staggered backwards, but shook it off and stalked quickly back in. He caught Samuel with a vicious right to the eye that dropped him.

The crowd had become quieter now. Their audience had grown doubtful, ashamed, even, as if witnessing something obscene, something no longer sporting. Girls clutched each other and covered their eyes, too frightened to leave. *That's enough, Sam. Stay down. It was never a fair fight.*

Samuel was so dizzy he stumbled sideways when he tried to stand, but stand he did. 'Stop it,' yelled Annabeth, but Samuel stalked forward again. Even Charleyboy wasn't sure what to do. He looked to his friends for advice, but nobody said a word. He walked back to his corner and squatted on his heels, watching Samuel with great interest. It was no longer clear to the crowd, or to him, who was winning.

'Queensbury rules', announced Johnny Lam. 'You've got to finish him.'

Annabeth began to cry.

Charleyboy advanced. With enormous effort, Samuel brought his hands up. Charleyboy had time to think about it, to pick his punch. He settled on a left hook and stepped in, pivoted on the ball of his foot and swung his hips into it. Samuel's knees buckled instantly and he hit the dust. Charleyboy knelt beside Samuel. 'Stay down,' he said quietly. 'You're gonna get killed.'

But Samuel didn't stay down. It took him thirty seconds to get back to his feet. 'It's not over,' he blurted, but Charleyboy had already left the ring.

Unable to declare a winner, Johnny Lam had returned all bets and stepped back inside the store. The crowd filed silently away.

'It's not over,' yelled Samuel, staggering sideways.

After a while, he stopped swaying and stood with his chin on his chest like a man asleep on his feet, covered in sweat and dust and blood.

Josh Hartford shoved aside the packing crates and ran into the ring. He guided Samuel by his elbow to the shade of the verandah where Annabeth wept and fussed over his cuts with her handkerchief. 'He needs a doctor,' she cried. 'Somebody get Dr Halliday, please.'

But it wasn't Dr Halliday who attended. Charleyboy opened the screen door and sat down heavily on Samuel's other side. He passed Annabeth a rag and a bottle of iodine. He glared at Josh Hartford and Josh backed off. Then he handed Samuel a Coke. Samuel squinted at him through his swollen eyes. He took the ice-cold bottle and held it to his eye. Then after a while, he drank.

Charleyboy drained his soda in one long pull and pitched the bottle across the ring. He belched loudly. They sat there for a while in silence, Annabeth fussing, her frock smeared with tears and blood.

A crow had spied the bottle glinting in the sun and it swooped down to peck at it. Its beak made a clink, clink, clink on the clear glass. Charleyboy leaned and spat into the dust and turned to Samuel. 'What's your name?' he said.

'Samuel Hewitt.'

Charleyboy nodded. 'You're crazy, Samuel Hewitt. You know that?'

'Hold still,' said Annabeth. She tried to clean a cut on Samuel's lip.

Charleyboy started to laugh, a low chuckle that made Samuel grin. Annabeth backed away. She scowled at them both.

Pretty soon the boys were laughing together, wincing and holding themselves around the ribs.

Annabeth slammed the rag and iodine down on the boards, got up and stormed off.

Samuel and Charleyboy rode through the cooler afternoon without encountering a soul. By evening they cleared the gorge and made camp on a small rise that commanded a view of the valley. They hobbled the horses and stood looking west the way they'd come.

'We did it, didn't we?' said Charleyboy.

In the bronze light the scorched browns of dried bunchgrass and the pale greys and greens of baked clay and sage became saturated with deeper, more definite hues.

'Why do you think they've not followed us?' said Samuel.

'I think they have. They're just not dumb enough to follow us through that.'

Samuel walked off a ways and found the limbs of a blasted pine hiding among the bunchgrass and dragged one back.

'Are you sure you want to do that?' said Charleyboy. 'How far away can they be?'

Samuel dropped the tree limb and began snapping kindling from the narrower branches.

'They're not coming,' Charleyboy said.

Samuel fetched the matches from his saddlebag and squatted on the ground to gather the kindling. He cleared a circle about three feet across and made a wigwam of the sticks and struck a match. The bunchgrass he'd balled beneath the pyramid lit instantly.

'Your mom put a stop to it.'

Smoke rose into the darkening sky. Samuel reached for a tree limb and broke it violently over his knee and piled the wood onto the fire. By no means had the evening grown even remotely cold, but he snapped another and piled on more wood anyway.

'Hey,' said Charleyboy. 'Look at that.'

They watched two jackrabbits dive down a hole a short distance away.

'There's another hole over there where I found the firewood,' said Samuel.

'Then let's trap us a rabbit,' said Charleyboy.

'You brought wire?'

'Don't need wire. Just poke a burning branch down that hole.'

When Charleyboy found the exit to the warren over by the blasted pine, he squatted above and behind the tunnel, out of sight, and made a circle of his thumbs and forefingers a fraction narrower than the circumference of the tunnel.

Samuel dragged a smoking branch out of the fire and shoved it down the hole. They waited. After a while, a rabbit bolted out of the exit directly through Charleyboy's grip and hightailed it over the plateau, zigzagging in between the stands of bunchgrass and kicking up small clouds of dust. 'Did you see that?' yelled Charleyboy.

'Yeah, I saw that.'

Charleyboy laughed and squatted again over the hole, tightening his finger trap a little. The next rabbit to exit was a huge male that Charleyboy snared around one hind leg. He stood up with the rabbit flailing wildly in his grip, secured both its feet in one hand, seized its long ears in the other to stretch it out and in one swift motion cracked its back on his kneecap. The rabbit jerked and twitched and Charleyboy dropped it in the sand like a hot potato. One foot was still twitching. He watched its toes curl up into a ball and relax and then stop moving altogether. 'Goddamn,' he said.

Samuel drew the branch out of the hole and returned it to the fire. He could hear Charleyboy whooping. He had picked up the dead rabbit by the feet to hold aloft and was performing an improvised victory dance there in the sand.

'You're out of your mind.' Samuel laughed.

Charleyboy skinned and quartered the rabbit while Samuel fashioned a makeshift spit over the coals with green wood he'd found down by the river. They took turns rotating the meat, watching rabbit fat drip and hiss into the fire.

'You know what?' said Charleyboy. He was lying with his head on his saddle and his boots crossed. 'I could get used to this.'

Samuel leaned and turned the meat. 'I might be wrong, you know. They might be waiting for us at Kamloops,' he said.

'And they might not.'

'We could go somewhere else,' said Samuel. 'We could head south from here.'

'America? That's a long way.'

'Everywhere's a long way. What's stopping us?'

Charleyboy gestured at the stallion. 'The longer we hang on to that stolen horse, the more likely we are to get shot.'

Samuel stared into the embers of the fire. The coals popped and settled. Charleyboy was right. His mother may have placated Beckinsale for now, but they needed to fence that stallion as soon as possible. 'You ever think about that?' Samuel said.

'Not until yesterday.'

'Not just getting shot. About dying.'

'No.' Charleyboy sat up and took a skewer off the fire. The meat smoked. He blew on a hindquarter and pinched it, then put the skewer back on the spit. 'Sometimes I do,' he said. 'I think the only thing wrong with it is you might not be ready. Like maybe there's something you've always wanted to do and your death comes too soon.'

'What do you want to do?'

'Join the circus, like I said.'

'I mean it.'

'So do I. I had a uncle ran away with the circus,' said Charleyboy. His eye was opening at last, like a dark flower. 'Wanted to be a trick rider. Got a job as a groom, to begin with. Had a real way with horses. He'd spend the winters in a shack up on the reserve, drinking mostly. Didn't work. Made enough in the summers to just sit. I asked him once what he liked so much about the circus and he said, besides the money? I said sure. Besides the women? he said. I said sure. He said the best thing about it was being just one other freak among many. No one gave him a second glance. Said he felt like he belonged there.'

Samuel removed his skewer and stuck it upright in the sand to cool. 'What's right with it?'

'Huh?'

'Dying. You said "the only thing wrong with it"?'

'Aw, son,' drawled Charleyboy, smiling sideways like Gary Cooper, 'you don't want to live forever now, do you?' He lay back again on his saddle. 'What about you? What do you want to do?'

Samuel shrugged. 'I always wanted to see the Rockies. But hell, I'll join the circus. I'm a natural clown.'

Samuel pulled his skewer off the fire and blew on the meat to cool it. After a while he ventured a bite. It was stringy and tough and took him a long time to chew. 'What did Beckinsale say to you?' he said.

'When?'

'When you asked for your money?'

Charleyboy sat up and leaned in to retrieve a skewer. 'He said he wasn't going to pay an Indian what he owed and told me nobody'd believe me if I spoke up.'

Samuel searched the desert for where he'd last seen the horses. When his eyes adjusted to the darkness he saw them standing stock-still amid the bunchgrass on a small rise. They had drawn together for company at last, their heads bowed, moonlight glinting off their backs, as if darkness and the stars they stood among had levelled whatever discrepancy there was between them as to breeding or otherwise.

'That is one hell of a horse,' said Samuel.

Charleyboy was still chewing his first mouthful. 'How's your dinner?' he said.

'Pretty awful.'

Charleyboy nodded. 'Mine too.' He looked at it. 'It's still raw in the middle.'

Charleyboy ate what was cooked and returned the skewer to the coals. He lay back on his saddle. 'You're no clown, Sam,' he said. 'You got book smarts.'

'There's more than one variety of clown.'

'You could be a teacher or something, like your dad.'

Samuel laughed. 'Yeah. Well, maybe that's what I'm afraid of, Charley-boy.'

CHAPTER FOUR

Near Seattle, Washington

Inside the Romani *vardo*, a young woman sat before a mahogany bureau unwrapping her grandmother's tarot cards from a black silk scarf. A hard rain rattled the roof, and through a crack in the joinery, water plinked into a tin washbasin. The bowtop wagon bolted to the flatbed had been crafted by William Wright in 1898 and shipped from Yorkshire to America at the ringmaster's expense. Helena, the ringmaster's daughter, had adapted the vardo to the modern motorcade.

'You can't save this circus with a deck of cards, Helena,' said her father, from his place folded into a red velvet armchair. By the light of the kerosene lamp on Helena's desk his ringmaster's riding habit showed its age. It was patched with leather at the elbows, and the black velvet collar was losing its nap. He tugged off his polished black boots. 'At this rate we'll be eating our own animals.'

They were en route to Seattle from Portland, Oregon, where the circus had not come close to selling out.

Helena shuffled the cards and cut them, then cut them again and laid out a pattern face down on the green baize. She sat back. The swivel chair creaked beneath her. 'A deck of cards never changed anything,' she said, after a while.

'Then what good are they?'

She turned her placid face toward him. 'I beg you to leave those boots at the door,' she said. 'Not only are they covered in mud but they smell like … like—'

'An orangutan's arse,' conceded her father, wrinkling his nose.

He rocked once, then again to gain momentum and heaved himself out of the armchair. He carried his boots to the back door and stood them on the mat. Then he shambled back and sat down. 'And how fares our main attraction this evening?'

'Unruly,' said Helena.

'She's a spirited girl,' said her father. 'Not unlike someone else I knew, at her age.'

Helena leaned forward and flipped over the first card, the following two in quick succession. Then she settled back. 'Josephine wants what any girl wants,' she said. 'She wants to be kissed. She wants romance, she wants…'

'To be free to make her own mistakes,' said her father.

'Yes,' said Helena. 'She wants to be free.'

'So?'

The old man perched along the edge of the cushion. Beneath the light of the lamp his bald crown shone. The three inches or so of white hair above his ears lent him the look of a tonsured cleric, though the old rogue was anything but holy. Devoted, by all means, but not to God.

'So our future is uncertain,' said Helena, at last. 'There will be a suitor,' she added.

Her father nodded. He looked down at his hands.

'A fool,' said Helena.

'Jolly good,' her father muttered.

On the eve of his seventy-fifth birthday, three years ago, her father had abdicated his role at the helm of the circus. The business was now hers to manage. The old dissembler clung to his involvement by costume only, and with a grip growing ever more frail. His memory was a jigsaw puzzle losing pieces week by week. Within the year, she predicted, there would be no pieces left at all. She hoped, for his sake, that he would pass before that happened, but her compassion extended no further. As a father he had rather fallen short. He'd always claimed that Emily, her mother, was the love of his life, but she was by no means the only woman he'd ever loved. Helena knew she had one other sibling, at least, a girl much younger than her, and she had long ago accepted the likelihood that somewhere in these United States flowered one or two others.

She reached and overturned another card. Out the corner of her eye she saw her father raise his head. He collapsed into the cushions and looked up at the roof. The rain was beating harder still. It sounded like the galloping of horses. 'Bah,' said her father, 'I'm an old fool myself. What do I know? When it rains this hard, and for this long, in June, why not trust a deck of cards? Like your mother always said ...'

He trailed off, lost. Helena had grown used to it. 'Do you want to talk about it?' she said.

'About what?'

'Why she fell off that horse?'

Her father answered so quietly she had to strain her ears to hear.

'That was twenty years ago,' he whispered. 'Why would I want to talk about it?'

'It was twenty years ago tomorrow. That's why you're here, isn't it, and not sleeping in your own caravan?'

The ringmaster pursed his lips. He rolled his head toward the wall. His daughter had filled one side of the vardo with a rogue's gallery of photographs. His wife's image hung front and centre, framed in silver. She posed beside her favourite horse, smiling in her satin getup, forever young. A monkey they'd named Woodrow Wilson sat grinning on the saddle of her Palomino. 'She fell off that horse,' he said, eventually, 'because her work was dangerous. People die every day doing less perilous things for a living.'

The wagon lurched from side to side as the driver swerved to avoid a collision, perhaps. Either that or he was sleeping at the wheel. Helena reached and steadied the lamp without taking her eyes from the cards.

'What's the name of that Gypsy you've got driving this contraption?' said her father.

'Dimitry.'

'He doesn't talk much, does he?'

'I've never heard him say a word.'

'How'd you find him, then?'

Helena shrugged. She turned over another card. 'Same way you find anyone in this business,' she said. 'They find you.'

Her father closed his eyes and composed his hands in front of his belt. He let out one long breath. 'So where are we going?' he asked.

'North,' said Helena, surprised by her own answer.

'What's farther north than Seattle?'

'Canada.'

'Bloody hell. Canada,' he said quietly. 'Has it come to that?'

CHAPTER FIVE

At dawn the boys rose and rode east along the broadening river valley with their hats pulled down low over their eyes against the rising sun. On the north side of the valley they could see in broken lines like writing the ruins of the wooden flumes once built to irrigate the benchlands. To the south of the river ran the train tracks, and before long the first freight train they'd heard since leaving town came howling round the corner hauling tomatoes from Beckinsale's cannery. They sat their horses and watched the train pass. Charleyboy offered Beckinsale a facetious salute. They waited until the screech of steel on steel was no more than a lagging echo and the train had disappeared around a bend as if the whole caravan, caboose and all, had been swallowed by the sun. Then they rode on.

The river had broadened and slowed, fashioning shallow, sandy pools through which the horses waded safely to their bellies. They splashed through these turnouts for the balance of the morning, leaning from their saddles to gather water with their hats. The day was already very hot and they rode with their shirts drenched and clinging to them, water dripping from their saddles and tack. In this manner, like freshly minted Baptists, they came upon the ruins of Walhachin.

The remains of a main thoroughfare were barely visible, like the ghost of a road, bordered with fragments of a river-stone wall that led to the skeleton of what had once been an English village green. Lured by genteel notions of Utopia, some two hundred Englishmen had settled Walhachin at the turn of the century only to abandon it ten years later when the country proved intractable. Modelled on the crossroads of a Cotswolds hamlet, the village green, long since returned to bunchgrass, formed a diamond around which the main road flowed. In the spring of 1911, a maypole had been erected and decorated with ribbons, around which had danced the youngest daughters of Walhachin's landed gentry. A greased piglet had been released into the crowd with a one-dollar bounty. The Morris dancers tossed their hankies, and the sounds of their hoorahs and their hobby-horses and their wooden swords a-clacking had drawn forth the yellow- and the brown-skinned people from their servants' quarters to witness agog this transplanted ritual. Rendered absurd by its surroundings, the custom was gorgeous for all it was fragile, like a rose that might bloom once and once only, for a single afternoon, then wither without passing to seed.

All Samuel and Charleyboy found now was the skull of a horse, bleached white by the sun. Their own mounts would go nowhere near it. The rest of the bones had been scattered by coyotes up the track. Its rib cage like an overturned boat, half buried by sand. Vertebrae like puzzle pieces.

They rode past a blasted peach tree still supporting a single panel of the pantry wall against which it had been espaliered. A broken plough. Fence wire of a kind they'd never seen. The only thing with four walls was the church. The tall entry doors had been looted, allowing Samuel to ride right into the vestibule. He sat his horse among the fallen roof timbers and looked up at the sky.

'You want to stop?' said Charleyboy.

Samuel turned. Charleyboy would not follow him inside.

'No,' Samuel answered. 'I don't want to stop.' He reined Ignatius around. He knew churches made Charleyboy nervous. 'My dad told me about this place,' Samuel said. 'He used to joke it was the only church he'd ever consider attending.'

'Because there's no churchgoers.'

'Because there's no roof.' Samuel rode Ignatius back through the archway. 'My mom was the churchgoer. They used to fight about it. We were sitting down by the Bonaparte one day, my dad and me, and he started talking. Back when he used to,' said Samuel. 'He told me that *if* there were a God he didn't think he'd live beneath a roof. When I pressed him about that he just reached into the river, handed me a stone and didn't say another word. Which I thought was just more of his craziness. And proved by what came after.'

'Your dad's not crazy,' said Charleyboy dismissively.

They rode side by side until the road gave out and the desert spread uninterrupted before them. The heat rose up in waves.

'Your dad can look after himself,' Charleyboy added. 'There's nothing wrong with him.'

'You don't think it's odd he stopped talking? He stopped washing?'

'That doesn't make him crazy.' Charleyboy shrugged. 'He's just sad.'

What Samuel missed about his father he also missed in himself: his clowning around. His dad used to make them laugh until it hurt. He did the perfect impression of his father-in-law, the taciturn Scottish gent. 'Caroline,' he'd pronounce, in a spot-on Scottish brogue, 'you've married beneath ya. I warruned ya to stay away from the Welsh. They can sing, I'll grant, but they're all soft in the head.'

Or the time he took the scarecrow apart and dressed up in its clothes, ran the pole up the back of his shirt and waited for his wife in the garden. He stood there perfectly still for ten minutes, silent while she weeded the strawberry patch, making faces at Samuel until Samuel couldn't take it anymore. When his mom asked Samuel what he was laughing at, his dad simply ambled away without saying a word. Caroline was speechless. She had fashioned an arbor at the entrance to her walled garden for which the pole was too tall. Trying several times to pass beneath it, his father kept banging away at the frame, like a bee at the window glass, until in the end he scratched his head, raised his index finger in a gesture of victory, and crawled through on his hands and knees.

Samuel and Charleyboy made their way back to the river and found shade under some cottonwoods. They turned the horses loose and sat watching them wade into the shallows. The horses drank. They raised their heads to watch the cottonwoods toss in the wind and then they drank again. Charleyboy leaned against the trunk of a tree and took off his boots.

Samuel had been to fetch food from his saddlebags and when Charleyboy set his boots down Samuel gathered up his wax paper packages and moved to Charleyboy's other side.

'What are you doing?'

'Sitting upwind of those things,' said Samuel. He wrinkled his nose at Charleyboy's boots.

'Aw, come on now, brother. I'll bet yours don't smell any better.'

'I don't take them off while you're eating.'

'What have you got for me?'

'I got nothing for you.'

'Give me some of that beef jerky, why don't you?'

'Why don't you go spear yourself a fish?'

Charleyboy took off his socks and stuffed them inside his boots. 'Spear myself a fish,' he said. He took off his shirt as well and folded it and laid it aside. Samuel had already done the same, and for the first time Charleyboy noticed the chain and silver disc Samuel wore round his neck.

'What's that?' Charleyboy said.

'What, this?' Samuel lifted and looked at the disc.

'Yeah.'

Samuel removed the chain and balled it up and pitched it to Charleyboy. Stamped into the disc was the image of a bearded saint surrounded by a halo of flames. 'Who is it?' Charleyboy tossed the chain back.

'Jude,' said Samuel. He placed the chain back around his neck.

'What's he the patron saint of?'

'The desperate.' Samuel shrugged. 'Lost causes.'

'They've got a saint for that?'

'They've got a saint for everything.'

Samuel unwrapped some cheese and cut it and handed half to Charleyboy. 'Here,' he said.

Charleyboy sniffed it. His face wrinkled up in disgust. 'Smells worse than my boots.'

'Eat it.'

'White people eat strange things.'

'It's just goat's cheese.'

— 51 —

'Exactly.' Charleyboy got up. He hobbled down to the river in his bare feet and squatted in order to drink. He scooped up some water with his hands and then stopped. Two men on horseback were coming up the riverbank. Both boys stood. The horses whinnied.

The men pulled up before Charleyboy and sat with their hands crossed on the pommels of their saddles. Their shirts were threadbare at the elbows and filthy, and their knees poked through their jeans. They wore boots bound together with rawhide twine and their horses were half wild. The saddles looked older than their riders.

Samuel hurried down to the riverbank. Charleyboy hadn't said a word. One of the men was very heavy-set. He was bearded and dark. The other was tall, fair, and for all his raggedy, almost comical deshabille, had shaved that day and had clearly taken pains to slick his hair back in the manner of a silent movie star.

'Is that your horse?' said the heavy man.

Charleyboy didn't answer.

'Yes, sir, that's his horse,' said Samuel.

'You got papers for it?'

'Sure.'

'Let me see them.'

'We don't carry them.'

The man leaned and spat into the river. 'That ain't your horse,' he said.

'I believe what my colleague implies,' said the taller man, 'is that a couple of young runaways like yourselves look unlikely to be owners of such a fine stallion. Not to mention the equestrian saddle.'

'How do you know we run away?' said Charleyboy.

The Englishman ignored him. 'Now, being men of honour and justice despite these desperate times, we would feel obliged—a citizen's duty if you like—to return that horse to its rightful owner.'

Charleyboy looked at Samuel. Charleyboy was ready to make a run for it.

'With all due respect, sir,' said Samuel, 'I assure you the horse is his. May I introduce you to Little Rabbit, world famous trick rider and I, his humble squire, Robert Barnes.'

The Englishman grinned. His teeth were yellow and very crooked. 'Well, Mr Rabbit,' said the Englishman, 'this is indeed an honour. And why, pray tell, does a celebrity of your stature find himself in this infernal place? And without his boots?'

Charleyboy bit his lip. The man waited. He grinned again. Then he spoke to him in Salish. Charleyboy's jaw stiffened and his face became dark. He glanced at Samuel. Samuel didn't know what to say.

'Just shoot them both, Sheldrake,' said the other man.

'No can do,' said Sheldrake. 'Mr Beckinsale's orders, I'm afraid. "Shoot the Indian only," he said, "if need be."'

Sheldrake reached into his waistcoat and withdrew his pistol. It was a colt .38 automatic and the only thing he carried that did not look antique.

'Let him have the reins, bud,' said Samuel.

Charleyboy didn't move.

'Go on.' Samuel stared at Sheldrake. The heavy man drove his horse forward and took the stallion by the hackamore. Phaeton tossed his head and reared, nearly unseating the man from his own horse. Charleyboy still hadn't let go. Sheldrake squinted down the barrel of his pistol. 'What a tragedy,' he said. 'World famous trick rider found floating down the river.'

'Go on, bud,' said Samuel.

Charleyboy relinquished the reins. The heavy man led the horse away and turned and sat looking at them.

'First rule of the road, boys,' said Sheldrake, 'never trust a fellow traveller. Especially not the one you travel with.' He levelled the pistol at his companion and shot him through the head. The heavy man fell sideways from his horse and began spinning downriver in a slow fan, blood gushing from his head and eddying like a scarf.

Sheldrake stuffed the pistol behind his belt. His gesture had been so swift the horses hadn't even flinched. He leaned and took the reins of Beckinsale's stallion and the reins of his dead companion's horse and led them both out of the river. Without a backwards glance, he walked the horses along the riverbank at a companionable pace, proclaiming in song his love of sweet Molly Malone.

Charleyboy waded out of the river. 'Son of a bitch,' he said, hands clasped behind his head. 'Son of a bitch,' shouted Charleyboy, pacing back and forth along the riverbank.

Samuel sat. His mind's eye replayed in slow motion what he'd just seen. The bullet had barrelled through the man's skull and exploded the right side of his head. Following the bullet, shattered fragments of bone and the darker matter of his brains had belled out and sprayed twenty feet away, only to be swept away instantly by the swift river current.

'Hey, bud.'

Samuel didn't answer.

'Bud?'

Samuel ripped off his boots. He stood and fumbled with his belt buckle, hauled down his pants and waded out into the river to his waist. His hands shook so badly he couldn't feel them. He could still see the dead man spinning away. Samuel watched until he disappeared around a bend and then lowered his hands into the river and clumsily splashed water over his face and neck. Then again, the same number of times, as if by this improvised ritual he might erase what he had just witnessed. After a while he walked back into ankle-deep water and simply sat and held himself about the knees.

'Sam,' said Charleyboy. 'He's gotta sleep sometime.'

Samuel didn't move. He looked down at the water. Trails of moss attached to flat river stones flared electric green in the sunlight. Across the river, where the current was swiftest, a freight engine's length of the bank collapsed with hardly a splash and was swept away.

'Son of a bitch,' said Charleyboy. He was pacing again.

At length, Samuel stood and turned around and walked out of the river. He tried to put his clothes on but his hands were still trembling and he struggled with the buttons on his shirt. Charleyboy caught the gelding and led him over. He handed the reins to Samuel. 'You want to double me?'

'Yeah.'

'Bud.'

Samuel looked at him.

'That horse is all we got.'

Samuel nodded and tried climb into the saddle but his knees were shaking and he failed to stand up.

'Let me go first,' said Charleyboy. He climbed up and made way for Samuel. 'You just take your time,' he said.

Samuel tried to calm himself. He breathed deeply. After a while, he leaned his forehead against his horse's shoulder. Ignatius turned his head and blew.

'All right,' said Samuel.

'All right?'

'Yeah.' Samuel put his foot in the stirrup and stood up. His shock was passing into anger. 'Let's get this goon.'

The river ran straight for a mile before swinging north through a shallow gorge. They followed the Englishman at a distance, speeding up as he approached the bend lest they lose him. But before he'd turned the corner Sheldrake stopped. He turned all three horses around.

Samuel halted Ignatius.

'What do you want to do?' said Charleyboy.

'Keep going. Look.'

Sheldrake sat with his hands held out beside him, palms upward, in a gesture akin to benevolence.

'His gun's in his belt,' said Charleyboy.

'He won't shoot us,' said Samuel.

'He won't shoot *you*,' answered Charleyboy.

When they rode within earshot Sheldrake folded his hands over the pommel. He cocked his head slightly to one side. 'Gentlemen,' he said, 'I do believe you are following me.'

Samuel did not stop the horse. 'We're not following you. We just happen to be travelling in the same direction.'

Sheldrake grinned. He reached for the pistol. He cupped one elbow in the palm of the opposite hand, leaned forward and dangled the pistol from his wrist.

Samuel halted the horse.

'All roads lead to Rome, boys, I'll grant you that.' He gestured at the riverbank. 'This is the route I have chosen.' He levelled the pistol. 'Now. Find another one.'

Samuel backed Ignatius up and Sheldrake lowered the pistol. 'Adieu,' he said, but did not ride on. He hovered until Samuel had turned the horse and ridden back downriver.

'What now?' said Charleyboy.

'We ambush the son of a bitch.'

'With what?'

'I don't know.'

Charleyboy jumped off the horse and picked up a rock, hefting it in one hand. 'With this,' he said.

Samuel swung down. He led Ignatius over to a cottonwood and looped the reins around a branch. 'We need to split up,' he said.

Where the Thompson took its northward turn there was cover among the cottonwoods. Charleyboy said he'd make for those while Samuel should take the higher ground. On his signal they would stone the Englishman from both sides.

'How are you going to get ahead of him?'

'You leave that to me,' said Charleyboy.

Samuel left the river and scaled the low cliff. He cut across the plateau to head the Englishman off. At what he figured was sufficient distance he dropped to his knees and crawled on his belly to peer over the edge. He was sweating and he tried to steady his breathing.

Sheldrake was maybe thirty feet ahead of him, close enough that Samuel could see the pistol glinting in his belt. The stallion followed quietly behind. 'Why do you pick now to be led like a lamb?' Samuel said.

Sheldrake meandered beneath the shade of the cottonwoods trailing the other horses with a slack rope like a gentleman enjoying the country of a Sunday afternoon. Samuel fell back, cut ahead another fifty feet or so and then crawled again to the edge. Before he had time to think he saw the man twist in his saddle. He stopped singing. Charleyboy had struck him in the ribs and was throwing more stones. The Englishman waved his pistol but he didn't know where to aim. Charleyboy hit him again and the effect was almost comical. The man let out an odd, high-pitched howl and flinched, shielding his head with one arm and shooting ineffectually at the cottonwoods as if at a swarm of bees.

The silt and gravel slope that Samuel had scaled did not hold much in the way of rocks, but the first one that came to hand was about the size of a baseball. Samuel pried the rock loose, took aim and gave it a shot.

He figured by its arc he'd heaved the rock well over Sheldrake's head and he was already scouring the cliff's edge for another when he saw, out the corner of his eye, the man drop from his horse like a dead weight. Charleyboy had struck his horse's hindquarters at the same time, causing the animal to rear and spin. One of Sheldrake's feet held fast to the stirrup, and Samuel watched the panicked horse rake her erstwhile rider over the stony ground like a rag doll, bouncing him along in a wide arc until, with a crack like a snapping branch, the man's femur popped from its hip socket. When at last the horse came to a stop, Sheldrake's leg was wrenched completely the wrong way.

Samuel ran down the slope and near the bottom slid on the scree he'd dislodged. He fell on his ass and lost his hat. 'Holy ... Jesus!' yelled Samuel, scrambling back to his feet. 'Did you see that?'

The two other horses stepped nervously. Charleyboy seized each one by the reins and tied them to a tree. When Sheldrake's horse had stopped tossing her head Samuel advanced with his hands outspread to reassure her. He palmed the reins and spoke gently to the horse and stroked her neck until she bowed her head. Only when the horse was calm did he look down at Sheldrake. He'd struck the man flush in the temple. Blood trickled out of one ear and pooled beside him, floating the cotton and staining it carnation pink.

Charleyboy pried Sheldrake's foot out of the stirrup and turned out his pockets. He carried nothing but tobacco and a few small coins, no more bullets. He picked up the pistol, took the reins from Samuel, led the horse down to the river and turned her loose.

Samuel stared in fascination at the dead man. One side of his face had begun to bruise horribly. Blood had seeped into his eyes and coloured the irises red. Samuel crouched beside his head to take a closer look. Sheldrake's mouth hung open as if in a frozen scream, exposing the rude pucker of his gums where some medieval dentist had torn out three of his teeth.

'Well done there, Dizzy Dean,' offered Charleyboy.

'You told me to stone him!'

'I told you to stone him, not kill him.'

Samuel turned away from the dead man, holding his head in his hands.

'Dropped him like a ton of bricks.' Charleyboy laughed.

'It's not funny, Charleyboy.'

'Aw, come on, we got our horse back, didn't we?'

Samuel couldn't bring himself to look any more. 'So what now?' he said.

'We throw him in the river,' said Charleyboy. 'Like he did to his buddy.'

'You don't think we should bury him?'

'Why?'

'I don't know,' Samuel blurted.

Charleyboy leaned and spat. He couldn't stop laughing. 'Damn,' he said, at last, 'that leg is like something out of a sideshow.'

They dragged the dead man by his armpits into the river and let him go. He drifted a few feet and got snagged on a sand bar.

'You're kidding me,' said Samuel.

Samuel waded in to drag him farther out. Sheldrake spun in the deeper current and sank at first, then bobbed up again in the rapids face down, but with the toe of one boot pointing skywards.

Charleyboy sat on the riverbank rolling himself a cigarette with the dead man's tobacco. 'I wish I'd killed the son of a bitch,' he said.

'What did he say to you back there? He said something in Salish.'

Charleyboy lit his smoke and shook out the match. He smothered a cough and contemplated the end of the cigarette. 'You remember my little sister Ruth?' Charleyboy took a long drag and exhaled a plume of blue smoke that disappeared into the wind. 'He said he'd fuck me, too, and then drown me, just like he did my sister.'

'You think he did it?'

Charleyboy shrugged. He picked a loose leaf of tobacco from the tip of his tongue. 'Him, or someone like him. My sister, someone else's. Son of a bitch deserved to die. He killed his buddy. He would have killed us.' Charleyboy leaned and spat again. 'So don't ask me to feel sorry.'

Samuel bent and picked up his hat. He sat and pulled on his socks and reached for his boots.

'And don't let this eat you up, either,' said Charleyboy.

Samuel pulled on his boots. 'You ever killed a man, Charleyboy?'

'Like I said, I wish I'd done it.'

'But you didn't. What if he's got a family?'

'Everybody's got a family.'

'Children, I mean.'

'Well,' said Charleyboy. 'That's a whole other topic. Sometimes children wish their fathers dead.' Charleyboy drew deeply on the cigarette.

Samuel knew some of what Charleyboy had seen, growing up. Samuel's dad had tried to step in once, and had been warned away. Robert called it the Flanders blues. The blind rage. The bad dreams. He and Charleyboy's dad, Raymond, had both fought in France.

'I watched your dad in a fight one night outside the Central,' said Samuel, after a while. 'He beat the hell out of some guy. Big guy, too. He probably would have killed him if someone hadn't broken it up. He just kept hitting him. After your dad split I heard someone say he was the toughest Indian he'd ever seen.'

'Nah,' said Charleyboy. 'My mom's tougher. She put up with all that *and* raised six kids. Kept us out of the mission school, too. Used to hide us when the priest would come knocking. Every fall we'd spend a week in a lean-to, up in the hills.'

'Your dad ever talk about the war?'

'Never. Yours?'

'No.'

'You ever wonder?'

'All the time,' said Samuel. 'What did you do with that gun?'

Charleyboy smoked his cigarette down to the nub. 'I tossed it.'

'No bullets?'

'He shot 'em all up at the trees.' Charleyboy laughed and exhaled at the same time. He flicked the burning butt into the river.

'I didn't know you smoked,' Samuel said.

CHAPTER SIX

Helena Ballantyne, known as the skipper to her crew, maintained attendance records for every town they played. She made a study of where—and even when—one stream of revenue might prove more lucrative than another. In Seattle, for example, tattoos were two a penny and exotics landed daily from across the seas. The sideshow didn't draw the same crowds on the coast as it did in the Bible Belt, say, or even a mere hundred miles inland, where folk were more God-fearing and more inclined to gawp. The height of the summer was the best time for them, the freaks, when the nights were long and hot and the rubes lingered round the lot into the wee hours, well after the big top had emptied. Sultry weather was also a boon to the showgirls, some of whom would supplement their wages turning tricks.

The showgirls' exploits lent a seedy edge to entertainment billed as 'fit for the whole family' on the circulars, but Helena had to admit the sequins and leotards performed more than just a practical function. Husbands could sit comfortably beside their wives and children and get an eyeful of more than just a can-can, or a nifty aerialist's trick. Helena couldn't bring herself to judge, so she turned a blind eye. God knows those showgirls weren't paid much.

The sideshow, on the other hand, did very well for itself—relatively speaking—owing to a collective agreement that they would supplement their wage with a percentage of the door. They had formed themselves into a union of sorts, and their spokesperson was Ethel Banks.

The skipper was very fond of Ethel. Ethel had been born with no legs, and her gig was 'sitting' on a pedestal—the kind you might employ to showcase an aspidistra—while smiling demurely. She stood, as a matter of fact, because she had ordinary feet at the end of each foreshortened femur, but her dress kept them from view and nobody knew. Like Helena, Ethel was a southerner, and she had a sharp mind. Like many others in her company, Ethel was possessed of a serenity developed from overcoming an affliction most people feared. She had passed her test in life.

The circus convoy had driven through the night and had halted that morning in an abandoned lot southeast of Seattle, a no man's land of wrecked automobiles and refuse and torn canvas flapping from the toppled posts and barbs of a bellied wire fence. Helena and Ethel sat together outside the vardo. Dimitry had set up a folding table and four chairs—an apple crate on one chair for Ethel—and had answered Helena's request for tea.

Ethel came prepared to negotiate. It seemed she had also been keeping attendance and knew that Seattle, where they had planned to perform next, was not the brightest prospect for her and her motley comrades.

'Ethel, honey,' said Helena, 'I don't suppose I have to remind you that the sideshow is not the only revenue stream at Ballantyne's.'

'Helena, my darling,' drawled Ethel, 'I don't suppose I have to remind *you* that without a sideshow your precious elephants wouldn't eat.' Ethel lifted her pinky as she sipped from her teacup. 'Per capita we're much more valuable. Heavens, by bodyweight those elephants hardly pay at all.'

'By that logic, my dear, our precious midget and his wife are worth more than you and all the sideshow combined.'

'But you understand my objection.'

'I do. I understood it in California. And in Florida before that.'

'Well, somebody's got to keep you honest.'

'I resent the implication.' Helena pretended to be shocked.

'All I'm saying is that I think it's time to head inland.'

'How's your tea?'

'Tolerable. Although I haven't had a decent cup since Boston.'

Helena returned her teacup to its saucer and sat back. 'Tell me the gossip,' she said.

Ethel rolled her eyes. 'You do not want to know.'

'Oh, but I do.'

Ethel sipped her tea, then again, keeping Helena in suspense. 'Our midget has grown jealous,' she said eventually. 'He claims his wife has been flirting with Fat Teddy.'

'But Teddy weighs half a ton!'

'I believe our midget might be correct. Teddy's smitten with her, I'm sure of it.'

Helena reached for her teacup. 'How marvellous.'

'And that's not all. Everyone's favourite albino wants to cut his hair.'

'But he mustn't.'

'You try and tell him that. He says long hair makes him look spooky.' Ethel reached for a biscuit and bit into it. She brushed the crumbs from the front of her dress. 'But you can't blame him. You can't blame any of us. You know, for wanting to pretend we're normal. Once in a while.'

'Oh, Ethel, what's normal?'

Ethel shrugged and took another bite of her biscuit. 'The rubes know what's normal—and what's not. And let's face it, we depend on them maintaining the distinction.'

Just then the ringmaster shuffled past. He wore a singlet and his jodhpurs but no boots. His suspenders hung below his waist. Ethel and Helena watched him go. He appeared to be deep in conversation with himself. Dimitry and Helena exchanged a glance. Dimitry nodded and followed him.

'That is worrisome,' said Ethel.

'Everybody gets old.'

They quietly sipped their tea.

'So,' said Ethel. 'Are we playing Seattle or crossing the Cascades?'

Helena looked after her father. 'I think we should cross,' she said. 'I don't know about you, but I've always wanted to see Canada.'

'Canada?' said Ethel, draining her cup. 'Now there's a grand idea. We'll be one giant freak show up there.'

The convoy crossed the Cascades in the shadow of Mount Rainier, the Mack trucks whirring up the mountainside in first gear and making slow progress.

The pride of the fleet were two six-ton Mack BQ series six-wheelers hauling two trailers apiece that carried the menagerie cages, including both elephants. At full capacity, and on level ground, they boasted a top speed of forty miles an hour, but up the steep mountain roads they barely made ten. The other trucks were smaller—Macks again, mostly four-ton BMs—hauling passengers and canvas only, but even they made slow going. The mechanics were concerned, and in jogging conference with Helena, who rode up front with Dimitry, decided they would not cross this way again.

When they crested the summit at Wenatchee and turned north, the drivers all breathed a sigh of relief. The descent down the leeward side toward Okanogan would present its own challenges, but at least nobody would roll backwards. The dry grassland they entered was the same Sonoran desert that hugged the eastern slopes of the Cascades all the way from Mexico through Arizona, California, Oregon and Washington, and crossed into Canada at Osoyoos.

The advance man had scouted several potential border crossings and had chosen the most remote. He warned the rookie border guard they were coming and filled in any necessary paperwork, but not necessarily with the truth. There were fourteen trucks altogether, not four, twenty-four horses and three zebras, not a 'handful of animals'. Ballantyne's travelled with two elephants, six lions, one tiger, two orangutans, an ibex, four camels and three llamas—eighty-nine souls the last time they made payroll and fewer than twenty were possessed of a passport.

The rookie border guard had been warned, then, but he had never seen anything pass his kiosk that could have possibly prepared him for what was coming down the road. If there were rules concerning travelling circuses entering the country he didn't know them, and he was in a dither by the time the first trucks came rolling up. In order to glamour him, the various overseers—sporting glossy hair and big smiles—rallied around. They stepped down from the wagon they travelled in to point out unusual details of some of the more garishly decorated trailers, relating anecdotes of their history with other circuses. They halted the tiger truck so the border guard could peer at the fearsome beast through the wooden slats, then introduced him without pause to the performers, who swaggered down out of the convoy like royalty to shake his hand and assure him a first-rate performance. All the while the convoy rolled quietly past.

In the end, they pressed into his palm a dozen tickets to the show, knocked off his cap with hearty pats on the back and foisted a cigar on him even though the guard protested that he didn't smoke. They left him standing beneath the barrier with the tickets in one hand and his cap dangling from the other, gazing after the vanishing convoy with an expression of utter astonishment.

CHAPTER SEVEN

They camped that night beside the river and made no fire. Samuel couldn't sleep. He lay wrapped in his blanket recalling with hallucinatory clarity what he'd seen and heard that day: bolls of cotton floating on a puddle of Sheldrake's blood, the aubergine colour of his shattered skull. The loud, hollow pop when his femur dislocated, like a cork being drawn from a bottle. At first Samuel winced inwardly, but the more his memory replayed each image or sound the more immune to the horror he became, until he began to appreciate in the violence a terrible beauty.

He watched the moon, thin as a rib, rise over the rim of the valley. He listened to coyotes on the plains yip and keen in plaintive chorus and he thought about his father, of what he must have seen in France that had silenced him. One day, when Samuel was ten years old, a blackbird had flown into the parlour window. He and his father had hurried outside only to find the blackbird bleeding from the beak and unable to fly. His father agonized over what to do, whether to let the blackbird die in its own time or to end its suffering. He asked Samuel. Samuel didn't know what to say. In the end, his father placed the point of a broom handle on the blackbird's back and leaned on it with all his weight. The blackbird's wings flared sideways in its dying and its neck arched back. Its beak opened wide and its eyes closed slowly. *Death is the mother of beauty*, his father had said, softly, like a prayer.

When Samuel at last fell asleep he dreamed of the raven. Dreams follow their own logic, and it made sense that Sheldrake led him limping up the stairs with his one

leg twisted backwards. It made sense that Samuel should have shattered his
temple again with a rock as the raven wept and wailed upon the wall, new blood
oozing from its wounds. Sheldrake lay dead upon the floor and his mouth would
not close, would not close, frozen open like a silent scream. Like an accusation.
Killing does something to the heart, *Samuel said.* Doesn't it?

The raven wearily lifted its head.

In the morning they left the Thompson and crossed the dry, barren plains of
the Skeetchestn reserve. The next water they reached was the Deadman River
flowing south out of Vidette and they nooned in the shadow of the canyon
walls and ate what was left of their food. Behind them, emblazoned in red
ochre on the copper-coloured cliffs, were crude likenesses of fish, bizarre,
long-legged birds and what looked to be hands or perhaps rising suns that
traced in petroglyph the history of those who had lived and died beside that
river a thousand years ago. A hot wind had pursued them all morning, making
uncanny music through the hollows of the canyon like a choir of crying
women. Even the horses appeared uneasy. They resisted the rich, riverside
grass and listened, grazing only when the cacophony subsided.

Samuel and Charleyboy caught the horses and rode on. The afternoon
had grown so hot that when they reached Savona at the head of Kamloops
Lake, they undressed without a word and rode their horses into the water up
to their bellies and dove off their backs and laughed like children, forgetting
themselves for a spell. The water was so clear and still that when they opened
their eyes they could see their shadows, unattached to their bodies, treading
water like doppelgängers on the bottom of the lake.

Refreshed by their swim, they put on their clothes without drying off.
They caught the horses and rode east for three miles up the steep Kamloops
road. When they crested the long hill they stopped to look down at the lake,
cradled like a sapphire in the dun cupped hands of the mountains.

They quit the road for fear of other traffic and began the long descent
through an ancient ponderosa forest rich with the scent of vanilla. Fires had
scorched their trunks and annihilated small shrubs and saplings, but in their
wake had fashioned a parkland of bunchgrass between veteran trees that two

months before had rioted with arrow-leaved balsamroot and squaw currant. As the evening wore on, the cicadas creaked their final chorus and they could hear, as they rode under the open canopy, the click of spotted bats hunting moths and farther off, up the mountainside, the bassoon of an awakening owl.

By dusk they saw the lights of the city at the east end of the lake. They halted the horses and sat.

'You want to make camp?' said Charleyboy.

Samuel's horse shifted beneath him. 'Not yet,' he said. 'But I don't want to ride in there in broad daylight either. Not with two stolen horses. Do you?'

Half a mile farther down they chanced upon a narrow road bordering a swath of pastureland that rolled northwards to the lake. A single, slat-ribbed heifer bedded along the fence raised her head to watch and struggled up as they drew closer. With a bawl of protest she limped off into the meadow, stopping to look over her shoulder from a safer distance. They followed the fence until they came to a gate with a massive pair of elk antlers mounted to the crossbeam. On either side of them the words 'Brandt Ranch' were burned into the wood. Down the dirt track they spied a huge barn with a corral of unpainted railings and a round pen for breaking horses, but the barn door was open and the corral was empty.

'That's quite the spread,' said Charleyboy.

'It's abandoned.'

They turned between the gates and rode slowly down the track. The house was modest by comparison, a small wooden structure with a front porch and four windows facing the road. They helloed the house but no one answered. After a while they got off their horses. Samuel pushed open the door. They found nothing but a cast-iron stove in the kitchen at the end of the corridor, and upstairs a mattress on the floor of one room. The mattress was pancaked with dust, but beneath it they could see a rust-coloured bloodstain in the shape of a giant carnation. A birth, perhaps. Or a murder. When they flipped the mattress dust rose and swirled like fiddleheads in the last of the day's light.

They searched for food in the pantry attached to the kitchen but found none, not even a tin of beans. They found no lamp or candles either and so withdrew to the bedroom and lay down on the mattress with aching bellies. In the shadow of the mountain the room grew very dark.

'What do you think happened here?' asked Charleyboy.

'Lots of people lose their farms. The banks foreclose.'

'I meant the bloodstain.'

Samuel didn't answer.

'You want to sleep outside?' said Charleyboy.

'We've got a mattress in here. Go to sleep.'

Charleyboy let out one long sigh. 'Something evil happened here,' he said.

Charleyboy had rolled up his jeans for a pillow and he got up and pulled them on. Then he sat back down on the edge of the mattress and wrapped his blanket round his shoulders. 'It's true what they say about Coltrane, Sam.'

'That's what all this is about? You leave Coltrane to me.'

'He's the devil, Sam.'

'He's Beckinsale's enemy. That makes him our friend.'

'I'm sleeping outside,' said Charleyboy. He sprang off the edge of the mattress.

'Suit yourself.'

Charleyboy fumbled for the door. Samuel heard his footsteps on the stairs, heard him open and close the front door. They'd found hay in the barn and stabled the horses before turning in, and when Samuel heard the stallion whinny he knew where Charleyboy would be.

Coltrane was an obstacle to be negotiated. One more Cyclops they had to confront. Tomorrow they'd be rid of the stallion, and Daniel Beckinsale would lose.

Samuel's belly cramped with hunger. He breathed deeply until the pain went away, then after a while he fell asleep.

'Water,' said the raven. 'Please.'

The black bird nodded to a corner of the room. Tucked into a niche behind the door stood a font chiseled from stone, tapered in the shape of an eye …

* * *

They left in the morning before first light and abandoned the road to follow the rail tracks down by the lake. Twice they were forced on to the verge by passing freights, and each time they sat their horses to watch the caravan pass. Scores of homeless men heading for the coast and the same number riding east watched them from atop the boxcars with baleful expressions, their faces caved with broken hopes. Samuel raised a hand the first time, but not one of them waved back.

They rode on, and before long the ammoniac reek of manure filled their nostrils. They rode to the railroad terminus, where, beyond the stationed freights, among a loose clutch of outbuildings, they came across some two hundred head of cattle corralled in four separate pens, flicking away with their tails a plague of flies. The sun was up now and the stockyard was in full swing. Amid the din of bawling livestock upwards of two dozen men were busy counting cattle and loading freights. With one exception, every one stopped what he was doing to watch the two boys and the stallion approach. A shirtless man with a broken nose and a tattoo of an eagle on his chest continued to lead a horse and cart across the yard. A punctured barrel of water affixed to the cart trickled its contents to settle the dust. Samuel asked him where they might find Coltrane. The man still didn't stop. With an unwelcoming stare he simply pointed to a row of low wooden huts beside the water tower and kept on working.

Samuel and Charleyboy rode through the shadow of the water tower and dismounted in front of the first hut that looked occupied. Dirty yellow curtains hung behind the windowpanes and behind them, an electric light burned. The boys tethered the horses to a rail and Samuel knocked on the door.

The man who answered opened the door only halfway. He rolled a toothpick from one side of his mouth to the other. He smelled of whiskey and tobacco. Samuel asked the man, 'Are you Coltrane?'

'Who wants to know?'

'Is he in there?' said Charleyboy.

The man looked at Charleyboy, then back at Samuel. 'Mr Coltrane don't like Indians,' he said. 'Neither do I.'

'Just tell him we got a thousand dollars' worth of horse out here,' said Samuel.

The man looked over Samuel's shoulder at the horses. He removed the toothpick from his mouth, leaned and spat tobacco onto the porch. Then he stepped aside and nodded for Samuel to enter.

'I'll be right here,' said Charleyboy, locking eyes with the man.

The man shut the front door behind Samuel and knocked on another at the back of the office. He muttered a few words Samuel didn't catch. Then he sat down at his desk. It was a palisander partner's desk inlaid with green leather and bordered with gold leaf. There were two inkwells built into it but no bottles of ink. It was a piece of furniture worthy of a lord and it looked preposterous in that ramshackle cabin. Behind the man hung a pin-up of a girl selling soap and a wall clock that had stopped ticking. The man leaned back in his chair and put his boots up on the corner of the desk. He rolled his toothpick from one side of his mouth to the other and stared at Samuel.

After a while, a tall, dark-haired man with very pale blue eyes entered the room from the back. He walked with a cane as thick as a small tree. One side of his face was caved in. His right eye, without the carriage of its socket, gazed absently at Samuel's knees. Coltrane fixed his one good eye on Samuel and waited.

Samuel glanced at the man behind the desk.

'Does he speak?' Coltrane asked.

'I have some horses to sell,' said Samuel.

'Horses?'

'Yes, sir.'

'This is a cattle yard. You see any horses out there?'

'One of them belongs to Daniel Beckinsale,' said Samuel.

Coltrane limped over to the window and pulled aside the curtain. He let the curtain fall and turned. 'How long ago?' he said.

'Three days.'

Coltrane nodded. 'I know Beckinsale well,' he said. 'We're like brothers.' He smiled. 'The fact that you're still alive is a testament either to your courage or your dumb luck. Judging by the company you keep, I'd wager it's the latter.'

'How much will you give me?' said Samuel. 'For all three?'

'Other two ain't worth a damn.'

'That's a good work horse I'm riding.'

Coltrane crossed the floor and sat down on the front edge of the desk. The tabletop creaked beneath him. He turned, smiling, to the man in the chair. The seated man laughed.

'What good's a workhorse, now,' said Coltrane, turning back to Samuel, 'when nobody's got any work?'

Samuel didn't answer.

'I'll give you two hundred dollars.'

'I could do better at the knacker's yard.'

'You're trying my patience.'

'Eight hundred.'

Coltrane grinned. His teeth were the colour of old parchment. 'Come here,' he said. He limped over to the window again and drew the curtains aside. 'I say the word,' he continued, 'those boys out there in the yard? They make you disappear' he snapped his fingers—'and that stallion your redskin's riding is mine for free.' He reached into his pocket, counted out two hundred dollars and held it up. 'On account of your age, I'll forgive the impertinence.'

'Four hundred.'

The man behind the desk dropped his feet off the edge of the table and jumped out of his seat but Coltrane waved him back. He counted out another hundred and stuffed the money into Samuel's shirt pocket. 'I can respect a man who drives a hard bargain,' he said. 'For that you'll include the saddles and tack.'

Samuel took the money and glanced at the man behind the desk. The man was staring at him without blinking. Samuel opened the door and walked onto the porch. Charleyboy took one look at Samuel and knew he'd been screwed. He turned and started emptying the saddlebags. 'The saddles, too?' he said.

Samuel nodded. They took their belongings, such as they were, and wrapped them in their blankets. Samuel and Charleyboy said a few words of farewell to the horses, then made their way back through the yard.

It was only when they reached the road that Samuel spoke. 'Son of a bitch,' he said.

'Hey,' said Charleyboy. 'Before you say another word, just consider your-self lucky you're still walking. You know that feeling you get when you're somewhere you're not supposed to be?' Charleyboy glanced back at the yard. 'I don't ever want to see that place again.'

'All I got's three hundred dollars.'

Charleyboy pursed his lips and nodded. He kicked a stone that went skit-tering into the roadside grass in a cloud of dust. He shrugged. 'Well,' he said, 'that's three hundred dollars we didn't have this morning.'

'Son of a bitch,' said Samuel.

Charleyboy turned again and watched the road behind them. 'I'm gonna buy myself a steak,' he said.

Samuel pulled the money out of his pocket. He counted it and handed half to Charleyboy.

'You look after it,' said Charleyboy.

Samuel held the money up. He stared at Charleyboy.

'I mean it.'

'What if I lose it?'

'You won't lose it.'

Samuel put the money back in his pocket.

Charleyboy began quietly to laugh. 'I'm gonna buy myself a steak and eggs, a whole pile of potatoes, and as much coffee as this Indian can drink.'

They ate at the Good Eats Diner on Victoria Avenue and made plans over end-less cups of coffee. Charleyboy ordered cherry pie to follow his steak. Then he ordered a slice of lemon meringue. When they could eat and drink no more they paid their tab, left the waitress a generous tip and staggered out into the noonday sun.

'I don't feel so good,' said Charleyboy.

'I'm not surprised.'

'I'm sweating all over.'

'It's the coffee,' said Samuel. 'I got the jitters myself.'

'What did you think of that waitress?'

'She kept filling our cups, didn't she?'

'I don't mean that way. She was looking at me.'

They started walking west up the avenue.

'She's old enough to be your mother,' said Samuel.

'She was fine looking.'

'And fat.'

'Yeah.' Charleyboy nodded.

Victoria Avenue was a wide boulevard of false-fronted stores boasting rollback canvas awnings that made a shaded arcade of the sidewalk. Model A Fords, Buick Coupes and pickup trucks lined the tarmac parked at angles to the curb, and men on horseback shared the roadway with dogs and delivery trucks. They marvelled at the sign for the Strand movie theatre, a column leaning over the sidewalk two storeys high, dotted by a hundred bulbs, and in front of the box office a singular sight caught their eyes: a Bennett-buggy parked beside a Cadillac passenger sedan, sign of the times. The buggy was an old Model T drawn by two mules. One of the mules had just dropped its dung and obliged the woman in the passenger seat of the Cadillac to wind up her window. She stared straight ahead and fanned herself with a magazine.

Samuel and Charleyboy stopped and asked a shopkeeper for directions to the nearest post office and CPR ticket counter. He sent them two blocks farther up the avenue. Their plan was to send some money home to their families and then buy third-class tickets on the next train to Kelowna where they hoped to get jobs picking fruit.

'The Okanagan,' Charleyboy mused, savouring each syllable. 'The fruit is so heavy it just falls from the trees. They don't even pick half of it up.'

They passed the stone edifice of the bank with its heavy, brass-handled doors. A rich-looking man in a gabardine suit danced down the steps, walked over to the Cadillac, opened the driver's-side door and climbed in. Charleyboy joked he'd come back to Kamloops a rich man, carry the fat waitress back to Ashcroft and marry her.

They found the post office and went in. Charleyboy bought an envelope, stuffed some money into it and addressed the package to his mom. Samuel bought the same and some writing paper as well. He borrowed a pen and wrote a hurried note to his father:

Dad, I promised you I'd send you some money and here it is.

You will have heard some things about me and Charleyboy by now.
It's true we stole Beckinsale's stallion, but he had it coming. He stole from us.

I'm sending you enough that you can quit the stamp business for a
while, but if you don't, promise me you'll blow out the candles.

—Samuel

P.S. We'll be back when the dust settles.

He stuffed three twenties into the envelope and scrawled his address on the front. He asked the clerk to stamp it. Then he walked back outside to join Charleyboy. He had added the postscript as encouragement, but it rang hollow. Beckinsale would string him up for sure.

They walked on. At the next intersection, kitty-corner from the CPR ticket office, a handful of men shot craps against the wall of an abandoned building. They'd seen out-of-work men loafing up and down the length of the avenue, wearing their indolence like a badge, but the two men throwing the dice looked familiar.

Coming up on their left was an alleyway. Samuel and Charleyboy walked more slowly, eyeballing the men. They had both sensed something. Then Samuel recognized the men and stopped. The taller of the two was the tattooed, broken-nosed driver of the dust wagon and the other was Coltrane's right-hand man, sans toothpick. They straightened when Samuel and Charleyboy stopped. The tattooed man brought his fingers to his lips and whistled. Two men they hadn't seen leaped out of the alley. They grabbed Samuel and Charleyboy by their shirts, dragged them into the shadows and threw them hard against the brick wall. Samuel took an uppercut to his belly and another just under his solar plexus that left him gasping. The man jerked his knee up and loosened one of Samuel's teeth. The blow knocked Samuel up against the wall. He bounced back swinging but his attacker only ducked and sidestepped, artfully catching the boy in the ribs with a short hook. Samuel buckled, and an elbow to the back of the head flattened him.

From where he had fallen on the cobblestones he could see another man laying into Charleyboy. Charleyboy was holding his own, landing blows as they rolled over the floor, but by now the two men from the corner had joined in and the tattooed man started kicking Charleyboy. Samuel got to his knees, but the last thing he saw was the lace of the other man's boot. Everything went green and purple, then blinding white.

He came to in a pool of his own blood. He tried to stand but fell over. When he looked up he saw Charleyboy on his hands and knees, leaning against the alley wall for support. He held himself around the middle and vomited and spat. 'Charleyboy,' Samuel managed, and staggered over to sit down beside him.

'You all right?' said Charleyboy.

'I don't know.'

'Kicked the shit out of us.'

Samuel searched his pockets for the money but he knew, he just knew, it wouldn't be there. He wanted to cry but he willed his face not to betray him. 'Can you move?' he said.

'Yeah.'

'I don't know if I can move.'

Charleyboy looked at him and then looked away. 'They got you pretty good,' he said.

Samuel tried to get to his knees but the pain nauseated him. He sat down again. 'Charleyboy,' he said.

'Yeah.'

'I got to sit here for a while.'

'Okay.'

'Just for a little while.'

'We got to find you a doctor.'

'That bad?'

Charleyboy didn't answer. He heaved himself up to stand leaning against the wall.

Samuel sat looking at the blue strip of sky between the roofs of the two buildings. 'Coltrane,' he said.

'No,' said Charleyboy. 'If he'd wanted to beat us up he would have done it back there in the yard.'

Samuel rolled his head to one side. He spat blood. 'Son of a bitch,' he said. He looked up at Charleyboy. Charleyboy was checking the integrity of his jaw.

'Is it broken?'

'You think you can walk?'

'Yeah.'

Charleyboy found his blanket but nothing else.

'Charleyboy.'

'What?'

'They took the money.'

Charleyboy nodded like he already knew. A short distance away he found Samuel's blanket as well and rolled it up. He stuffed it under his arm and turned and held out his hand. Samuel reached for it and Charleyboy heaved him to his feet.

They wobbled like drunkards down the alley and out the other side into the sun. The few people they passed on the sidewalk gave them a wide berth. Two well-heeled women in sun hats crossed the street when they saw them approach. One of them hesitated at the curb and turned around, but her friend took her firmly by the arm and led her away.

They staggered down to the river and approached the hobo jungle from the east. It looked like the entrance to hell. A dog on a chain ran at them, bristling and baring its teeth. They smelled woodsmoke mixed with sewage, and when they made it beyond the first shanty they began to see figures squatting about their cook fires, wreathed in smoke.

Samuel and Charleyboy's vanquished appearance among those broken, unemployed and homeless men caused hardly a ripple. They warranted no more than a cursory glance until Charleyboy stopped one man and asked him to help them. He was kindly looking, about the same age as Samuel's father, and he took a long look at both of them before answering. They offered no explanation, nor did the man ask for one. 'Come with me,' he said. 'Name's Mitchell.'

They followed Mitchell through a labyrinth of huts and lean-tos hammered up out of mismatched planks and sheets of tin or cardboard. One resident had patched his roof with a woolen coat. Another used a butcher's leather apron for a door. There were upwards of a hundred such structures, each housing two or more men. There were no women or children. As if in some parody of the world beyond its borders, the jungle was segregated by race. The Chinese, they noticed, had fashioned an entire Chinatown down by the river, separated by a gate of woven willow limbs hung with lanterns made out of old tin cans. The Italians had cleared a small soccer pitch and bound tree limbs together for goal posts, but in the heat of the day nobody played.

Forlorn men shuffled past without speaking. Somewhere farther off they heard shouting, a single voice. The cry sounded like a woman's name, three syllables, maybe Rebecca. Mitchell led them on without a word. The screamer's lamentations grew louder.

After a while, they arrived at the screamer himself lying prostrate in his shanty with an empty bottle in his hand. Mitchell stopped. He knocked on the doorjamb. 'Doc,' he said.

The drunk muttered something under his breath.

'Two boys here need your help.'

The doctor raised his head and squinted at them, then lay down again. 'What's the matter with them?' he said.

Mitchell waited for them to speak.

Samuel tried to speak but his lips were badly swollen. He sounded like his mouth was full of bread.

The doctor sat up and glanced at the empty bottle. He threw it past them out the open door and rubbed his eyes with the heels of his hands. 'What's the matter with you?' he said. 'Don't you speak English?'

'We got beat up,' said Charleyboy.

The doctor squinted at Mitchell. 'Bring me some water,' he said.

'You want hot water, doc?'

'No, for Christ's sake, I need some water to drink, my eyes have dried up in my head.'

Mitchell went away.

'Sit down,' said the doctor.

Samuel and Charleyboy sat down in the shade. They winced as they leaned against the shanty wall.

'This damn heat is infernal,' said the doctor. He held his head in his hands. His beard was at least two weeks old and his clothes were filthy. 'Who beat you up?'

'We don't know,' said Charleyboy, before Samuel had a chance to say.

The doctor nodded. He looked at Charleyboy. 'Don't worry, son, I'm just making small talk. W A T E R,' he yelled.

After a little while Mitchell returned with a quart jug of drinking water. The doctor drank all of it in one long draught that left him breathless. He wiped his mouth with the back of his hand and looked at them as if for the first time. He handed the jar off to Mitchell and nodded.

'You need some more, doc?'

'Yes, please.' He seemed a more gentle man already. He rubbed his bloodshot eyes and studied the boys more closely. 'Now,' he said. He looked into Charleyboy's eyes. 'You have a concussion.'

'I been knocked out before.'

The doctor nodded.

'It's my buddy here I'm worried about.'

The doctor ignored him. 'Where else did they hit you?'

'In the belly, I guess. My ribs.'

The doctor put his hands on Charleyboy's belly. He nodded. 'Did you vomit?'

'Steak and eggs.'

'Was there blood in it?'

'No.'

'Okay,' he said. 'You'll be all right. You're definitely concussed. And if it's not the first time it's more serious. If you won't go to a hospital then you'll be staying here a few days.'

'I feel okay.'

'Don't argue with me.' The doctor turned his attention to Samuel. 'You too,' he said, looking into his eyes. He examined Samuel's ribs and kidneys. Samuel winced. Then the doctor felt his belly. He nodded. 'Good,' he said. 'You've only broken a rib.' Then the doctor looked at his face. 'And you need stitches, which I don't have. But I can clean you up.'

He sat back and let out a deep breath. 'After I've quenched this devil in the river,' he said.

The doctor struggled to his feet. He took himself down to the water's edge and stripped. He was very tall and pale-skinned, and stooping to splash water across his arms and neck he looked like some kind of featherless egret bathing there among the reeds. He returned with his hair brushed back off his forehead wearing only his underwear and hung his clothes out to dry from a line erected for that purpose between his shanty and the next.

He kept his medical bag high on a shelf inside his hovel. He reached for it and squatted before Samuel on an overturned bucket. He poured iodine onto a gauze and began wiping his mouth. 'You've lost a tooth,' he said. 'Do you have it?'

Samuel shook his head.

'Shame. If you replace them right away they've been known to knit.'

He poured iodine again and disinfected the inside and outside of Samuel's mouth. 'Good,' he said. 'Good. You're not a bleeder. You have to keep this clean,' he said.

Samuel studied him. He seemed a different man altogether from the one they had found lying in drink not ten minutes ago. His eyes had cleared. He reeked of liquor still, but his gestures and his general bearing did not betray it. He placed his leather bag back on the shelf and turned to them.

'Thank you, sir,' said Charleyboy.

The doctor waved these words away. He shuffled to the door of his hut and stood contemplating the river. 'The devil visits me in liquor,' he said, 'and is most persuasive. But an act of compassion is the one thing he fears. 'Tis like holy water to him. And so it is I,' he said, turning to them, 'who must thank the two of you for delivering me from his grip this time. You can stay here as long as you like.' He nodded. Then he bid them a good day, and strolled out of his shanty into the sun.

CHAPTER EIGHT

The ringmaster leaned against the painted wooden doors of his daughter's vardo and closed his eyes. The circus had driven north all day long and everyone was weary. Even the animals were asleep. He could hear the faint ratcheting sound of his daughter winding the clock on the sideboard. She drew aside and then closed the curtains that concealed her bed. Then it was quiet. It was quiet inside the wagon and it was quiet in the lot.

He leaned forward to knock the ashes from his pipe onto the top step. Reaching into his inside jacket pocket, he took out a pouch of tobacco and opened it. He stuffed the bowl, lit the pipe and sat smoking thoughtfully.

When they had required twice as many men to run this circus, the last thing he would hear at night was the fiddle music of the Gypsies and the women laughing. An accordion, perhaps a Flamenco guitar. The rhythm of clapping and boot heels stomping the boards laid out for a floor.

The blacks they hired now were a watchful lot, wound tight and ready to run. They had their music and their dance but mostly kept to themselves, making camp away from the others because that's how they'd been raised: never let the boss see you do anything but work. And work hard. Whenever he requested to join their campfire they always made space, but with silent, well-rehearsed deference, he suspected. With suspicion. So. Their tribe was divided now, and much the worse for it, he thought.

But who could afford to pay white folks these days? Unless they were winos, or fresh out of prison. Or both. The blacks they paid less than everybody else and yes, they were taking advantage. Ballantyne's paid them more than other circuses, but still. It wasn't only the economy though—the reason John Robinson had folded and Gangler's was selling off its animals. Even the Ringlings had combined with those charlatans Barnum and Bailey, their archenemies of old. For the first time a child raised in the circus was just as likely to leave and find a job in a city somewhere, or on a fishing boat. Heaven knows, even join the army. What exactly did it mean, he wondered, that the world no longer thirsted for marvels? For mystery?

Old folks everywhere bemoaned a golden age that never was. Of that he was certain. It just seemed to be happening so quickly these days, this … innocence lost. This unwillingness to wonder. He blamed the war. An entire generation either died or never truly came home and he couldn't say which was worse. All that anger, the lack of trust. Men throwing their medals in the cut. Their sadness was the reason he'd never returned to Europe.

Ballantyne drank the dregs of his coffee cold and lit his last bowl of tobacco before bed, and then rose and walked stiffly down the steps. Three, four, maybe five fires he counted out in the darkness. Thirty years he'd run this circus. It wasn't because he wanted quit of it that he had handed the reins to his daughter. He had bowed out because of his mind's dark undertow, exacerbated now by his lapses in memory, his terrible old age.

Excessive melancholy—and its opposite—he had always fought with, never able to decide which of two extremes was worse. When he was on top of the world he felt invincible, charismatic, but also reckless and indifferent, and he often hurt the ones he loved. When he was down like a dog, with what he called 'dust in the blood', he was in danger of hurting himself. There had always been a balance, however unpredictable, and between the extremes an exquisite peace and quiet. But lately the dark times were lasting longer, and the respites of ecstasy had grown so few and far between the scales had shifted, he thought, beyond any conscionable balance.

His occupation had always been his saving grace. In his riding habit, under the lights of the big top, he knew exactly where, and what, he was. But once the patrons filed away, the clowns washed off their makeup and the janitors took up their brooms he was an unused puppet, and growing ever more diffident.

He drew deeply on his pipe. The tobacco flared and faded. A storm front had barrelled north up the valley and the night had turned cold. No rain yet, at least. People imagined if you owned a circus it was all romance and the open road but it wasn't. It was winters spent in rented rooms. It was financial instability. It was backbreaking work. Literally, for some. There was a genius of the trapeze or the tightrope dead in every state in America, buried in an unmarked grave, farther from home than he, or she, had ever imagined. And his beloved wife was one of them. He drew once again on his pipe but it was no longer burning. He tapped out the ashes on his boot heel. He tucked his pipe into the pocket of his jacket and stood watching the closest campfire, the flames sawing sideways in the wind, sparks rising skyward. Then he closed his eyes.

'Oh, Emily,' he said.

CHAPTER NINE

Samuel sat beneath a tree on a hill that commanded a view of the shanties, watching heat rise in waves off the corrugated tin. The sun was well advanced when Charleyboy found him. Charleyboy made his way slowly up the dusty slope and stood before his friend.

'Somebody told me once,' said Samuel, 'that if you lean against a tree it will absorb what's on your mind.'

'Is it working?'

'No.'

Charleyboy sat down, but it was no longer the same boy from Ashcroft, the good schoolmaster's son, that he sat beside.

'I'm angry,' said Samuel.

'You've always been angry,' said Charleyboy. 'You've just never known who to blame.' He fished the last of the Englishman's tobacco from his shirt pocket, rolled a cigarette and lit it. 'At least they didn't steal this,' he said. He inspected the tip of his cigarette. He smoked.

'What do you want to do?' said Samuel.

'About what?'

'About getting that money back.'

Charleyboy took a long drag and exhaled a plume of blue smoke. 'I think you need to know when you're beat.'

Samuel shook his head and looked off at the dry, brown hills beyond the river. 'You're not the first person to tell me that.'

'Then maybe you ought to pay attention,' said Charleyboy.

Samuel's eyes welled up. He would not meet Charleyboy's gaze. 'That money was supposed to set us up,' he said.

Charleyboy smoked. He flicked ash into the cuff of his jeans. Men in the ghetto below drifted along the alleys in twos or threes. Some Chinese were laundering their clothing in the river, standing naked to the waist, bending to slap their Zhongshan suits on broad, flat rocks.

'You won't get your revenge,' said Charleyboy. 'Not this time.' He shifted to ease the pain in his ribs. 'This isn't Beckinsale.'

'I'm not afraid of those guys.'

'You should be.' Charleyboy smoked his cigarette down to the nub and stubbed it on the heel of his boot. He flicked the butt down the slope. 'What would your plan be anyway?' He chuckled. 'Ambush 'em with their pants down? Those guys were killers.'

'Tell Coltrane who did it. Let him punish them.'

'You wouldn't get your money back though, would you?' Charleyboy was losing his patience. 'Listen. My old man's been kicking my ass as long as I can remember. Kicking someone else's don't make you feel better.' Charleyboy winced to his feet. He was calm again. He brushed the dust from the seat of his jeans. 'I'm going for a swim.'

Samuel watched him turn and walk a few paces and then called out to him. 'So what next then?' he said.

Charleyboy turned. 'Go to the Okanagan, like we said. Pick fruit.' He shrugged. 'Go see the Rockies. Why do you need a plan?'

'It's all been for nothing, Charleyboy.'

Charleyboy feigned defeat. He let his chin fall to his chest. But when he looked up again he was smiling. 'You take all the time you need, Samuel Hewitt,' he said. Then he turned and walked away.

That night they found Mitchell down by the cook fires with a dozen other men, and when he saw them, Mitchell gestured for them to come over. The men shifted sideways to make way. As he tended the fire, Mitchell told Samuel and Charleyboy he had farmed a quarter section in Saskatchewan and abandoned it after five years of drought. 'I watched my land just disappear,' he said, 'the topsoil turned to dust and blown east one day, then south the next, into the Dakotas.' The other men around the fire quieted and began to listen. 'Drifts of fine soil higher than fence posts. Land so scoured a man would be lucky to raise Russian thistle in a creek bed. I don't need to see the deserts of Arabia,' Mitchell continued, with an ironic smile. 'I've seen them from my back doorstep, right there in the Palliser Triangle.'

Other heads around the fire nodded in commiseration. 'The Palliser Triangle should never have been broken to the plough,' one man said. 'Those grasslands supported buffalo for centuries and grazing land it should have stayed; the subsoil was too loose. But that's all hindsight now. Who could have reckoned on five years of no rain and a wind that wouldn't quit?' The other men murmured their agreement. They stirred their various dinners in their tins.

'And grasshoppers,' said a man across the fire. 'I've seen hoppers blot out the sun. Billions of them. Trillions. I've seen an ordinary kitchen broom leaning up against the side of a granary where we was crushing oats, when the hoppers was done with was no more than a chewed-up stick. Only thing they couldn't eat was the metal band that held the bristles.'

Samuel looked from one man to the next. The firelight deepened the creases in their brows, the lines that failure and consternation had etched around the corners of their mouths and eyes.

'I was travelling the CPR toward Napinka,' said a small, bespectacled man. He leaned over the coals to stir the thin gruel in his tin. 'Ran into a plague of grasshoppers. They smashed into the side of the boxcar, greased up the tracks until that train slowed to a crawl for lack of traction. I tell you it was biblical. Frightening. The windows all smeared. My glasses fogged over. I took them off and there was this oil on them.'

'Tobacco.'

'That's right. It was the mist of a million crushed hoppers the wheels of that train was sending up as spray. Grasshopper-'baccer mist. Ruined the ladies' dresses. Oiled up everything.'

'Went out once after the hoppers had been by,' joined another. 'What little crop I had was gone, of course. Damn things ate the leather seat off my John

Deere. But that tobacco. That brown juice they'd leave when they flew into the side of your barn.' The man shook his head. 'I knew I was all but ruined. I threw my gloves against the barn door and they just stuck there. That's when I knew I was beat.'

Mitchell picked his tin out of the coals with a pair of greenwood sticks. He placed the tin between his feet and reached into his jacket for his spoon and a small packet of salt.

'So what are you eating there, Mitchell?'

'What does a man eat these days?' He stirred his thin stew with a spoon. 'A few vegetables. Some oats. What say we dish up a little for the boys here,' he said.

One of the men handed Samuel an empty tin. 'You can use my spoon when I'm done.'

'Thank you,' said Charleyboy. He knew it hurt Samuel to speak.

'Met a fellow on the prairies,' said one man. 'Lived on gopher pie.'

Mitchell stopped eating and looked at the man. Then he continued.

'Now you might laugh but that man didn't starve. Nor his family neither. I used to watch them. The whole family would go out together with a couple of scruffy-looking dogs. Mama in babushka. Her sleeves rolled up. Old Vaynerchuk would pour water down a likely-looking hole, set the dogs and his wife to watch over the other holes and they'd whack 'em as they came out the exits. The dogs would kill them with a couple of shakes and Mama, she'd just unload with this big stick.' The man shook his head. 'Pretty crazy-looking scene. The kids would go around afterwards and pick them up. Everybody knew they was doing it. Making gopher pie. But the funny thing is—and this'll tell you just how hard these times can be on a man, on his pride—when me and the wife were invited one night—we were neighbourly enough, though we couldn't understand most of what they were trying to say—old Vaynerchuk sits us down and out comes this pie. When I asked him how gopher season was treating him he got all hot under the collar and informed us we weren't about to eat no gophers. He said it was squirrel pie, from squirrels his boy had shot up in the woods. As if that made any difference.

'I don't know,' the man said. 'It makes you wonder.'

'How did it taste?'

'About like you'd expect.'

Another man spoke up. 'Sounds better than that dried codfish we were sent.'

'Who sent you codfish?' said Mitchell.

The man shrugged. 'Came from the Maritimes on one of them relief trains. Bundled together like shingles. Tied up with twine. There was a story going around that Billy MacIsaac had tried to shingle his outhouse with 'em but the nails had bent.'

Mitchell handed the boys his tin and the other men added a spoonful or two of their own food to it.

'Thank you,' said Charleyboy. 'Thank you.'

'Well. I was in Vancouver a few days ago and I'll tell you this for free. I'd rather eat gopher pie than them crabs they all eat down there. Damn things scuttle about the harbour eating garbage. And worse. The man I was travelling with said he'd seen a dead body dredged up from under the bridge just covered in about fifteen big crabs, all gnawing away on him.'

Three more men joined the fire. They wore ten-day-old beards and dirty clothes, like any other, except one man's boots were black and looked brand new. The polished toes shone in the firelight. Their arrival caused a silence to fall over the company and one of the Saskatchewaners—a boy not much older than Samuel—gave up his seat to the big man in the boots. The newcomers nodded gravely. Their leader rolled a cigarette and lit it.

'There's no work in Vancouver, then?'

None of the three men answered. They sat staring into the embers of the fire, as if among those shifting coals were writ some kind of consolation to their fruitless wanderings. The man smoking the cigarette was the first to speak. In his Irish lilt he announced: 'Anybody planning to ride the rods would do best to settle down and wait.' He blew a thin plume of smoke at the fire, his gaze still fixed upon the coals. 'The bulls will be out for blood, and no mistake.'

'What happened, Bartlett?'

'Did one of those devils finally get what was coming to him?'

'And then some,' said Bartlett. He smoked. ''Tis enough to make a man contemplative.' He smiled, but there was no joy in it. 'Somebody crucified themselves a railroad cop,' he said.

'D'you mean they killed one?'

'I mean they crucified one,' he answered. 'Strung him up and nailed his hands and feet to a boxcar. Me and the boys found him with his billy club stuffed up his arse.' He took a long drag on his cigarette and blew smoke at the fire. 'Which makes you wonder,' he said, flicking the ash from the end of it, 'did they administer that before they killed him, or afterwards?'

The prairie men glanced at the big man's boots, but Bartlett had anticipated the question. ''T'weren't any one of us, lads,' he said. 'Jezza just took the man's boots.'

'Do you think they'll come looking?'

'I wouldn't be surprised. Though Jezza here reckons his new boots are worth it.'

'They won't come looking,' said Jezza. 'That bull I recognized. Even his bosses were scared of him. Son of a bitch killed two men I know of.'

'There wasn't much left to recognize,' said Bartlett.

'I've been on the wrong end of one of those billy clubs myself,' said one farmer. 'But who would do such a thing?'

Bartlett shrugged. 'Desperate times,' he said. 'And we all know who's to blame for that.'

The talk turned to R.B. Bennett and the calumny of his government. Every man about that fire claimed to know what was wrong with the country—and how to fix it.

Samuel studied Bartlett by the firelight. The man seemed cut from a different cloth, more worldly than even his colleagues, who themselves had ridden the rods twice from Halifax to Vancouver and back again. He sat on an overturned apple cart with his legs crossed and one elbow atop his knee rolling a cigarette in one hand. The double-breasted Saxony-wool suit he wore was soiled but fit him as if tailor-made. He wore his shirt open at the neck and a handkerchief of matching lilac in his breast pocket that lent him the unlikely look of a ruined dandy.

Bartlett caught Samuel watching him and offered him the cigarette he'd just rolled. Samuel refused, so Bartlett gestured to Charleyboy. Charleyboy leaned forward and took it. He thanked him and lit the cigarette from a burning coal and exhaled a long, luxurious plume of blue smoke.

Five days later they were loitering by the rail lines outside Kamloops city limits, waiting for the freight train to Kelowna. The terminal had been crawling with bulls, and because they would now have to dash to catch the train, Bartlett had advised them to carry nothing. Samuel and Charleyboy buttoned their extra shirts over the ones they already wore and stuffed their food, such as it was, into the pockets of their jeans and strapped their bedrolls to their backs like haversacks.

The moon was full and high and their shadows lay squat across the polished tracks. A man named Pocock paced nervously up and down the rail ties like a quail in a cage, muttering quietly to himself. He wore a complete gabardine suit beneath his overalls as well as two cable-knit sweaters. Tied around his neck by the laces was his better pair of shoes. It was a warm, windless night in late July, and Pocock was sweating like a sinner in church.

The other three paid him no mind. Samuel and Charleyboy's wounds were halfway healed and they felt optimistic, expansive, if not a little drunk. They toed the gravel packed between the rail ties trading tall tales with Bartlett, who had taken a shine to them, and passing back and forth a bottle of cheap whiskey.

The far-off whistle of the train leaving the station pierced the silence of the night. Pocock froze. All except Bartlett turned and searched the tracks. Bartlett rolled himself a cigarette and sat down on a rail. He lit the cigarette and extinguished the match with a plume of smoke. Samuel and Charleyboy double-checked their belongings, refastened their bedrolls and waited for Bartlett to instruct them, but Bartlett was suddenly quiet. The tip of his cigarette flared more frequently than usual.

The train was picking up speed. The valley side amplified the pneumatic hiss of the pistons. Pocock was beside himself. 'For Christ's sake, Bartlett,' he cried, 'it'll be here any second and it's only you knows the ropes! A little instruction, man, if you please.'

'I'd be happy to help, Mr Pocock,' answered Bartlett, 'if I'd done this before.'

'You've not jumped a train?' Pocock said.

'Not this far from the station,' replied Bartlett. 'However,' he assured him, 'while the mathematics might be different, the principle is more or less the same, I'm sure.'

Pocock stared at Bartlett like he was mad. 'You don't know what you're doing? Good God,' said Pocock, clutching his head in his hands, 'I knew I should have bought a ticket.'

Samuel put his foot on a rail. It had begun to hum. Bartlett reached into the inside pocket of his jacket and removed his pewter flask. He took a long pull and offered the flask to Pocock, who refused, at first, and then thought better of it. He snatched the flask out of Bartlett's hand and drank.

Bartlett grinned, smoked his cigarette down to the nub and dropped it onto a crosstie. He twisted his boot onto the burning end as he stood up. He exhaled the last drag through his nostrils and stared intently down the tracks. 'All right, boys. You run like hell as the train gets close,' he said, 'like you're in a relay race, about to receive the baton. The ladders'll rush by your ears. You make up your mind to jump at the third one that passes, or the fourth, or whatever you want, so long as you stick to your count.'

They saw the long headlamp of the freight now sweeping the south side of the valley. As it rounded the corner, the outward reach of its beam began to play upon their shapes, resolving out of the night the endless tangle of sumac and milkweed in the deep run-off ditches and flushing from its roost a ptarmigan that went skittering up the embankment and back again.

Bartlett stared intently at the oncoming train. 'She's moving,' he muttered. 'Twenty-five, maybe thirty.' He turned to the others. 'Anybody here can't run ten miles an hour won't make it,' he declared.

'How does a man know how fast he can run?' demanded Pocock. 'You've timed yourself, have you?'

Bartlett didn't answer right away. He stepped off the crossties, secured his hat and watched the train. 'Fifteen miles an hour is the speed of a John Deere tractor going full-throttle,' he said flatly. 'You're a farm boy, aren't you, George?'

'No.'

'No? You never raced a tractor back to the barn? What do you do for fun in Vancouver?'

'We swim.'

Bartlett nodded. 'Shame you're not catching a boat, then,' he said. 'I suggest you get yourselves ready, boys. Spread out now. Not all these boxcars got ladders up the sides.'

The train came howling down the line. The ground beneath their feet shuddered. The headlight was blinding now and they had to shield their eyes to see. Through his fingers Samuel saw a man leaning out of the engine room window. Above his head the boiler smoke billowed from the chimney in thick white columns that curled in on themselves as the wind sucked them backwards and upwards in disbanding whorls.

'RUN, BOYS, RUN,' yelled Bartlett.

When the engine erupted into Samuel's peripheral vision, the rush of air swept the hair from the nape of his neck. Bartlett was already aboard. He gestured to Samuel frantically from his ladder. When he began to count and the second ladder passed, Samuel edged closer to the tracks, preparing to leap, only to see Charleyboy hanging on with one hand halfway up the ladder he was aiming for, whooping and pumping the other fist. He counted again—one, two, then launched at the third ladder.

When his hands found the metal rungs the momentum of the train flung him nearly horizontal. He swung his legs forward until his boots found a foothold. His broken rib ached brutally. His chin had struck his shoulder and opened the cut on his lip. He crouched close to the bottom of the ladder catching his breath with the air sweeping the hair back from his forehead, the deafening screech of the wheels in his ears and the metallic taste of blood flooding his mouth. Between his feet the creosoted rail ties flashed past in a blur. When the pain had abated a little he spat and looked up. Charleyboy was climbing his ladder. Behind he saw Pocock still running, apparently unsure when to jump, his shoes bouncing about his ears and his inflated figure becoming smaller and smaller as the train sped away.

The boxcars themselves were all locked, as Bartlett had predicted, so they sat atop the train and watched the landscape pass. Charleyboy had jumped back three cars to join Samuel, and then Bartlett strolled over, flask in hand. After a while, Pocock joined them also. He had lost his brogues and was most dejected about it. 'First thing a woman looks at is a man's shoes,' he said. 'Tell me how I'm going to win her heart now.'

But the others only laughed. 'Consider yourself lucky you didn't lose your legs,' said Bartlett.

'You've seen that happen?'

Bartlett turned to Charleyboy. 'At not half that speed, either.' He laughed. 'But aye, I've seen a freight train cut a man's head clean off,' he said. 'One old boy from Winnipeg. Three sheets to the wind, mind, but lost his grip, got his boots caught in the rungs. Poor sod dangled upside down cursing for a furlong, likely broke both his ankles, until he untied his boots and fell out of them. Landed headfirst on the tracks.' Bartlett made a guillotine motion with the edge of his hand. 'Railroad bulls caught one man as the train was pulling out. Tried to yank him off the ladder by the back of his britches 'til the eejit unzipped them. Stepped clean out of one leg, but got his foot caught in the other.' Bartlett shook his head as if the image were too painful. 'The way the bulls pulled him he fell under the wheels. Train sliced him lengthwise,' he said, 'right through his family jewels.'

The two boys instinctively covered their crotches with their hands and rocked forwards. 'Man,' said Charleyboy.

They laughed again and watched the night roll past. They listened to the rhythm of the train. Samuel lay back with his hands beneath his head. 'We lost all our money in Kamloops,' he said. 'Got robbed. That money would have seen us both through the winter.'

'Where'd you two get money?' said Pocock.

'Sold some horses,' said Samuel.

'You've met Padraig Coltrane then,' said Bartlett. 'Who robbed you?'

'Coltrane's men,' said Charleyboy.

'Without Coltrane knowing?'

'We think so,' said Samuel. 'Why would he go to the trouble of paying us first, and *then* robbing us?'

'Coltrane discovers *that*,' said Bartlett, 'and your thieves won't see Christmas.'

Bartlett fished tobacco and papers from his pocket and began rolling another cigarette. He licked the gum along the edge of the paper, sealed the cigarette and put it in his mouth. He shook his head. 'Man that ruthless becomes legend,' he said. He lit his cigarette inside the cover of his jacket. 'There isn't one of us who isn't capable. Of evil, I mean.' He exhaled the first drag. 'But the man who takes that road as far as it goes—knowingly, now—and can live with himself that way? Well. He doesn't answer to anybody. Not even God.'

'You blaspheme, Bartlett,' said Pocock. 'God will take his revenge. He always does.'

Bartlett glanced at him sideways. 'It's what a man believes shapes his world. Look at you, Pocock. You jump a train for love.'

'Aye,' said Pocock, 'but the love of God no man can escape.'

'Have it your way,' said Bartlett. He turned to Samuel and Charleyboy. 'What about you, boys? What do you believe in?'

Neither had a ready answer. Bartlett smiled good-naturedly. 'Not to worry,' he said. 'We'll call it a rhetorical question.' He smoked down his cigarette and stubbed it out. 'How come yous had horses in the first place?'

'The gelding belonged to my dad,' said Samuel, 'who won't be missing it. One we inherited, and another we stole.'

'Sounds like the start of a folktale.' Bartlett laughed. 'Or a joke. You're sure you're not Irish?'

'A gelding, a nag, and a stallion.' Samuel grinned, warming to the theme.

'The stallion belonged to a crook,' said Charleyboy. 'Sam here killed the man he hired. With one throw of a rock.'

'It was an accident,' said Samuel.

'Dropped him like a ton of bricks,' said Charleyboy. 'One throw.'

'Who owned the stallion?' asked Pocock.

'Daniel Beckinsale,' answered Charleyboy.

Pocock raised his eyebrows. 'You stole a stallion from Daniel Beckinsale?'

'You've heard of him?'

'Who hasn't?'

'That was Sam's doing as well,' said Charleyboy.

'You're the one eared him down, Charleyboy.'

Bartlett burst out laughing. 'You eared down a stud horse,' he said. He reached into his jacket and pulled out his pewter flask. 'To the Ballad of Sam and Charleyboy,' he toasted, taking a pull and passing the flask. 'May your souls be in heaven half an hour before the devil knows you're dead.'

At first light, after passing an uncomfortable night upon the roof of the boxcar, they sat wrapped in their blankets watching with bleary eyes the sun rise above the distant city lights of Kelowna.

'Honolulu beckons, boys,' said Bartlett. 'Honolulu and its orchards. All you've got do to,' he added, 'is jump off this freight before the bulls get you.'

'It slows down, though,' said Samuel, 'as it gets near the yard. Right?'

'Some,' said Bartlett. 'It slows down some.' He was eyeing the oncoming city with that same calculating air.

Samuel checked the laces on his boots. 'You ready, Charleyboy?'

'Sure.' Charleyboy yawned. 'I could eat a horse,' he said. 'But other than that.'

Pocock rolled up his blanket and tied it and slung it over one shoulder. 'May the Lord be with you boys,' he said. He started walking back down the boxcars to pick his spot.

'Spread out now,' said Bartlett. 'Yard's coming.'

Bartlett walked forward one boxcar. Charleyboy jumped one back. He turned, looked at Samuel and grinned. All four of them climbed down to the end of their ladders.

Samuel took his cue from Bartlett. He watched him swing off the bottom of the ladder like a trapeze artist and scissor his legs, so that when he struck the gravel he was already at a run. Samuel watched him slow to a jog and then stop, still holding on to his hat. Samuel looked down at the gravel speeding past. He could feel the train slowing, hear the brakeman with his levers applying pressure to the wheels. Looking back he saw Bartlett in the near distance make a gesture with his arm like he was throwing a lasso. Samuel hung off the bottom rung. He swung once, twice, to gain momentum and then let go, hanging motionless in thin air for a moment as the train sped on. He landed and ran but not fast enough. He fell forwards, taking the blow on the heels of his hands. Somewhere behind him he heard Charleyboy yeehaw. Samuel lay where he was, spitting gravel, until Charleyboy ran up. Judging by a raw scrape on his arm, he had fallen also. 'You all right?'

Samuel sat up and loosened his blanket. 'Yeah,' he said. 'I'm all right.' He stood. 'Soon as I pick this gravel from my hands.'

Pocock came limping up behind them. He had ripped his overalls and one sleeve of his suit jacket, which was also soiled with creosote. He brushed the dust from his hair and cursed quietly. 'Where's Bartlett?' he said.

They found Bartlett sitting tailor-wise atop a rock. He was rolling a cigarette and watching the sun come up over the Monashees. 'The Lord has blessed us with a beautiful morning, has he not? What do you say, Mr Pocock?'

'You make a mockery, Bartlett.'

Bartlett smiled, exhaled a plume of blue smoke and leaped down off his perch. In the distance, above the din of the receding train, they could all hear the unmistakable sound of a brass band. It was almost as if Bartlett had conjured a fanfare to accompany his arrival. He tilted his trilby at a rakish angle and grinned. 'Follow me into the Promised Land, lads,' he said.

CHAPTER TEN

Samuel and Charleyboy parted company with their fellow travellers on the outskirts of Kelowna. Bartlett went north toward the hobo jungle, brogueless Pocock east to find his sweetheart. Persuaded by the music and the faraway sound of a crowd, the boys drifted south, toward the city. They could make out two distinct rhythms—one a brass band playing ragtime and snatches of a martial-sounding oompahpah that suggested some kind of parade.

'What do you think that is?' said Samuel.

'Can we find out after we've slept?' said Charleyboy. 'I see a perfectly good ditch right over there.'

When they turned onto the main road into Kelowna, however, they were jolted awake by the spectacle of city-bound traffic jammed a mile long, drivers and their passengers climbing out of their cars and trucks to perch along the running boards or on the hoods of their vehicles. There were office workers leaning out of second-storey windows, people running in the street, children bouncing on their fathers' shoulders, bankers and shopkeepers abandoning their posts without stopping to lock their doors.

'Are you seeing what I'm seeing?' said Charleyboy.

They were running now beside the line of parked cars, threading their way among the swelling crowd and they soon began to see, lumbering west through the intersection, above an ocean of trilbys and tilted Florentine hats, the massive, leathery figure of an elephant. A dancer, clad in little more than a leotard and a gauzy, sequined skirt that glittered in the sunlight like a hundred suns, turned pirouettes on the elephant's head. Hard behind galumphed another, even bigger bull elephant. Fastened to its back by embroidered straps was a roofed and bejewelled howdah rolling with the motion of the pachyderm's stride and inside, sequestered like royalty, a dark-skinned woman reclined on a divan of satin cushions and waved a lazy, tattooed hand at the crowd.

The crush of onlookers was seven rows deep. The boys stood on tiptoe and craned their necks to see better but it was no use. Samuel glanced around wildly. He struck Charleyboy on the arm and gestured to a lamppost. They pushed their way through the crowd. The lamppost rose from a square metal base wide enough for a boot sole, and the two boys clambered up and balanced there not unlike acrobats themselves, each with one arm wrapped around the pole. From there they could see with no obstacle. A flatbed truck followed the elephants, fitted with a cage painted gaudy red and green on each end. Behind its iron bars a tiger paced and glowered at the crowd with eyes like burning coals. Four ensuing menagerie wagons carried lions, a caracal, a leopard and a sorrowful-looking orangutan that tried to hide behind its hands. Next came the clowns, their faces painted into tragic masks or grins almost sadistic, cavorting like fools and tossing aloft entire fistfuls of confetti that rained down on the crowd like coloured snow: one in a bridal gown and one dressed like a cleric, a fat one framed by a papier-mâché goose, dwarves wardrobed with shoes as long as they were tall and one leading a pig by a long sausage link. And at last, at the tail end of the cavalcade, six white horses sporting feathered plumes drew a glorious bandwagon wrapped entirely in gold leaf. The slowly turning wheels were carved to look like smiling suns, and a pair of swans applied in bas-relief to the sidewall panel nuzzled beaks so the incline of their necks framed the shape of a heart. Flowers and fruiting vines drew the eye upwards to a pair of cherubs, embossed in opposite corners, who coyly drew their bowstrings back with fat fingers. And seated in four rows of three atop this travelling stage a band of twelve black men dressed in green-and-white-striped jackets and straw boaters played ragtime with their clarinets and brass, tapping their brown-and-white brogues in time to the music and swaying in unison from side to side. The bandleader stood before them with his cornet cradled loosely in his fingers. With his other hand he held his hat over his heart, as if to hedge in its swelling. He trembled and wept with his face tilted heavenwards like a sexton at an evangelical gathering.

After the bandwagon departed, the crowd of onlookers poured into the street from both sides like a grey sea swallowing the fin of an extraordinary, luminous fish, and a small but enthusiastic crowd—mothers and small children, unemployed men, boys Samuel and Charleyboy's age—pursued the cavalcade down to the lake.

But for the dots of confetti drifting in the gutters and the few circus flyers littering the sidewalk, the city street appeared unaltered. Merchants returned to their stores. Traffic flowed as before.

Ballantyne's Travelling Circus had assembled its itinerant village in a cottonwood grove, still within the city limits but on unimproved land. The advance man had arrived two days prior, secured feed for the animals and paid off the local officials. By the time the cavalcade returned, the majority of the company were settled. Laundry snapped on lines bellied sideways by the wind. Lanterns swung on wires attached to neighbouring trailers, and canopied living rooms complete with carpets and armchairs and coffee tables—like bourgeois parlours without walls—had been erected to make comfortable the elderly and those most senior among the company.

The menagerie wagons parked downwind of the sideshow and the elephant tents. The drivers climbed down out of the cabs, chocked the wheels and began setting up stakes and rope before the cages. If the rubes didn't have something to hold on to they would press closer and closer to the bars until the front line was flattened up against the cage. The lions were liable to reach out and rip someone's head off.

Already the enormous red-and-yellow canvas of the big top lay flat on the grass like a collapsed lung and a shirtless hammergang was at work driving stakes round the perimeter. Without exception the hammermen were black. The oval outline of the big top had been marked with long pins and two teams of four men apiece—as well as one huge, heavily muscled man who worked alone—drove four-foot stakes into the clay beside their markers. They sang a cappella as they worked; one man hollered a phrase, the others answered in unison, and the clink of steel striking steel provided an improvised beat.

The man who worked alone laboured with a fury that had drawn a small crowd. He swung a forty-pound mallet overhead as if it were a tennis racquet, twisting his wrists after the impact, raising and ramming down the mallet without pause. He timed his hammer blows to coincide with his companions' but he did not sing.

'Who do we talk to?' said Charleyboy.

Samuel watched the canvasmen flapping kinks out of the big top, pulling from all sides and stretching the sections flat as sheets. Gesturing in their midst was a big, barrel-chested man sucking on an unlit cigar. 'Him,' he said.

Samuel entered the stake line. 'Excuse me, sir,' he said.

'SHAKE IT, SHAKE IT, SHAKE IT,' the boss man bellowed.

'SIR,' said Samuel.

The man swung around.

'Do you have any work for a couple of young men, sir?'

The man snatched the cigar out of his mouth. He looked Samuel up and down, then turned and yelled another order before saying, 'I don't see but one of you.'

'Me and Charleyboy,' said Samuel.

The man squinted at him. 'Charleyboy, huh. He a nigger?'

Samuel bristled, but held his tongue. 'No. He's not.'

'That's good,' said the man. He wore a pained expression. He stuck the cigar back in his mouth. 'Goddamn hollering hurts my head. Always did.' He rolled the cigar from one side of his mouth to the other. 'Talk to the skipper,' he said.

'Where do I find him?'

'Her,' said the boss man. He snatched the cigar out of his mouth. 'The skipper's a her. You'll know her when you see her.' He looked over Samuel's shoulder. 'BAINES,' he yelled, striding away, 'for mercy's sake, quit standing on the canvas.'

Samuel searched the lot for a private wagon, something grand, perhaps set apart from the others. He drifted back to Charleyboy.

'They're feeding the lions,' said Charleyboy.

'We've got to find the skipper.'

'I thought you were talking to him.'

'That wasn't him. Anyways, it's a her.'

Charleyboy was impressed. He pressed down the corners of his mouth. 'Then you'll just have to flash those boyish good looks.'

Samuel scoffed. 'I was a lot better looking when I had all my teeth.'

Just then, an enormous man waddled by wearing a kind of smock sewn together out of several other shirts, or perhaps a bedsheet. He must have weighed a tonne or more. He was sweating and breathing heavily. Trotting several paces behind followed a miniature but otherwise fully formed man dressed in a three-piece suit who regarded them through his monocle with an air of supercilious disdain.

Samuel and Charleyboy stopped talking. They both turned to watch. The midget reached barely to the fat man's knees. The fat man reached the fly tent of the cook shack first, received his mountain of food, squeezed on to the middle of a bench and commenced to eat his dinner with impeccable manners, availing himself of his serviette every now and again to dab the corners of his mouth. The midget also climbed on to the bench to hover beside him, and was much animated. He appeared to be scolding his companion.

'We got to find this woman,' said Charleyboy.

Samuel turned and scanned the lot. 'I don't know what she looks like.'

'Boss man didn't tell you?'

'Said I'd know her when I saw her.'

Charleyboy glanced at him. 'Is she a freak, too, or something?'

'He didn't say.'

Charleyboy nodded. 'She's probably eight feet tall.'

Samuel didn't answer.

'Or tattooed. Maybe she's got a tail.'

'I see her,' said Samuel.

A tall woman dressed in a man's linen slacks and white shirt approached the Bengal tiger's cage. Her hair was bobbed short in the modern style, but slicked back. Except for the length of her neck and the slenderness of her wrists, from behind she looked much like a man. She reached between the bars of the cage and scratched the tiger under the chin.

A small crowd of townsfolk had gathered to watch, expecting a violent end. Secretly hoping for such. And their hopes were realized, to a point. The tiger seized the woman's hand in its mouth and stood. The onlookers gasped. But the woman didn't flinch, and when the crowd heard the roar of an angry lion two cages away and saw a handler prodding horsemeat through the bars with a chewed-up stick, they quickly moved on.

Samuel and Charleyboy hurried across the lot. Once they were within earshot, Samuel asked, 'Are you the skipper, ma'am?'

The tiger released the woman's hand and tested the air with quick, lifting motions of her massive head.

'Pilinszky sent you?' said the woman, without turning around.

'Yes ma'am,' said Samuel. 'Me and my friend here.'

'What are your names?'

'My name is Samuel Hewitt. This is Charleyboy.'

The woman glanced over her shoulder. She was of indeterminate age, more handsome than beautiful, and she studied them both in turn with very clear grey eyes.

After a while she smiled, then swung fully around. She folded her arms and leaned against the tiger's cage. 'You've run away then,' she said in a mellifluous southern drawl.

Samuel and Charleyboy didn't answer.

'You have run away because … "the homes you woke up to no longer mirrored your heart's architecture", as my father's fond of saying.'

'Ma'am?' said Samuel.

'But then he always was a bombast,' she added. The woman smiled again. 'We all have the same story here, Samuel Hewitt. We are at home among the homeless. Study Justice there.' She gestured to the huge man driving stakes by himself. 'A king on his own continent, to be sure, by the power of his arm. But in Mississippi?' She shrugged. 'A slave.' She studied them more closely. Took in their shabby clothes. Their tightened belts. 'When was the last time you ate?'

Samuel and Charleyboy looked at one another. 'I don't remember.'

The woman nodded. 'Will you work hard?'

'Yes,' said Charleyboy.

'Will you follow the rules?' She looked at Samuel. 'People get hurt when the rules are not observed.'

'We'll do whatever you tell us,' said Charleyboy.

The skipper nodded, though she appeared unconvinced. 'You will not talk to the sideshow. You certainly will not talk to the performers. And you will fraternize with … your own kind. Keeping the peace around here is a constant challenge,' she said wearily. 'Segregation is a necessary evil.'

She jutted her chin at the canvasmen. 'Pilinszky will give you a meal ticket for this evening. If I hire you it's two dollars a day, plus room and board. Until then'—she pointed beneath the tiger's cage—'under here is the safest place to sleep.'

'Ma'am?'

'You're not one of us yet,' she answered. The tiger pressed her face against the bars. The skipper must have felt the tiger's breath on the back of her neck. She appraised Samuel once more, then something in the village caught her eye. An old man wearing a singlet, old-fashioned riding pants and polished boots wandered over, looking lost. The skipper intercepted him, raised his arms to her shoulders and danced him round to face the other way. They walked off arm in arm a short distance, like partners in a three-legged race, and then, as if guiding a child, she let him go with a gentle nudge toward the village.

'They want to separate us, Charleyboy.'

'I get it. They don't like coloured people. They don't like them in Ashcroft, either,' Charleyboy said. 'Who's Pilinszky?'

'Man with the cigar.'

The tiger raised its head and sniffed. Charleyboy grinned. 'I never slept beside a tiger before. You wait until we tell them.'

'Tell who?' muttered Samuel, studying the tiger.

The hammermen had driven their last stake and were leaning on their mallets in the sun. Horses began to haul the big top off the ground. Down the alley of caravans, Samuel watched the skipper stop and talk to a dark-skinned man. He thought he saw her gesture in his direction. 'I've got misgivings about this,' he said.

'I'm going to get us that meal ticket,' Charleyboy said.

Charleyboy approached Pilinszky. Samuel watched Pilinszky snatch the cigar out of his mouth. He couldn't hear what they were saying, but he saw Charleyboy point in his direction. After a while, Pilinszky reached into his shirt pocket, produced two tickets and begrudgingly handed them over.

Before Charleyboy had made his way back, two young women walked by. They passed not six feet from where Samuel was standing, laughing and holding one another by the hand. They went barefoot, wearing loose summer dresses that clung to their figures. Their long, dark hair was wet from bathing in the lake. The closest girl turned to Samuel and smiled, sadly, he thought, though her eyes never quite met his own. She was very pale, very beautiful, and she carried herself with the lithe, seemingly weightless gait of an acrobat.

She turned, smiling once more over her shoulder before she and her companion moved on under the canopy of cottonwoods and disappeared among the clutch of circus caravans.

'You still got misgivings?' said Charleyboy.

Samuel was looking down the path where they'd gone. There was nothing there to see but he stood looking anyway. 'She's blind,' he said.

Samuel and Charleyboy stood last in line behind the hammergang, circumspect and silent now that their work was done. As they filed past the long board-and-sawhorse tables at which the labourers ate, it was not hard to see why. The vast majority of the unskilled workers were white and poor: hardlooking men dressed in threadbare shirts and dirty jeans, their faces seamed by knife fights; or toothless, stinking drunks with skulls dented by billy clubs. Samuel watched one of them take his teeth out of his mouth and lick the food off them before leaving the table.

The working men spoke sparingly, if at all. They ate with their eyes on their plates and their elbows propped up on the table to protect their food like convicts in a prison mess—which was, in fact, where many of them had learned this lesson. The overseers and performers, on the other hand, who sat farthest from the smoking stovepipes around tables laid with checkered cloths and condiments and glassware, laughed and ate noisily and enjoyed one another. The women at these tables looked like movie stars, their eyes heavily pencilled and their lips painted crimson. Some dressed in bathrobes and swimsuits as if fresh from the beach. Others appeared ready for dress rehearsal and reluctant to sit, for they strutted among the tables in costume and heels, waving conspicuously and kissing each acquaintance on the cheek.

The sideshow owned its own table. An obese pair of twins sporting matching cotton smocks and bows in their hair had joined the fat man and his miniature adversary. Across the table from them sat a pretty girl with no arms, just tiny hands like flippers poking out beneath the fabric of her cap sleeves. Straddling the bench to her left a shirtless man tattooed from head to toe stroked her hair and fed her with a spoon. He must have said something funny because the pretty girl laughed with her mouth full and the tattooed man grinned, wiping the food affectionately from her chin. A grim-looking albino with long hair to his waist sat ramrod straight without eating at all, like a baleful ghost, and beside him hunched a woman whose rough, puckered skin dipped and cracked like a crocodile's. Samuel couldn't help but stare, but when the crocodile woman caught him gawping, Samuel quickly looked away.

The boys received their food at last. They took their dented plates from stacks beside the entrance to the serving station and their cutlery from dirty wooden bins. One of the cooks scraped some stringy-looking meat from the bottom of a blackened pot and slapped it onto their plates. He spooned up beans and what appeared to be mashed potatoes and gestured for them to help themselves to bread.

With their plates full they surveyed the labourers' section to see where they might sit. Some tables under the fly tent were not entirely occupied, but not one man endeavoured to make room. The only space left was next to the hammergang, so they ventured from under the fly tent, squinting, to sit with them in the sun.

The blacks eyed Samuel with hostility. One or two of them stopped eating. Only Justice did not watch them. He chewed his food very slowly and stared straight ahead.

'You like to sit with niggers, boy?'

Samuel turned. With the sunlight in his eyes and smoke swirling from the stovepipes he couldn't make out, at first, who under the awning had spoken.

''Cause if that's how you feel you can sleep with them, too. We sleep two to a bunk around here.'

The boy who spoke sat with his back to the hammergang's table. He was about Samuel's age. Tattoos decorated his neck. The hammergang watched to see what Samuel would do.

'Well,' said Samuel, 'I guess it doesn't matter to me where I sit. We haven't eaten in three days. I had a mind to wrestle that lion for his horsemeat but he looked about as hungry as me.'

Stifled laughter broke the silence. The tension lifted momentarily, but Samuel held the boy's gaze longer than necessary. The tattooed boy took it for the provocation that it was; his face darkened.

When Samuel turned back he saw Charleyboy trying not to smile. The hammergang began to eat again. Charleyboy spooned some beans into his mouth. 'I'm watching the son of a bitch,' he said.

Samuel glanced down the table at Justice. For a man of such immense proportions he ate with surprising restraint. His fork made hardly a sound on the tin plate as he scraped up the last of his beans.

Before Samuel and Charleyboy finished their meal, the skipper crossed the lot toward them in the company of a man bigger still than Justice. The man walked with a platform shoe and the journey from his trailer had clearly taxed him, for he wheezed as he ducked under the fly tent and limped his way over to the serving station. If Justice stood six and a half feet tall, this man was taller by another foot. In every way a giant, from the lobes of his beefsteak ears to his hands like catchers' mitts. The cooks had saved him a choicer cut of meat and they had kept his utensils separate. They handed him an oversized spoon and a heavy china platter that could have carried a suckling pig.

Samuel and Charleyboy watched him. He made his way over to the sideshow table and sat opposite the fat man on a bench reinforced with iron. The skipper stood beside him, not quite eye to eye even so. Whatever they were talking about animated them both, for they laughed and gesticulated. Samuel could hear them clearly, but it was not English they were speaking.

Samuel turned back to his food. He glanced at Charleyboy. Charleyboy gestured with his chin. 'She just pointed over here,' he said.

'I don't want to turn around again,' said Samuel. 'I can feel that boy's eyes drilling into the back of my head.'

At Samuel's elbow sat a man named Henry Sweet. 'Best steer clear of him,' he said, without looking up. 'Cracker like that hunt niggers for fun.'

'We ain't niggers,' said Charleyboy.

The man looked at him. 'You is a nigger,' he said. 'White boy here just confused.'

A few blacks at the table laughed softly.

'Who is that guy anyway?' said Samuel.

Sweet stopped eating. 'Name's Lynch,' he said. He looked up. 'Which ain't even funny. And the boy don't work alone.'

Pilinszky came at last to the cookhouse. He shook his head when he saw them sitting with the hammergang and went directly to the skipper. He spoke in a low voice, but with much agitation. The skipper regarded him calmly. She drew him aside and when they returned he seemed mollified. He got himself a plate of food and sat down at one of the performers' tables.

Charleyboy asked Henry Sweet who sat at the top table, and Sweet said it was the stars, of course. He said the aerialists and trick riders and foot jugglers made the most money, then the animal trainers and the clowns, then the freaks at the next table down.

'What about the blind girl?' said Samuel.

Henry Sweet laid his fork in the centre of his plate and sucked his teeth. 'The blind girl,' he said. He did not look up.

The canvasmen were roused by Pilinszky to get back to work. The hammergang began to get up, as one, from the table. Samuel glanced again at Justice and Justice met his gaze for the first time. His eyes revealed no hostility, but no measure of welcome either. He simply looked at Samuel once, then got up and went back to work.

Pilinszky came and told them that he'd spoken with the skipper and she seemed to think that by tomorrow they'd be needing extra men. He said that they could watch the show tonight and report for work in the morning. Until then they should stay out of the way.

When they were done eating they carried their plates to the dish pit. Lynch had waited to follow them up and Samuel just knew what he was aiming to do. 'Charleyboy,' he said. 'I want you to promise me something.'

'What?'

'I want you to stay out of this.'

He turned and confronted Lynch, who came at him fists swinging. Samuel ducked the first blow but caught another in the stomach. He straightened and swung, striking Lynch on the side of the head with his elbow. They both went to the ground. Samuel had landed on top and he rained a few well-aimed punches at Lynch's face before somebody grabbed him and threw him aside. Lynch's nose was clearly broken, swelling and trickling thick ribbons of blood over his split lips. He rose and charged at Samuel, but the same man stepped in and held him back and advised him to cool it.

Charleyboy seized Samuel by the shoulders and hustled him down the stake line toward the tiger's cage. By the time they arrived he was stifling a laugh. 'Brother,' he managed.

'What's so funny?' said Samuel. 'That son of a bitch.'

'You got him good,' said Charleyboy. 'Did you see his face? Listen,' he said, 'maybe we'd better think this over. We could walk away right now.'

'No way.'

'That guy's not going to quit.'

'Neither am I.'

'What if next time it's a knife?'

'Then I guess I need one as well.'

Charleyboy shook his head. He looked away.

'This is what you wanted,' said Samuel. 'To join the circus.'

'Yeah. Not if it's gonna get you killed.'

'I'm not backing down, Charleyboy.'

'Oh, I know,' said Charleyboy. 'That's what I'm worried about. You still fighting with Coltrane's men?' he asked. 'With Beckinsale?'

Samuel couldn't look him in the eye.

'They're not worth it, Sam,' said Charleyboy. 'They're trash. They're all trash.'

Samuel shook the pain from his knuckles. The adrenaline and the punch he'd taken to the stomach combined to make him feel sick.

Charleyboy turned away while Samuel vomited. 'There you go,' he said. He shook his head, gravely. 'You're not even coloured.'

Dimitry had parked the vardo as close to the lakeshore as possible without miring the wheels in the sand, and Helena had thrown the doors wide open to receive the breeze. She dragged the red velvet armchair to the threshold, reclined into the cushions and closed her eyes. A suitor. So. Josephine would sample courtship, and the fate of the circus rested upon the success—or failure—of this young man's advance. A deck of cards never changed anything, and neither could she. Fate owned the patent to the future. Helena had learned that the hard way.

Without Josephine, however, Ballantyne's would be indistinguishable from any other travelling show. If she left, this would be their last season. Some eighty-nine souls would then have nowhere else to go. But to meddle would only guarantee the worst. This hero, Samuel Hewitt—this Parsifal—must be allowed to have his say.

Behind the velvet curtain, deep within the recess of the vardo, Josephine lay sleeping. They had argued again about loyalty, about love, about family, about sacrifice, and the battle had exhausted them both. Helena was about to fall asleep herself when her father, in full ringmaster's regalia and with a freshly lit cigar clenched between his teeth, erupted into her line of sight.

'Helena,' he announced, 'I had an epiphany while voiding my bowels. It was so magnificent my sinuses ran. One of those ... soul-cleansing shits that begins as a tingle in the sphincter and rises like a Kundalini up the spine to polish the resin off your third eye!'

'Dimitry,' called Helena, 'Daddy's manic again. Could you fetch him a tonic?'

'Don't patronize me, you pelican.'

'Squawk, squawk,' said his daughter.

'That's not the right sound at all,' called Josephine from behind the beaded curtain. 'It's more like a belch.'

'Aha!' said the ringmaster, 'the pelican's protégée. How apropos.'

'Do sit down, Father, you are ruining my view.'

Her father climbed the vardo stairs. He snatched the cigar out of his mouth and jabbed it like a weapon into the darkness. 'A pelican hatchling,' he began, much animated, 'feeds on what its mother regurgitates, at first, until she is of age to simply plunder what her parents keep stored in their pouch. And then, even when full, she performs what ornithologists call "throwing a tantrum".'

'Josephine, why don't you run along, honey.'

'Oh, I'm not finished,' her father declared. 'This tantrum,' he continued, 'consists of the chick prattling on and on and pathetically dragging herself round in a circle by one wing and a leg—'

'That's enough, Father.'

'Too late,' said Josephine.

'And its mother,' continued the ringmaster, appealing to the heavens, as if the crescendo to his parable might be etched upon the sky, 'will pick at her *own breast*,' he said, punctuating his exasperation by drumming on his chest with his fingertips, repeatedly, 'until she bleeds, so her chick might drink that down as well.'

'That is mythology, Father, not ornithology.'

Dimitry appeared in the open doorway, eating a sandwich. Helena waved him forward.

'And do you know what the learned bird-lovers believe is the reason for this ... *dramatic* display?' Ballantyne raved. 'She wants *attention*. She aims, above all else, to divert her mother's gaze away from any rival.'

'Dimitry, lead Josephine back to her caravan please.'

Josephine appeared from behind the curtain and felt her way along the wall toward the open door. 'You're such an ass,' she said, as she passed the ringmaster.

Ballantyne grinned and drew deeply on his cigar. 'Why don't you tell her,

Helena,' he said. 'Tell the pelican chick here how well you fared when you left.'

'She already knows. Calm down.'

Dimitry finished his sandwich and wiped his hands on his jeans. Josephine reached for his hand. He guided her down the steps and they hurried off.

Helena turned to confront her father, but the man who stood before her looked suddenly defeated, confused. He leaned to grip the back of the armchair with both hands, still holding the cigar. Sweat trickled down his temple. His breathing was belaboured, and he squinted at his daughter like he'd never seen her before.

'Your epiphany,' she queried, 'was about pelicans?'

'What?' Her father grimaced, genuinely at a loss.

So. It had happened again. The old ogre saved by his own advanced age. Helena felt cheated, her vitriol robbed of its target. She plucked the cigar from her father's knuckles, threw it onto the top step and extinguished it with a twist of her shoe. She descended the steps and stalked off toward the lake, arms folded. A pair of mallards gabbled along the shoreline, and she watched a brindle mutt belonging to one of the grooms run at the ducks and panic them. They spanked off across the surface of the lake until their wing speed lifted them clear of the water and they whistled away.

Her name was Sarah, the woman she loved. A showgirl. She and Helena had abandoned Ballantyne's to seek a life outside the circus. At first, they had imagined themselves to be like any other couple, though clearly they weren't. And the world never let them forget it. People were generally easier on two women who lived together than two men in the same situation—they could be sisters, after all—but the snickers and the stares and the questions, unspoken or not, eventually wore Sarah down. They moved, but the scrutiny they could never escape. Evil is other people. If she and Sarah had retreated to a desert island, Helena was certain they would still be together. And in love.

'They mate for life, mallards,' said Helena. 'Since we talk of birds.' She turned to her father, but he had not heard.

Her father sat on the edge of the cushion rocking backwards and forwards, weeping and holding himself around the middle. He would do this for a while, longer on some days than others. When he returned to his senses she would tell him what he'd said. He would apologize, do his penance, and carry on. Until next time.

'I want it to stop,' whispered her father. 'Please.'

How much clemency, she considered, does a daughter owe her father if her father has been absent from her life?

Helena took the steps two at a time, strode beyond her father into the vardo and opened her bureau. Beside her tarot cards she kept another box, locked, the key to which she hid in one of the many small drawers. She unlocked the box, unwrapped an ivory-handled Smith and Wesson from its chamois leather and slammed it onto the armrest of the chair.

Her father stopped rocking. He stared at the revolver for a long time until, at length, he looked up at her with his watery blue eyes. Clearly, he didn't know whether to be grateful, or outraged.

'Where did you get that?' he said at last.

'It was your wife's.'

'I know that. I never knew what happened to it. She was a bloody good shot, your mom.'

'How would I know?' said Helena.

Her father picked up the revolver and thumbed open the cylinder, saw that it was empty, and snapped it shut.

'The bullets are in the box,' said Helena.

Ballantyne handed her the revolver. On the floor beside his daughter's feet, he noticed his extinguished cigar. 'You ruined a perfectly good cigar,' he muttered, and with a long sigh slumped back into the cushions, utterly spent, like a defunct ventriloquist's puppet.

CHAPTER ELEVEN

Samuel and Charleyboy spied a place to sit about halfway up the bleachers near the centre of the ring. Good seats. The family they stopped beside smiled and squeezed closer together, making ample space at the end of the row. They thanked them and sat. Two angry-looking local boys across the aisle passed a bottle back and forth and sized them up. When one of the boys muttered something about Indians, Samuel and Charleyboy got up and moved into a different section.

Clowns infiltrated the aisles, some shaping animals out of long balloons and handing them to delighted children while others in shabby suits preyed on the stiffer patriarchs. Mimicking the patriarchs' pretensions, the clowns bent to brush dust off the empty seats beside them with enormous hankies pulled from up their sleeves, and spread their coattails before settling in with their noses held high, as if relieved at last to be insulated from the riff-raff. If their targets took it all in stride and laughed the clowns would shake their hands and move on, but if they stiffened and stared straight ahead, pretending that nothing was happening, the clowns would tease them mercilessly, much to the amusement of the crowd. One actually draped his arm around a woman in order to kiss her and was kicked into the aisle by her husband. The clown recovered and stood, pretending to be grievously offended.

While the clowns amused the audience, Samuel glanced up at the rigging above the ring. There were two swings attached to towers on opposite sides of the big top with ladders leading up to them. Three men at ring level were levelling the sawdust a final time with long rakes, and through a cavernous tunnel opposite the main entrance way, he could already see the shadowy outlines of costumed horses, performers in their sequins and feather headdresses, and more and more clowns of all types—character, whiteface and Auguste—gathering for their grand entrance like figures on the threshold of a dream.

'Ladies and gentlemen, boys and girls.' The same white-haired man they'd seen half clothed and doddering yesterday now strode into the ring dressed in a scarlet riding habit, a black top hat and leather boots that shone under the lights like dark glass. A riding crop nestled in the crook of one arm. 'We are proud to present,' he announced, with a wave of one arm toward the cave, 'the one, the only, the world famous, BALLANTYNE'S TRAVELLING CIRCUS.'

The band began to play as the horses and performers, the elephants, the animal trainer with the tiger on a chain, and the full charivari of jugglers and acrobats and clowns gambolled into the ring. Charleyboy elbowed Samuel in the ribs.

'I see her,' said Samuel. He grinned. 'Give me two weeks.'

Charleyboy scoffed. 'You won't get within ten yards, Romeo. You so much as look at her I'm going to find you in the river.'

The blind girl entered the big top on a white mare. She shared the saddle with a mustachioed man decked out like a Cossack. Samuel watched her as the mare cantered around the perimeter. Her hair was pulled tightly on top of her head and fastened with rhinestone barrettes. She was smiling and waving with her free hand.

'What do you think her act is?' said Charleyboy.

The troupe began to file out and the girl disappeared into the tunnel. Only the clowns remained. A sad-looking character with his hair standing straight up pelted his buddy with a rubber chicken, and with this slapstick the show began.

'She's a trick rider,' said Charleyboy, unequivocally. 'She's gotta be. Even blind she can feel a horse moving, right? In a pattern,' he added. 'The ring's only so big. Either that or she's the knife-thrower's model.' He grinned. 'She wouldn't see the knives.'

But the blind girl was neither of these. They had to wait until the grand finale to find out. When the last aerial act made its entrance they saw her again. As the safety net was raised the trapeze artists entered the ring hand in hand, perhaps to hide the fact that one among their number couldn't see. One of them was broken-nosed Lynch. Only after the ringmaster had announced them did he draw the blind girl aside, under a spotlight. He led her into the centre of the ring with great pomp and ceremony. 'And ladies and gentlemen,' he bellowed, 'this … beautiful young lady, this … monumentally brave and remarkable artist I stand beside, was born without the benefit of her eyesight. It is with the greatest pleasure that I present to you the star of Ballantyne's circus, the only blind trapeze artist in the world … MISS JOSEPHINE LYNCH.'

The audience erupted into an ovation of applause as the girl made her curtsey.

Samuel dropped his elbows on his knees and buried his head in his hands. Through a gap in his fingers he glanced up at Charleyboy, but Charleyboy wouldn't look at him. He just shook his head and stared tight-lipped at the ring.

Josephine and her two colleagues climbed the ladder to the platform high above the ring. Her brother, the catcher, scaled a hanging rope to the platform opposite using only his arms. The band gave a drum roll that lasted until the performers reached their positions. A hush fell over the crowd. Lynch was the first to swing out. He kicked forward at the apex of his arc and backwards into a pike above his platform. After this first swing he hung upside down with the trapeze behind his knees, his ankles wrapped securely around the ropes, and continued to build his swing using his torso alone.

The audience was so quiet they could hear Lynch's 'hep' calling his sister off her platform. The beauty of her swing was alone worth the price of admission. Her toes were pointed at the apex, her chin raised in her pike above the platform. She was graceful and proud and the lights fixed by the sequins of her leotard left a comet's tail of yellow in a sideways figure eight emblazoned against the dark roof of the tent. On her third swing she performed a simple, immaculate drop to her brother's hands and a pirouette return to her own trapeze. She landed back on her platform and acknowledged the applause.

Then she swung again. This time, a single layout and a double pirouette back to her trapeze. One of the other performers—a short, sinewy man—followed with a front somersault, then a layout with a full twist and on his return, at the lowest point of his swing, Lynch let go of the man's arms, dropping him into the net. The flyer fell in a swan dive, turning at the very last moment onto his back and bouncing high enough to regain his trapeze in mid-air. The audience went wild with applause.

But the finale was saved for Josephine. Her brother began his swing again. He called 'hep' and Josephine set out. She swung higher than before, and on the fifth swing, launched into a double twisting back somersault that left the crowd gasping.

When the show was over Samuel and Charleyboy sat waiting for the crowd to depart. They did not speak. They watched the same three men they'd seen earlier enter the ring with wooden bins and rakes and begin shovelling sawdust. Hired hands made their way between the bleachers gathering paper cups drained of lemonade and empty popcorn bags.

Assaulted by the smell of candyfloss and cigarettes and perfume, Samuel and Charleyboy passed, eventually, from the relative silence of the big top into the din of the Saturday night crowd. Barkers shouted like weary auctioneers, drawing rubes to their try-your-luck attractions. Candy butchers hawked pink lemonade and cheap taffy. Children screamed. The two boys drifted among the attractions until the crowd grew thin and things turned seedy. Circus folk began to outnumber the paying customers. Toothless bleachermen emboldened by drink leered at men's wives and young daughters. Girls in groups of three or four hurried past clutching one another. A few last rubes emerged from an unadorned slit at the back of the sideshow tent either greatly animated or oddly downcast, holding their hats stoically before them as if what they'd witnessed had given them reason to ponder the promise of a merciful God.

Weary from a poor night's sleep atop the train the previous evening, Samuel was all for turning in, but Charleyboy had other plans. He persuaded Samuel through the backlot to where the blacks had made camp. They had sequestered themselves a safe distance away and built a fire around which they squatted or sat and passed a gallon jug of whiskey. When Samuel entered the circle of light the blacks stiffened visibly. Above all they wanted no trouble. A couple of men got up to leave. 'Sit down,' said Justice. He looked hard at Samuel. 'You don't mean us no harm, do you?'

'No, sir.'

Justice nodded. The two men who had risen sat down again. Henry Sweet picked up a guitar. Sweet played his six-string wearing the neck of a bottle on the little finger of his left hand. The broken edge of it was worn smooth and round as if melted by fire, and the wailing tremolo it made as he slid it up the strings turned Samuel's skin to gooseflesh. The song Henry Sweet sang was nothing like the ragtime he was paid to play. It was a hard-driving blues so soaked with emotion the lyrics were all but lost. He kept time by thumping his foot on the ground and the solid, percussive style with which he plucked the strings made of that single instrument a drum orchestra in miniature and the slide a second voice.

He finished the first song and launched into another, one that his audience recognized: a blues about a man who had to keep moving on because a hellhound was hot on his trail. Sweet had laid aside the bottleneck and instead bent the strings with his fingertips. An eerie kind of atmosphere prevailed, as if the tune had beckoned from beyond the edges of the firelight some occult presence come to warm itself among them. In the vacuum that lingered after Sweet put down his guitar, one by one the men started to speak.

They traded stories of the first time they'd heard that song. Of the man they'd first heard sing it in Vicksburg, or Clarksdale, outside the very courthouse where he'd likely spent the night. One said the man carried a rabbit's foot around his neck and had sold his soul to the devil at a crossroads. That he didn't live long after that. Another said he spent his last days on earth blind and barking like a dog and at that juncture one old man spoke up. 'He didn't meet no devil,' said the old man. He pursed his lips and shook his head to emphasize his declaration. 'Ain't no devil where we all come from.'

The juniper piled upon the fire spat and crackled and the flames sawed sideways in the wind. Everyone waited for the old man to continue. After a short while, he said: 'The devil is the white man's invention. Fashioned in his own image. From some disposition within himself he can't stomach. When the old gods came with us from our first homes, there was one among them the white slavers feared as much as their own devil—for his ways were just as tricky—and that was Papa Legba, the deceiver.' The old man raised one crooked finger. 'But he was the one who also opened the way. And folk built his shrine at a crossroads.

'Man didn't sell his soul nowhere. He dug deep. Met Papa Legba.' He said it with great emphasis. 'Papa Legba gave his song the power.'

Somebody asked how this power was Legba's to give and the old man said that Legba was unique among the gods. That he was an advocate. He placed his hands palm-up either side of his hips in imitation of a set of scales. He raised one hand, then the other. 'He speaks to the gods on behalf of men and to men on behalf of the gods. He's neither here nor there.' He made a gesture with his hands like a magician making a coin disappear. 'He lives in-between,' the old man said. 'Neither god nor man but undeniably both and for that he suffers most of all. And so his home is at the crossroads. Between two places. Between heaven and earth.'

'But was not Jesus himself,' said another man, 'nailed at just such a place?'

The old man held out his hands and shrugged as if to say the answer was self-evident. In the firelight his face had taken on a tragic cast. 'White man's Papa Legba not the problem,' he answered. 'It is the *death* of that Legba in white men's hearts. In their churches. *That* is the problem.'

Then Justice spoke up. He told the story of two farmers who had once ploughed the land either side of a road. They were tolerable neighbours, but in secret they coveted one another's land. Then one day, as these two farmers were out working their fields, a very strange-looking man came walking down the road wearing a very strange-looking hat. One side of the hat was painted white, the other black, and the farmer who saw the white half called out to the other who saw only the black half, 'Hey, what did you make of that raggedy-man with the white hat?' The other farmer countered that the hat was black, not white. 'White,' said the first farmer. 'Black,' said the second, until the two came to blows. They killed each other on the road and Papa

Legba laughed out loud as he came back and stepped over their dead bodies.

The story caused the blacks, and Charleyboy, to fall about laughing. Fearing reprisal from the whites, Justice stood and made a motion with his hands like he was putting out a fire. The men contained themselves until they only grinned. The fire crackled and spat. Somebody lost his cool and laughter erupted again for a moment, but it soon subsided.

Samuel looked up and saw Justice smiling at him across the fire. The gallon jug of whiskey landed in Samuel's lap. He thanked the man beside him, raised the jug to his lips and drank. He passed the jug to Charleyboy and wiped his mouth with the back of his hand. When he looked up again, Justice had turned away.

Feeling alienated, Samuel told Charleyboy he was going to get some sleep.

Charleyboy finished his drink and passed the jug to the next man, who declined and quietly passed it on. 'All right,' he said. 'I'm going to stay.'

Samuel nodded. For a moment he doubted his decision. He looked at Justice, but Justice only stared into the coals. 'Don't get mugged stumbling home later,' Samuel said, as he got to his feet.

Blinded by the firelight, he stepped gingerly at first, until his eyes adjusted to the darkness. Soon lights from the village illuminated the grass. The first caravan he reached housed the family of foot jugglers. They lounged on the steps and on small wooden stools, smoking and listening to music amplified by a portable gramophone. The record was scratched and the song sounded both far away and unfamiliar, the rhythm incessant. The melody played fast and loose upon a multitude of violins so that it seemed to rise into the night like a cobra from a woven basket. The foot jugglers were Romanis and much used to the road. Their act and the great discipline it required was all that kept them loyal to the company. The women sat with their legs uncrossed like men. One of them caught Samuel's movement in the shadows. She watched him with her dark eyes and inhaled deeply on her cigarette. She blew smoke slowly from her nostrils and hissed and beckoned to him but he did not stop.

He passed deeper into the village, drawn again by violin music. This time live, and played solo. It was a melody both sweet and sad that reminded him of the ballads his mother used to sing. He walked on, past lanterns strung trailer to trailer. Past laundry pegged on lines. And so it was that Samuel found the blind girl, sitting alone on the steps to her trailer.

He scanned the lot for any sign of her brother, but aside from the Romanis on the outskirts and the blacks beyond the pale, the village was deserted, its occupants asleep.

He stopped and listened to her play. If she sensed his presence there she made no mention. She played her song to the end and as she put aside the fiddle he began, very quietly, to walk away.

'Who's there?' said the girl.

He kept going.

'Is that you, Dimitry?' she called out.

Samuel stopped. He turned. Her face was aimed directly at him, or a little to his left. 'Where did you learn that song?' he said.

Josephine stiffened. She adjusted her gaze.

'I've heard it before.'

'Who are you?'

'An admirer.'

'With no name?'

'Samuel Hewitt.'

'It is very impolite, Samuel Hewitt, to not announce yourself,' said Josephine.

'Forgive me, Miss,' said Samuel, 'but the rules say I can't talk to you.'

Josephine scoffed. 'The rules,' she said dismissively. She relaxed against the jamb. 'Come closer.'

Samuel stepped into the light. Through the open door he could see behind into the trailer she shared with her girlfriend. There were clothes strewn everywhere. A dresser cluttered with makeup and small, oddly shaped bottles of perfume. From wires strung under the ceiling, the girls had hung their costumes out to dry.

'Do you work with us?'

'I hope to.'

'You've met Helena then.'

'You mean the skipper?'

'Mmhmm. Let me guess. You were told not to talk to the sideshow. You mustn't talk to the performers, and you sure as hell don't mix with negroes,' she drawled, mimicking Helena's southern accent.

Samuel smiled and nodded. Then, remembering that she could not see, he said, 'Yes. More or less.'

'They're unjust, of course,' said Josephine, '*the rules*. Especially that last. They pay the black men less than everybody else. The others know it and fear for their jobs. Personally, I don't see colour.'

'Me neither,' said Samuel.

Josephine smiled. 'That was a joke,' she said. She tilted her head to one side. 'That was you, wasn't it? Down by the lake yesterday.'

'How do you know?'

'You make an impression.'

'Miss?'

Josephine laughed. 'Everybody has a signature,' she said. 'A presence they can't help but project. I can feel it.'

'What did you feel?'

'Sincerity. Come closer,' said Josephine.

Samuel glanced left and right, then stepped forward. It was disorienting staring into the twin shifting lenses of her dark eyes. 'So what's it like,' he blurted, 'you know—'

'Being blind?' said Josephine flatly. 'Being a trapeze artist? Being both at once?'

'You've been asked that before.'

'A thousand times. In every town we pass through. By every reporter Helena drags me along to talk to. I'm like a monkey on a chain,' she declared.

'I'm sorry.'

'Sorry for asking, or sorry for me?'

'For both.'

Josephine shrugged it off. 'We're all part of the sideshow here, Samuel Hewitt. Only the "freaks" make a meal of it.'

'The sideshow isn't beautiful, though,' said Samuel.

Josephine blushed.

'Red,' said Samuel. 'The colour of your cheeks. They're red.'

'Sit down,' Josephine said.

Josephine began to speak of her childhood, of growing up blind though born into the circus where a handicap of some kind was like a badge of membership. 'Popov?' she said, 'the tightrope walker? Is petrified of heights.' She laughed. 'Almost everybody drinks or suffers some ... mysterious illness that tethers them to their trailer for days. Ballantyne himself is the worst.'

Samuel asked her if she were ever afraid of getting hurt and she said at first, as a young girl, she had been, but her desire to fly had been stronger. 'Now that I've been practising for twelve years or so my desires have ... evolved,' she explained. 'In more ways than one. What I love most about trapeze, though,' she said, 'isn't the trick, but the swing. At the highest point of each upward motion there's a moment of weightlessness where time stands still. It's a feeling I associate with silence because the rush of air past my ears simply stops. Falling is also more fun than being caught,' she said. 'You know, I think it's because I care so little for the success of each trick that I always complete it?

'Besides, the trapeze is an exercise in timing,' she continued. 'And trust, not magic. It's a gimmick that I happen to be blind,' she said, dismissively. 'Everybody's blind when they're upside down. The pattern of the performance is set in stone. I'm more afraid of walking alone to the outhouse because it's never in the same place, unlike the hands that clasp my wrists in mid-air.'

'You mean your brother.'

'Yes. My brother.'

'He doesn't like me very much.'

'I'm not surprised.'

'Why not?'

'Because he's a bully. He's threatened by anyone with a shred of self-respect. Was it you who broke his nose?'

Samuel nodded. 'Yep.'

'Well,' said Josephine. 'I have no doubt he had it coming. Helena tore a strip off him, too. He put our performance at risk. Listen,' she said, 'you want to understand the trapeze, I'll show you.' She stood up. 'Come on.'

She found his shirtsleeve, then his forearm. She grasped his hand. He stood up.

'Close your eyes,' she said. She descended the steps and pulled him toward her. 'Don't open them.'

She turned him around to face the light and she let go of his hand and walked behind him. She placed her palms on his shoulders. He felt her move backwards until her arms must have been straight. Then she wasn't touching him at all.

'Are they closed?'

'Yes.'

'When I say "hep", I want you to fall backwards. Like a plank. With your hands by your sides.'

'But I—'

'I will catch you.'

'I'm heavy.'

'I am strong.'

He stood there for some time. His heart was racing. She did not speak right away and the longer she was silent the harder it was to believe she was still there. After a while, she said 'hep' and he took a deep breath and fell backwards. Hands by his sides.

He was almost horizontal when he felt her hands support his shoulders, and she lowered him gently the last two feet, cradling his head between her forearms. He didn't open his eyes. He could feel her face close to his, her breath on the bridge of his nose. He lay there pillowed by her arms until he felt her withdraw them and lower his head slowly to the ground. His mind flooded with memories of home: of his father declaiming the classics by firelight; of lying on that tartan blanket watching dragonflies in the sky; his father's laughter; his mother's laughter; her contralto as she sang her childhood ballads.

After a while, Samuel sat up. Josephine had returned to the steps unaided. She sat haloed by the light inside. 'Have you never yielded, Samuel Hewitt?' she said.

Samuel wiped the tears from his eyes. He was at a loss for words. He stood up and looked at her. 'So—so what now?' he stammered.

The girl gave a radiant smile. 'Is this not enough?' she said.

At first Samuel didn't answer. He laughed, looking into the blind girl's face. 'Yeah,' he said. 'Yes, it is. It's really something.'

Charleyboy was already asleep when Samuel returned to the tiger's cage. He slept no more than four hours before the sound of men and engines woke them both. Horses began to draw tent pegs from the hard-packed ground, and, trailing stakes and guy-ropes, the big top collapsed in a medusa of dust and debris. They crawled out from under the tiger's cage and stood yawning. The sun was up behind the Monashees, but the valley still lay in shadow.

Charleyboy was never at his best in the mornings, especially not hungover. Samuel slapped him on the back and wished him a boisterous good day.

'Why are you so damn cheerful?' said Charleyboy. He looked genuinely distressed. 'We barely slept. They're packing up already?' Charleyboy turned and looked at the tiger. 'Why are they packing up already?' The great cat lay sprawled among a scattering of bones and hay, still fast asleep. 'I'm with you, buddy,' he said.

'You'd better believe it.'

'I was talking to the cat,' said Charleyboy.

They found Pilinszky and the skipper in conversation with two detectives in grey suits. There were three squad cars parked at the edge of the village. Uniformed cops patrolled the lot. The air was thick with hostility. The cops watched the hammergang and the canvasmen, in particular the hammergang, who looked coiled and tense, ready to run.

After a while, the two suits closed their notepads and left. The skipper disappeared into the village and Pilinszky was left scratching his head. Samuel and Charleyboy approached him.

'Mr Pilinszky,' said Samuel. 'We were told to report to you this morning.'

Pilinszky looked at them without really seeing them. He shook his head and looked after the squad cars as they pulled out.

'Sir,' said Samuel.

'Thirteen-year-old girl was raped last night,' he said. 'Thirteen years old. What do you make of that?'

'I don't know, sir,' said Samuel.

'Well, there's hell to pay,' he said. Pilinszky took off his hat and looked into the crown of it. 'Two of our guys don't show up this morning.' He put his hat back on. 'Which happens all the time. Drifter joins us in Wyoming only to move on in Spokane. But the police, well, they put two and two together, don't they.' He looked at them again. 'Figured it must have been niggers until I told them they was all present and accounted for. They didn't like that. If it's white men, then it must be a couple of the ex-cons we do employ from time to time. But it never once occurs to the cops, not once, that just as likely it's a couple of good ol' local boys, some fat cat's son drunk enough to reason he's entitled.' He shook his head again and reached inside his jacket pocket for a pack of cigarettes. He shucked one out of the pack and lit it. 'For all I know it was you two.'

'No, sir,' said Charleyboy. 'Wasn't us.'

Pilinszky didn't look convinced. He exhaled a long plume of blue smoke. 'Either way,' he said, 'we run a skeleton crew and now we're two men short. You boys got yourself jobs.'

'Yes, sir.'

'She knew that too,' he said. He took another long drag.

'Sir?'

'Never mind. You report to Chauncey over there.'

'Yes, sir,' they said.

'We eat breakfast when the tent's rolled,' said Pilinszky. 'You don't pull your weight, you're off the train. You don't talk to the freaks. You sure as hell don't talk to the performers.'

'The skipper told us already,' said Samuel.

'And you,' he said, jutting his chin at Samuel, 'quit sitting with the niggers.'

Samuel nodded.

'Go on, then.'

'Yes, sir.'

* * *

They worked beside two veterans of the circus and learned how to roll and pack the canvas. Chauncey had been with Ballantyne's since the beginning, and with Barnum and Bailey before that. Accustomed to young men who worked only for a season he was unforthcoming, showing them no more than they needed just to get the job done, saying even less.

At breakfast, they sat on overturned boxes with their plates on their knees—by themselves outside the fly tent so as not to run afoul of anyone. They talked of the girl who had been raped. The news had spread through the company and there was little laughter.

Before they finished, the skipper called all to attention. She stood beside the giant with one hand on his shoulder, as if for support. 'Our advance man has returned from the next town west,' she began. 'I regret to say we are not welcome there. Bad news travels fast. No matter who actually committed this crime, it is we who have inherited the blame.'

The giant stared down at the table. Nobody spoke. Some of the performers shook their heads gravely.

'Every tribe has its scapegoat,' she continued. 'I don't need to remind you that, among the more … settled, the traveller engenders little trust. However unjust that may be. At any rate,' she continued, 'borders have a way of diluting bad news. We shall be heading back south, into the fifty-one states,' she concluded. A small ovation rose from the crowd.

By noon the tents were packed and the first of the trucks rolled out. Coloured were not permitted on the bus, so Charleyboy sat with the hammer-gang atop the canvas wagon. The whites rode inside, in the shade, but Samuel thought they were the worse for it. The unobstructed view would have been worth the sunburn.

The road south hugged the lake and the rail tracks for some time before climbing the valley side through stands of scattered ponderosa. Through the window, Samuel could see clear to Penticton. Okanagan Lake shone iridescent blue, and the valley became a patchwork of irrigated orchards that rose verdant and incongruous from those stony, sage-covered slopes like desert oases. The canvas wagon crested the hill and began its descent toward the breadbaskets of Penticton and Naramata on the eastern shore. They passed roadside fruit stalls piled high with golden pyramids of peaches and open trays of glossy red and black cherries at which, before long, the skipper demanded they halt and refresh themselves.

Samuel found Charleyboy among the crowd. They sat with their backs to a tree and spat cherry stones into the dust. Samuel scanned the company for Josephine but she was nowhere to be seen. When Pilinszky ordered everyone back onto their vehicles, Samuel huddled with the hammergang and climbed with Charleyboy on top of the canvas wagon. He hid in a corner until the trucks rolled out.

The black men spoke of Georgia peaches. They spoke of cotton fields. They told stories of drinking corn whiskey peddled in juke joints on a Saturday night and the barrelhouse piano they'd heard in Helena or in East Monroe. One man among the windjammers, the drummer, had played with Bessie Smith in Memphis for the 1929 winter season, and another boasted of travelling the delta north to south in the company of Son House. Justice took his ease among the parcels of canvas roped to the top of the truck. He smiled when the other men laughed and ate his peach very slowly. Samuel caught Justice studying him with an inscrutable gaze. He decided to return the stare but Justice only grinned, flashing his large white teeth as he bit into his peach.

The circus made camp that evening at Osoyoos, at the south end of the lake, and the two boys walked up into the foothills as the cooks began assembling the kitchen. The sun was about down over the western rim of the valley, sinking through reefs of red cloud. They left the blue shadow of the valley floor and climbed into the light. They sat silently among the black sage and rabbitbrush on rocks warmed by the sun, looking off toward the south, toward America.

'I'm going to stay out of his way, Charleyboy.'

'By riding with us? You know that'll piss him off more. You heard Pilinszky.'

They looked down at the encampment. The performers with their ramshackle trailers were beginning to arrive. Their rigs lurched and wobbled off the blacktop over the stony ground to the edge of the lake where their drivers parked them side by side, chocked the wheels and threw open the doors.

'I got a bad feeling,' said Charleyboy. 'Like this whole thing, all these people, they're eating dinner on the edge of a cliff and they don't know the cliff is collapsing. One wrong move—'

'I'll stop sitting with you.'

'We can still eat together,' said Charleyboy. 'Like we did at breakfast. But I don't think you should ride with us.'

Samuel picked up a stone he found beside his boot and hefted it in one hand. 'Charleyboy, there's something I've got to tell you.'

'I can't wait.'

'I ran into that blind girl last night.'

'You spoke to her?'

'Yeah.'

Charleyboy shook his head. 'First day of work and you're fixing to get fired. Or killed.'

Samuel threw the rock. It made an arc over the valley and clattered among the rocky slopes below. The last of the sun's rays crawled toward them up the foothills. Already smoke was rising from the cook fire.

'I think she wants out,' he said. 'Of the circus. She's sick of being put on display.'

'So what?'

'So they're using her.'

'That's none of your business. What are you gonna do, Gary Cooper, rescue her? Ride off into the sunset together?' Charleyboy shook his head and looked away. The wind had quit and they began to hear laughter from the encampment. Accordion music. The splash of people playing in the lake. 'You think you're the solution, Sam, but you're not. You're the problem.'

Samuel pushed down the corners of his mouth. He bent and picked up another rock and threw it.

Charleyboy let out one long breath. 'Quit trying to be a hero,' he said. 'Just follow the rules, why don't you. For once.'

'The rules are unjust,' Samuel said. He stood and brushed the dust violently from the seat of his jeans. 'Doing nothing is the same as agreeing with them.'

Charleyboy looked at him like he'd never seen him before. 'I don't even know what that means,' he said.

When they returned to camp, Pilinszky pointed at Samuel and beckoned him over.

'What's going on, Sam?'

'I don't know.'

The skipper whispered something in Pilinszky's ear. Pilinszky inclined his head and nodded. Then he met the boys halfway. 'Come with me,' he said to Samuel, without chagrin. 'Just you.' He mollified Charleyboy with an easy-going smile. 'It's all right, son. He'll come back in one piece.'

Pilinszky escorted Samuel to a trailer parked in the shade of a cottonwood, a short distance from the other trailers. It was an old-fashioned Gypsy caravan. The wheels had been removed and the decorated sidewalls of the wagon, once painted garish red and gold, were now faded, the paint flaking in places.

Pilinszky knocked on the back doors.

'Come in,' said Helena.

Pilinszky swung the doors outward and gestured for Samuel to enter. Samuel climbed the wooden steps.

The inside of the caravan was dark, and it took his eyes some time to adjust. It was much larger inside than seemed possible. At the far end he could see the edges of a bed behind a red velvet curtain. Armoires of polished wood lined one wall and above them hung framed photographs of circus folk, some so old as to be sepia tinted. Every face antique looking, larger than life. On the opposite wall hung a heavy, gilt-edged mirror and two sconce lamps shaped like lilies made of brass and smoked glass.

The skipper sat behind a small leather-topped table in front of which she'd placed a wooden chair. 'Please,' she said, gesturing for him to sit. A white tomcat leapt onto the chair.

'Don't mind the cat,' said Helena.

Samuel gently picked up the tomcat and placed him on the floor. When Samuel settled into the chair, the cat jumped into his lap and purred.

Helena gestured to a package on the table wrapped in black silk. 'May I read your fortune?'

'Ma'am?'

She unwrapped the silk package.

'While I tell you a story,' she said, removing from a small wooden box a deck of cards. 'A story that may save your life.' She pushed the deck across the table. 'The deck is Marseillaise,' she said. 'Older than I am.'

'We're playing a game?'

The skipper smiled. 'Yes. But we are not yet acquainted with the stakes.' She gestured at the deck. 'Please,' she said. 'Cut the cards.'

Samuel reached across the table and with one hand removed roughly half the cards. He laid them aside and placed the remaining half on top of them.

The skipper leaned forward. She picked up the deck. Slowly she laid out seven cards, face down, in the shape of a horseshoe. She laid the remaining cards aside and leaned back. 'Once upon a time,' she began, 'there was a girl. Her name was Iris. She was unusually talented, this girl. From a very young age she displayed ability and acumen well beyond her years. She was a dancer. A fabulous acrobat. She was born into the circus, as her mother and father before her, and with the circus she would remain.'

The skipper reached and turned over the first card. Pictured on it was a woman, a queen, seated on a throne holding a sceptre in one hand and a large golden cup in the other. Her robes were red and blue. Written across the bottom of the card in French were the words 'Reyne de coupe'. The skipper made no comment on the card. She looked at Samuel. She reached and turned over the next one. The picture was not of a person but of five golden coins arranged symmetrically and decorated, or separated, by vines, like the scrollwork of an illuminated manuscript. It appeared to Samuel to be upside down, for the 'five' in roman numerals was printed on the bottom of the card, closest to the skipper.

Helena continued her story. 'This girl grew up to become a star. A trapeze artist at the age of thirteen. A genius. She toured with the company all over the United States.'

'When do I get to play?' said Samuel, but the skipper only smiled. She turned over the third card. The picture was of an old man in dark blue robes holding aloft a glass lantern. He carried a staff. His robe was hooded but his head was uncovered. Again the card seemed to be upside down, from Samuel's point of view, because written across the bottom, closer to the Skipper, were the words 'L'hermite'.

The skipper leaned back in her seat. She formed a bridge with her fingertips upon which to rest her chin, her elbows on the armrests of the chair. 'In Michigan Iris met a man. She was fifteen years old. He was older. A towner. She fell in love.' She leaned forward and turned over the fourth card. It was seven swords. The number was facing the skipper. It appeared to perplex her. She considered the card for some time, then went on: 'This man toured the country with us. With Iris. He made no overtures of marriage, nor did he ask her to run away with him. He understood, perhaps, that without her family Iris would not make it. Would not know what to do with her life. How to act in the world outside the circus.' The cat rubbed its head against Samuel's belly. He stroked it behind the ears. 'I'm not talking of happiness here,' said the skipper. 'As you may have discovered already, the circus is a most melancholy place. But if Iris had left with him she would have perished,' she said, categorically. She turned over the fifth card. On this one were pictured three swords, the number this time facing Samuel. 'Which, alas,' continued the skipper, 'she did anyway, because this man, after a year and a half, went back to his family in Michigan. Back to the wife and child he'd left behind.' She cocked her head at Samuel. 'And what do you think happened next?'

Samuel did not answer. He stopped stroking the cat.

'Poor Iris. Her heart was broken. And so, one night, when she was high up on the platform, she thought she saw this man in the crowd. She had to perform, but she was … distracted.' The skipper turned over the sixth card. The picture was of another woman, seated similarly to the queen of the first card, crowned, but in robes more ecclesiastical in character. In her lap she held a book and behind her was a veil, or tapestry, hanging from the wall. The image was reversed, from the skipper's point of view. Written across the bottom were the words 'La Papesse'.

As if she had known what it would be, Helena did not even glance at the card. She kept her eyes fixed on Samuel. 'In brief'—she held out her hands—'she fell. Awkwardly.' Helena leaned back. 'A safety net is not a guarantee. She died.' She glanced at the photographs lining the wall. 'But Iris left behind two children.' Helena watched him. 'Fraternal twins. Perhaps you have put two and two together. Josephine and Oscar Lynch were raised by all of us, for better or worse. Their grandparents departed seven years ago, within weeks of one another. Being blind, Josephine required more than the usual care and attention. Her twin, relegated to second fiddle, ran amok.' Helena watched him. 'What do you intend to do?'

'She can make up her own mind,' said Samuel.

'She is seventeen years old.'

The cat jumped off Samuel's lap. 'That's old enough to choose.'

'She has never known anything else.'

'You just want to control her because she's the main attraction. Without her this whole thing would fold.'

The skipper sat back in her seat. She seemed to have anticipated his response. 'You give me far too much credit,' she said. She gestured at the cards upon the table. 'Our intentions are often well beyond our understanding. As a clown I once knew used to say, "Your life is none of your business."' She smiled, then leaned and turned over the final card. The picture was of a single large decorated goblet. The number 'one' was facing him. The skipper looked at the card and she looked at Samuel. Then she got up from her chair. Samuel watched her closely, but her expression was inscrutable. She held out her hand. 'I wish you luck, Samuel Hewitt,' she said.

Samuel stood. He looked down at the cards and he looked at the skipper. 'They're just pictures,' he said.

'Indeed,' said Helena.

'She wants me to save her.'

'She might want you to try.'

'And what if I do?'

'Oh, you will,' said Helena. 'What is not clear, however, is whether or not she will go with you.'

'She doesn't belong here.'

Helena looked at him wearily, like she might at a petulant child. 'Tell me then, Samuel. Where does she belong? With you? Out there?' She gestured beyond the doors to her vardo. 'You think you're in love but you're not. You're more like Oscar than you know. Two hotheaded boys with too much to prove. You have no idea who she is, or what she wants. You don't even know who *you* are,' she said.

CHAPTER TWELVE

'Ladies and gentlemen, boys and girls, we hope you have enjoyed this afternoon's very special matinee performance. And now, if you will please put your hands together once again for the daring, the delightful, the dangerous, Ballantyne's Travelling Circus.'

The ringmaster doffed his hat and bowed deeply as the clowns gambolled past him into the ring. He straightened, replaced his hat and, with a flourish of his coattails, turned swiftly on his heels and strode imperiously toward the jostle of horses and performers and other animals and their handlers awaiting their turn in the wings. They made way like the parting of a glittering, sinewy sea, and he stepped from under the shade of the canvas into the heat of the day, past the ticket booth and the candy butchers and the sideshow tent all the way to the main road where he turned west and walked toward the sun.

They had pitched the big top along the Siuslaw River in a farmer's field between Florence and North Bend, Oregon, about two miles from the coast. The ringmaster followed the river all the way to the dunes, sweating dark crimson stains beneath the armpits of his riding habit and soaking the inside of his hat. He unbuttoned his habit and opened his shirt but it was no use. When he climbed to the top of the first dune and saw the ocean crashing half a mile away he began to hurry, like a lusty swain, throwing off his clothes piece by piece leaving a trail of discarded livery behind him in the sand.

By the time he reached the first line of foam retreating down the beach he wore nothing but his cotton shorts and top hat. He stood looking at the breakers for a long time, the cold sand giving way beneath his feet, so still a handful of sandpipers landed within arm's reach, pecked at the wet sand when a wave withdrew and took off *en masse* before the hem of the next robe of foam reached them. There was nothing before him but water and light. No boat. No other bird. Just a heaving mass of blue and white all the way to the horizon, where a thin ribbon of mist separated sea and blue sky. When he was a young man, travelling the counties of England as a pantomime actor, his favourite places to perform were the seaside resorts—Blackpool, Brighton, Weston-super-Mare—and not for the guaranteed crowds, but for the glory of the beaches: the shingles of Chesil, the golden sand and windy cliffs of Bournemouth. In Bournemouth, when the wind was strong, the sand would blow so far inland the path that wound down through the Alum Chine would drift and ripple like a desert highway. He remembered swimming all day long when the sun shone, diving through the breakers and bodysurfing back to the beach. Afterwards, collapsing on a towel, he would sleep and never dream at all. What on earth had happened to that innocence? That simplicity?

He extracted his ankles from the sand and stumbled forwards with his eyes closed, surrendering everything but the will to put one foot before the other. He waded into water past his knees, past his thighs, flinched when the water shrank his balls, but pushed on. In the end, it was the icy shock of the Humboldt Current crashing into his belly and chest that stopped him. He gasped. His eyes opened. Standing beside him in the breakers he saw a blond-haired boy.

Since Helena had read his fortune—seven days ago now—Samuel had spoken with Josephine only twice. Angela, Josephine's roommate, kept a close eye on her, and if it weren't for Angela turning the occasional trick, Samuel would never have found Josephine alone. Both times they had spoken in secret, stealing away from the village under cover of darkness to hide in an orchard or behind a farmer's barn to laugh and trade stories, their burgeoning courtship all the sweeter for the larceny of time, and for the transgression.

On the second night, Samuel told her about his mother and father, about Beckinsale and the stallion he and Charleyboy had stolen. He told her about Sheldrake and Coltrane and confessed how killing a man, even by accident, had done more than end his innocence; he felt *heavy*, he said—there was no other word for it—and he now found far less humour in the world. Josephine told him, in turn, how her brother had murdered a man in Waco, Texas. A black man. Because Oscar was a performer, however, and important to the survival of the circus, the tribe had closed ranks and hidden him. She told Samuel that her brother was dangerous, unstable, and she made Samuel promise not to provoke him.

Samuel didn't tell Charleyboy he'd been seeing her. Charleyboy had made friends with the grooms, who respected him for his knowledge of horses. One of the riders had even shown him a trick or two. Charleyboy told Samuel he might get promoted.

During the daytime he and Charleyboy ate together, just the two of them, on overturned buckets among the menagerie wagons, but Samuel, unlike his friend, had become an outsider among outsiders, travelling with the other whites but not otherwise seeking their company.

Lynch travelled in a different, more comfortable bus. Their paths rarely crossed. And if Samuel did see him coming, he turned and walked the other way.

All of which was why the ringmaster, on Florence Beach, did not die that day. Sitting beneath a tree across the road from the encampment keeping his own company, and out of Lynch's way, Samuel was the only one to notice the ringmaster leave the lot. He observed in Ballantyne's stride a purpose reserved only for his role under the big top but never, so far as Samuel could tell, for when the show was over. Samuel followed him at a discreet distance, gathering the trail of discarded clothing and reaching the beach just as the ringmaster walked into the waves. Discarding his own shirt and jeans and paperboy's hat, until he was all but naked himself, he waded out to watch over the old man. Familiar with the privacy—the eccentricity—of grief, Samuel knew better than to speak. He had shadowed his father the same way many times.

The water was very cold. Samuel was shorter than Ballantyne, and the waves lifted Samuel off the sand. They stood together for a while in silence. Seagulls careened above them in the wind, their cries all but drowned out by the surf.

After a while, the ringmaster turned to Samuel. 'Are you Death?' he shouted, as a wave collapsed about Samuel's ears. It knocked Samuel underwater, and when his feet again touched the sand, he stood up to find himself five paces behind. He wiped the salt out of his eyes and fought to stand beside the old man.

The ringmaster looked out at the waves. 'Because if you are,' he continued, 'it appears I'm not ready. Not yet.' He took off his hat. He handed it to Samuel. 'Do you know the story of King Canute? Some say it's apocryphal but they're missing the point. All history is fiction anyway. Canute hung his crown off a cross when it became clear that even he, a mighty king, could not hold back the tide. I don't mean to be a blowhard. God knows I'm no philosopher. It just seems to me that such is the value of all our achievements.' He looked at Samuel. 'Can I persuade you to hold your horses?'

'I'm not Death, Mr Ballantyne,' shouted Samuel. 'But unless you'd like to meet him for real, we'd better get out of the cold.'

The ringmaster nodded, pinched his nose between thumb and forefinger and ducked under the waves. He erupted from the surf shaking his head. He wiped the salt from his eyes and let out one short laugh. Then he took back his hat, and the hand Samuel offered, and together they struggled out of the surf.

When they made it past the reach of the waves they sat down in the sand. Samuel offered the ringmaster a flask of water. The ringmaster accepted with a nod, unscrewed the cap and drank. Handing back the flask, he noticed the scar on the boy's lip, his missing tooth, the chain and silver disc he wore around his neck. 'What's your name?' he said.

'Samuel, sir. Samuel Hewitt.'

'You've been in the wars, I see.'

Samuel pursed his lips and nodded. He looked out at the breakers. 'I don't believe the wars can be avoided,' he said.

'Quite so. We like violence, don't we? Our species.' The ringmaster reached for the flask again and drank. 'I've always thought there was no hope for us.'

'Have you changed your mind?'

'No. But that's no reason to go to hell in a hand basket.' The ringmaster handed back the flask. 'I've seen you around,' he said. 'You and your Indian friend. You've been mixing with the black men. Why is that?'

'Because I don't see why we can't sit together,' said Samuel.

'You've not made too many friends then.'

'No.'

'Nor been warmly embraced by the hammergang, I would imagine. You can't blame them for that, you know.'

They were silent for some time. The wind was still very strong. The tide was coming in, and it obliged them to rise and move farther up the beach.

'What is it you do for us?' said the ringmaster, sitting heavily back on the sand.

'I pack the canvas.'

'You're Chauncey's man.'

'Yes.'

'We'll have to change that.'

'Sir?'

'Crawford Chauncey's one of the worst. Hails from a family of slavers. Do you like animals?'

'Sure.'

'Good. Then you'll work for Van Winkle. He's a reasonable man. The menagerie crew keeps separate quarters. You'll be safer there. You should eat with them as well.'

'What about my friend Charleyboy?'

'Has he made the same enemies?'

Samuel seized a handful of sand and watched it run through his fingers. He wiped his hand against his thigh. An enormous wave flung foam right up to their ankles and Samuel didn't answer until the foam withdrew. 'No,' Samuel said. 'He fits in fine with the hammergang. It's just me. I'm the one making enemies.'

The ringmaster searched the beach for his clothes.

'I gathered them,' said Samuel. 'They're over there.' He pointed behind where they sat to the base of a dune.

'Good lad,' said the ringmaster. 'Though it wouldn't be the first time I've been found in my birthday suit.' He smiled. 'I'm quite the liability, it seems.' He stretched his back and turned his arms over a few times. 'Don't grow old,' he said at length. 'There's no purchase in it.'

'Ripeness is all,' offered Samuel. 'As my father would say.'

Ballantyne sneezed. He sneezed again and wiped his hand on his shorts. 'Every boy begins his life a hero,' said Ballantyne. 'Aside from a few rare exceptions, we all end up as villains or fools. Or both,' he added. 'What's that icon you wear?'

'Jude. My father gave it to me.'

Ballantyne smiled. 'He sounds like a wise man, your father.'

'He fought in the war,' said Samuel. 'I don't think he ever came back though.'

'None of them really did. Those who survived became mere shells of men, still fighting in their minds, their memories. It was like the Dark Ages in England. No more trust. I believe it takes more than one generation to overcome that.' Ballantyne glanced at Samuel. 'I don't suppose he talks about it.'

'No.'

Ballantyne nodded. 'Well,' he said, 'perhaps there are some horrors for which words are not adequate.'

'Can I ask you something? This whole notion that a lad like me, a labourer, can't talk to a performer, why is that so set in stone?'

'Why? Who have you fallen for?'

But Samuel only shook his head and wouldn't tell him.

'Oh dear,' said the ringmaster. 'You are in trouble, aren't you?'

'I don't understand it.'

'Well, get used to that.' Ballantyne studied him again. 'So it's you,' he said. 'The suitor.'

'Sir?'

'Never mind.' He smiled. 'Josephine is not a damsel in distress,' he said. 'Far from it. You wouldn't be the first to mistake her blindness for a handicap. But I'll tell you what,' said Ballantyne, 'I'm not going to stand in your way. My daughter might, but I won't. I'm done worrying. If this whole thing folds, so what. Have at her, Samuel Hewitt,' he said.

Samuel reached for the canteen and drank. 'I never said it was Josephine,' he muttered, but the ringmaster only laughed. He struggled to his feet and smoothed the hair back from his forehead. 'Once more unto the breach, dear friends,' he hammed. 'Once more.'

'You're gonna do what?'

'Sweep up elephant shit, I don't know. But it means I bunk with the menagerie crew.'

'A promotion,' said Charleyboy.

Samuel had taken his place in line beside Charleyboy. They spoke quietly and stared straight ahead. 'The hammergang likes you,' said Samuel. 'They've accepted you.'

'They've accepted you, too.'

'They'll never accept me, Charleyboy, not like you.'

They shuffled slowly forward.

'Okay,' said Charleyboy, after a while. 'It's an opportunity for you.'

'I'll still come to your campfire.'

Lynch was watching them. 'Yonder's your buddy,' said Charleyboy.

'I see him.'

They took their plates and cutlery and the cook spooned beans and some kind of stewed meat onto their plates. 'Pass me one of those scones,' said Samuel.

'Biscuits,' said Charleyboy. 'They're called biscuits.'

Samuel went to sit with the menagerie crew but one by one they got up and left. Only Van Winkle—a tall man with a handlebar moustache—stayed behind. He sat at the other end of the table, as far away from Samuel as possible. Samuel began to eat. The meat was tough and stringy and took a long time to chew. Van Winkle was likewise occupied. Neither spoke.

Samuel looked up from his plate. Lynch and his cronies were gathered just under the awning, two tables away. They ate in silence with their eyes fixed on their plates. Two tables behind Samuel sat the freaks. Most of them had eaten already and now had fallen into animated conversation. Occasionally they glanced at him, then leaned in to continue talking. Beyond them sat the performers on their raised platforms, including one entire table that seemed very downcast to a man. Samuel asked Van Winkle who they were. Van Winkle looked up briefly from his meal and said, 'Clowns,' and then went on eating.

'Why did those men get up and leave?' said Samuel quietly.

Van Winkle looked at Samuel for the first time. He sucked his teeth. 'It took them three years to sit at this table,' he said. 'You've done it in under three weeks.'

'The ringmaster arranged it,' said Samuel.

'Exactly,' said Van Winkle. He stood up and gathered his plate and headed for the dish pit.

When Samuel was done he waited for Charleyboy and the hammergang to get up. He rose with them, and it was only the presence of Justice, who rose last and stood at the back of the dish-pit line, that stopped Lynch from attacking Samuel again.

'I see you, boy,' said Lynch. 'This here nigger won't always have your back.'

Samuel bit his lip. The cooks and dishwashers became silent. The sideshow turned to watch.

Justice turned and drilled Lynch with a stare. Lynch took a step back. Then he tried to recover. 'A blade cuts through black hide as easily as white, nigger,' said Lynch.

Justice eyed him a while longer, then turned back around.

'That's right,' said Lynch. 'You be a good boy, now.'

The hammergang moved off as one with Samuel sticking close. It was only when they made it back to their camp that Charleyboy drew Samuel aside.

'You need to get the hell out of here,' said Charleyboy.

'Not yet.'

Charleyboy squinted. 'Don't tell me it's the girl. I heard you been see-ing her.'

'It's not the girl.'

Charleyboy raised his eyebrows.

'It's not *only* the girl.'

'Aw, brother, after everything?'

'We're still in this together, Charleyboy.'

'That's what I'm afraid of.' Charleyboy gestured at the hammergang. 'That's what *they're* afraid of, too.'

Samuel couldn't meet his eyes. 'I know what I'm doing.'

Charleyboy shook his head. He looked at Samuel askance. 'You can't mean you want to take her with you.'

Samuel didn't answer.

'Aw.' Charleyboy turned away.

'She's a meal ticket for these people. Nothing more. She's trapped.'

'So you keep saying.'

'I think she'll come with us.'

'Have you asked her?'

At first Samuel didn't answer. 'She'll come with me,' he said after a while.

Charleyboy laughed. 'You know who you sound like, don't you? Daniel goddamn Beckinsale. You can't just take whatever you want.'

'It's not even close to the same thing, Charleyboy.'

'Oh no?'

'No. She's not married, for one.'

'Would it matter?'

'It's not the same,' said Samuel.

Charleyboy raised his hands in a gesture of surrender and walked away, shaking his head, as if he'd finally witnessed something to challenge his grip on the character of a man.

Before that evening's performance, and alone in his trailer, the ringmaster rose purposefully from his armchair and slipped his scarlet jacket off its hanger. He put it on, stepping before his full-length mirror to fasten the buttons and adjust his cravat. He pinned to his lapel the white paper carnation he favoured and donned his top hat. In the yellow light of the table lamp the polished buttons shone like gold florins, the boots like black glass. Within the gilded plaster scrollwork of the mirror's frame, white gloves in hand, he looked every inch the ringmaster, he thought. Every inch the fool.

Outside the sound of horses, the laughter of equestriennes. Performers of all kinds made their way among the caravans to the big top, gossiping in foreign tongues. The ringmaster stepped away from the mirror and flung open the doors. He descended the steps of his caravan and crossed the flattened grass of the backlot in the last of the day's light, past the sideshow and the menagerie all the way to Clown Alley, a long tent set up closest to the big top's back end. It was a glorious evening; the tent flap of Clown Alley was tied wide open.

When he ducked under the entranceway all twenty-seven clowns fell silent. They glanced up from the buckets and stools and packing trunks they used for seats. Their makeup was in various stages of application, their costumes and props strung on clotheslines above them. 'Boss,' said one of the clowns. 'Mr Ballantyne,' said another.

'Friends,' said the ringmaster, 'forgive me, but I wonder if one of you might spare me a spot of paint?'

No one spoke. For quite some time the clowns simply stared, arrested in their various attitudes: their fingers full of paint, mouths bristling with pins, faces doubled in small hand-held mirrors. They remained motionless until the ringmaster himself broke the spell by clearing his throat. Then clowns large and small came forward, stumbling over one another, thrusting jars of all varieties into his hands.

'Thank you, friends, thank you.'

The ringmaster selected one jar each of red, black and white. 'Thank you,' he said again, then ducked back under the tent flap and retired to his trailer.

Half an hour later he washed his hands and dried them before putting on his gloves. He opened the doors to his trailer. He descended the steps and strode down the aisle of caravans to the back entrance of the big top, still immaculately dressed in his jodhpurs and his hat, his scarlet coat and cravat, but, with consummate skill, he had painted his face to suit his station. The broad white band around his reddened mouth sloped gravely downwards and his painted eyebrows arched so high he looked surprised at his own misery, or perhaps horrified.

The entire retinue was assembled. When they saw him coming they made way like courtiers at the coronation of a king. Some of the clowns bowed.

None spoke. The ringmaster swaggered past them, chin held high, and with all eyes upon him he strode through the gaping maw of the big top's back end and proceeded, for the last time, toward the bright lights of the ring.

Later that night, as the crowd was filing out of the front end, Samuel made his way around the side of the big top. It was dark beyond the light cast by the multi-coloured bulbs, and when he rounded the corner and stepped back into the light, he found the rear end of the big top in total pandemonium. One of the ponies had spooked and her wrangler had been dragged through the dust trying to hold on to the catch rope. The little mare reared up shrieking and kicking the air with her hooves. Two clowns and a groom danced around her perimeter waving their jackets in an effort to corral her, but her panic was unsettling the herd. Eleven other mares bunched against the crossbars at the far side of the enclosure, rolling their eyes and running their heads along each other's necks. When the little mare shot out one leg and screamed, the mares began to climb over one another and break up and to move along the fence in both directions.

There were men yelling orders in three different languages, people running everywhere, and the ringmaster in the middle of it all, balanced on a stool, gesturing broadly with his riding crop like the maestro of a demonic orchestra. The elephants were shrieking and the big cats, driven mad by the panic of the horses, paced the length of their cages without cease, thumping the boards as they turned until the chocks began to rock loose and the wheels creaked.

And just when it seemed the whole show might capsize, the ringmaster climbed down off his stool and calmly positioned himself before the panicked show pony. He stood dangerously close but unflinching with his hands held out beside him in a gesture of benevolence, or perhaps apology. And then, as if Ballantyne had waved a magic wand, order was restored. The show pony settled and Ballantyne kissed her nose. He reached for the reins and handed her off to a groom.

The foot jugglers, the acrobats and the clowns ambled past Samuel on the way to their trailers. One or two cast him a cursory glance. One clown stopped and insisted Samuel take his shabby hat and red nose. When Samuel grinned and shook his head the clown got down on one knee, weeping for deliverance, until two of his colleagues gathered him up under the armpits and carried him off.

It was only once the horses had been safely corralled and the backlot was all but empty that the trapeze act made an appearance, minus Lynch. Josephine was in the lead. It seemed she had once again been talking to the press, for two photographers followed her out of the big top, calling for one more shot. The skipper walked beside her. Josephine held the skipper's elbow with her thumb and forefinger and smiled for the cameras. When the photographers were done and had unscrewed the flashes from their cameras, the skipper thanked them and began to lead Josephine back to her trailer. The skipper saw Samuel standing there, but said nothing. Helena left Josephine on her doorstep and sauntered off. Josephine firmly shut the door.

With her brother absent for now, Samuel seized his chance. He crept round the back of her trailer. The lights were on inside and he could see her pass before the window every once in a while. Her roommate did not appear to be with her.

He knocked upon the window glass. 'Josephine,' he said. 'It's me. Samuel.'

Josephine opened the window. 'What do you want?'

'Same thing as you. Let's get out of here.'

Josephine did not answer.

'Josephine.'

'How can I?'

'Get Angela to help you when everyone's asleep. There's a bridge up the river. She can lead you there.'

'Samuel.'

'Will she help you?'

'Samuel—'

He heard Lynch's voice. 'I've got to go,' he said. 'Will she help you? Josephine?'

'Of course,' she said, flatly. 'Always.'

He followed the river to the bridge and waited. An hour later it started to pour. He found shelter under the bridge and wrapped his arms around his belly and looked out at the rain.

The rain fell heavily for another hour and soon the river rose to a level that threatened to evict him. Then the rain stopped. He guessed it was midnight. The circus would be asleep. Josephine would sneak out soon, when nobody was around.

He waited but she didn't come. It started to rain again. He huddled and watched the river, brown now with the downpour. After a while, the advance man's vehicle rumbled overhead. He could see the axle spinning through the wooden slats. It was going on one in the morning, but still she didn't come.

Half an hour later he crawled out from under the bridge and slogged his way back along the riverbank. He walked to her trailer and carefully climbed up the slope. The lights were off.

He stood in the rain outside her window and he stood there for a long time. He went over their conversation of a few hours ago. 'How can I?' she had said, which he'd taken to mean one thing. 'How can I?' she had said, but meant another.

Samuel woke before sunrise and took a long walk. Walking had always helped clarify his feelings, but not today. On his way back through the village, he happened upon the ringmaster dithering among the menagerie wagons. Ballantyne appeared to be searching for something. Flakes of dried makeup still clung to his face. The sun was not quite up and it was cold, yet the ringmaster wore nothing but his singlet and drop-seat long johns. He carried with him a jar of white greasepaint, cupped affectionately in both hands.

Samuel followed the ringmaster, intending to steer him back to his trailer. Clearly the man was in some distress. He was muttering to himself, but Samuel couldn't make out what he was saying. When the ringmaster reached the last cage down the wagon line—a smaller one belonging to the caracal—he ducked around the back. Samuel waited but he did not reappear. He could still hear him muttering.

The sun came up. The caracal's cage had once been painted fire-engine red, and in the first rays of the sun it flared like polished copper. Samuel waited for a while, trying to make out what the ringmaster was saying. It sounded like a sacrament, like Latin. He crept around the back of the wagon.

He found Ballantyne standing before the rising sun. He was naked now but for the long johns that he'd wrapped around his waist. The legs dangled down in front to hide his manhood. He had smeared himself from head to toe with the white greasepaint and had made a chain of dandelions with which to crown himself. Another he had snapped off at the neck and tucked into his navel. He stood there with his eyes closed and a smile that creased the corners of his mouth.

Sensing his presence, the ringmaster turned to him and opened his eyes.

'Are you all right, Mr Ballantyne?' Samuel asked.

The ringmaster smiled more broadly. He motioned to an overturned crate. 'Sit down,' he said.

'What about you, sir?'

The ringmaster waved this away. 'I think I'll stand. I have all of eternity to take my ease.' He rolled his neck from side to side and bunched and flexed his fingers like an actor backstage. He took a deep breath. Then he began: 'Once upon a time there was a troupe of players,' he said. 'They travelled the byroads by horse and cart and stopped not on the outskirts of town where their audience was guaranteed but whenever they got tired of travelling—sometimes at a crossroads, sometimes at a well, sometimes just the edge of a farmer's field.' He looked at Samuel, briefly, to make sure of his audience's attention, then went on. 'There they would roll out the painted backdrop, string the lanterns from whatever rigging was at hand, erect the stage, don their costumes and masks and perform to any audience they could draw from whatever place their weariness had required them to camp. Mummer's plays, mostly. Morality tales. Pantomime that literate and illiterate alike could understand. They chose their roles randomly at first, and then repeated them for ease: a tyrant, a virgin, a martyr and a clown. And no matter what story they elected to tell, the tyrant would get his comeuppance at the hands of the clown.' He paused for a while, as if lost in thought, or perhaps recollection. 'Grandiloquent gestures,' he continued, with a flourish of his arms. 'Very clear-cut. The audience booed, the audience cheered, and all went home satisfied.' He raised one finger.

'Except the actors.' He paused. He began to pace. 'The man who played the tyrant began to grow weary of dying nightly at the hands of the clown and began to demand that, from time to time, they be allowed to change roles. The virgin and the martyr even tried each other on for size. For his part, the clown was happy to oblige, to keep the peace, to die once in a while. But power went to the other man's head. After this first victory, he began to rule the company with an iron fist, demanding they press on beyond weariness into the cities where more money could be made. He drove them against their better instincts by threatening to leave them to their own devices and to the vagaries of the open road. So.' Again the ringmaster paused, to good effect. He became still. He turned to Samuel with a conspiratorial glint in his eye. 'One night the clown—the first one now, in his original role—climbed onto the stage with a genuine blade, and when, at the very end of the pantomime, it came time to kill the tyrant he did—for real.' The ringmaster mimed tugging back a man's head by the hair to expose his throat and, 'He cut his throat,' he continued, slowly passing the imaginary blade along the imaginary jugular, 'in front of an audience of seven or eight, and watched the tyrant's body collapse, lifeless, to the boards, his blood staining the stage that would never again be used. There was a smattering of applause, then the audience quietly got up and left.' The ringmaster turned back to the sunrise. 'Why did he do it? Not because of injustice; a clown can never be a hero. And not out of jealousy, or spite. No. The clown killed the tyrant because he knew that when a man and his mask become one, he cannot be much longer for this life.' The ringmaster looked at his hands. He turned them palm up, then down again.

Samuel shifted in his seat. The rough planks of the crate creaked beneath him. 'What happened to the clown?' he said. 'What happened to the company?'

'What happened, indeed,' said the old man. He turned and looked at the wagon, ablaze with the full rays of the sun. His name was stencilled on the side in paint faded to grey and flaking at the edges. 'She never should have tried that … impossible trick, my wife. My Emily. I was untrue, you know,' he muttered, 'unfaithful. I fooled myself that she hadn't noticed, but she knew.' He looked at Samuel with fear in his eyes. His bottom lip quivered. 'It doesn't fall to every man to kill a genius,' he said.

The ringmaster took off his dandelion crown and stood looking at it, shivering now with the cold.

Samuel removed his coat and placed it around the old man's shoulders. Ballantyne didn't refuse it, but the gesture appeared to diminish him. He looked lost, as if he didn't know where he was, why his limbs were painted white, nor who this blond-haired boy might be.

Samuel took the old man by the elbow. He led him back to the village, where the circus was beginning to stir. The company had thrown open their doors to let in the morning light. He heard a teakettle whistle, a whisper of quiet laughter. The man he'd seen attending to the skipper—a dark-skinned man with a sad face—tied on his boots and ambled over. He nodded a thank-you to Samuel and took the old man by the hand.

Later that morning, sweeping bones and hay out of the tiger's cage, Samuel spied Josephine and the skipper walking through the village arm in arm, leaning in to share intimacies, laughing and exclaiming as if they were the best of friends. Samuel had stopped to watch them go, and his co-worker—a middle-aged man with a chip on his shoulder—had ordered him back to work. When Samuel threw his broom against the wall, he and his co-worker came to blows.

Nursing his broken nose around the fire that night, his swollen lips, Samuel conceded the violence wouldn't end until he'd quit.

Charleyboy sat silently, staring at the coals. Through the firelight, Justice watched them with calm, impartial regard. Henry Sweet passed Samuel a jug of whiskey, which Samuel refused at first. Then he changed his mind. He drank, but the liquor burned the cut inside his mouth.

Sweet took out his six-string and the broken bottleneck and sang a hair-raising song that personified the darkness around them, the darkness within. When he was done, Charleyboy asked him the name of the song but Sweet did not answer. He only shook his head as if he would not name it.

'I got to go, Charleyboy,' said Samuel.

Charleyboy nodded. He took a pull from the whiskey jug. 'Where are we headed?' he said.

'You don't have to come with me. You've a reason to stay.'

The irony made Charleyboy smile. 'You've said that to me before,' he answered.

'She used me as leverage,' said Samuel. 'She never intended to leave.'

'Leverage for what?'

'I don't know.'

'So what are we waiting for?' said Charleyboy.

'Our paycheques.'

'To hell with our paycheques. What good is money if you're dead in a ditch?'

'How else do we get back to Canada?'

They decided to line up first for their pay, but to hide in plain sight. Pilinszky distributed the money from the back of a ticket booth by the big top's entrance, under the coloured lights, while rubes still lingered round the lot. When they took their leave of the windjammers and the hammergang, back beside their fire, Charleyboy got a warm send-off. Henry Sweet embraced him and called him Choctaw Boy. The black men shook hands with Samuel, too, but with more circumspection.

They left the fire and headed for the highway, but before they'd made it very far, Lynch and three others confronted them. They were still within the perimeter of light cast by the campfire, and the steel blades the men held beside their legs winked in the firelight. Lynch singled out Samuel. 'I'm gonna cut out your tongue,' he said flatly.

'We're leaving right now,' said Charleyboy, tugging at Samuel's arm.

'Too late, nigger.'

Lynch began circling to Samuel's left. He kept the knife at waist level and waved it back and forth before him in a slow arc. 'You think we've not seen your kind before?' he said. 'Mixing with niggers. Trying to take what don't belong to you.' With the firelight behind him he lunged and passed the blade twice before Samuel's stomach. Samuel arched his back like a cat but he did not raise his elbows high enough and the blade cut him deeply on both forearms. Lynch circled again. He feinted. He grinned as Samuel jumped back.

Charleyboy took off his shirt. He threw it at Samuel and Samuel spun it round his wrist and caught the loose end in his fist.

'Keep the nigger out of the way,' said Lynch. 'And shut him up.' The three men closed in. Charleyboy kicked and punched but two of the men held him and the third held the knife to his throat. 'At least give him a blade,' said Charleyboy. One of the men punched Charleyboy in the stomach.

By now the blacks had begun to leave the fire. The laughter had stopped. There was no music.

Samuel watched Lynch very closely. Lynch circled again, still grinning, then stopped and circled back the other way. 'I heard what you tried to do,' said Lynch. 'My sister tells me everything.' He waved the knife before him in the same slow figure eight, the blade winking now in the firelight.

Samuel thought his only chance to survive was to catch the other boy's arm as he lunged and wrestle the knife from his grip, but Lynch was too quick. Lynch feinted left then fell to one knee and passed the knife backhand across the front of Samuel's shirt. Samuel gasped. He staggered backwards. Charleyboy struggled but the men only tightened their grip.

Lynch circled again. He seemed to be in no hurry. As he circled he looked into Samuel's eyes.

The front of Samuel's shirt was drenched in blood. He felt hot and sick to his stomach. Lynch feinted again and then drew back. He feinted once more and Samuel stumbled and fell to his knees. Lynch rushed in. Samuel glimpsed the wink of the blade an inch from his left eye. It passed so rapidly across his face that his hands grabbed at nothing at all. He heard the other men laugh at what must have been a clownish gesture—the dying boy grasping at thin air. Blood dripped into his eye. It ran into his mouth as he tried to staunch the wound in his chest with the shirt and it occurred to him that he was going to die in this place. He was going to die and he would never see his family again. He would never see Charleyboy. He looked up at Lynch. From somewhere far away he heard Charleyboy call his name. And then, like some incarnation of the darkness, a massive black arm wrapped itself around Lynch's throat and picked him up off the ground. Lynch's legs kicked. Samuel couldn't be certain what he was seeing. He saw Lynch drop the knife and claw at the man's arm. He saw the men who'd held Charleyboy come running. Then he didn't see anything at all.

CHAPTER THIRTEEN

Samuel woke in total darkness and it was only when he tried to move that he knew for certain he was alive. The pain was unbelievable. He gasped, and it only got worse. He felt as if his lips had been sewn shut. He lay there breathing through his broken nose, and for a while could focus on nothing but the pain. Then he remembered Charleyboy.

He tried to call out his name but on his swollen lips the word was unintelligible. The pain made him wince, but he tried again. There was no answer. He tasted the metallic flavour of his own blood. His upper lip had split like an overripe plum. He waited but no one came, and then after a while he passed out.

He woke, and slept, and woke again. Each slumber was a sinking into water black as pitch, each waking a struggle to the surface, short of breath. And every time, the room in which he lay took on more definition: he could make out the white hospital blankets, the metal frame at the end of his bed, and beyond it, a door through which, from a small window three-quarters of the way up, a faint grey light emanated. He called out again for Charleyboy. The pain made him sick to his stomach.

Someone opened the door and approached his bed. She turned on a small electric light and hovered over him. 'Charleyboy,' he said. The nurse went away and came back with the doctor. He heard them talking. The doctor told him he needed to sleep, and soon he felt a needle enter his arm.

It was daylight when Samuel woke next. A young, bespectacled doctor stood at his bedside. 'Can you hear me?' said the doctor. 'Just blink.'

Samuel did so.

'Good.' The doctor smiled briefly. 'You have lacerations on your chest and arms. And on your face.'

Samuel tried to say Charleyboy's name.

'You mustn't speak. You've popped the stitches in your lip already.' The doctor's face straightened. 'I heard from the nurse you've been asking about your friend?'

Samuel blinked.

The doctor said, 'He was admitted along with you. He'd been stabbed. Here.' The doctor pointed to his solar plexus. 'It was a very serious wound, and we did the best we could to save his life. I'm sorry, but he didn't make it.'

It was the nurse, a while later, who filled him in on what had happened. She said that an old man and a younger woman had brought him and his friend to the hospital. That another, badly beaten man with tattoos on his neck had arrived some time later, but that he'd been discharged already. She asked him if there were any connection, if Samuel had, perhaps, been the one to wound the tattooed man, but Samuel shook his head. 'Justice,' he said.

'Sorry?' She leaned in.

'Justice.' He could form the word without moving his lips.

'I don't doubt it,' said the nurse. 'If he was the one who did this to you. And your friend.' She looked at him with great concern. She was young and pretty, and he wondered for the first time just how he must look. She said that his friend must have been stabbed trying to help him. He blinked and began to cry. The nurse wiped the tears from his eyes. She said in two weeks he would be able to go home to his family. Did they live in Oregon? But Samuel only turned his head away and closed his eyes.

He did not see the pretty young nurse again. When next the doctor came he brought with him another, much older nurse who ministered to him with a stern efficiency.

By Samuel's third day in hospital, he could speak, though not without agony. By the fourth day he could move himself around in bed. After a week he demanded to see Charleyboy. The doctor hesitated. Then he nodded and said that as soon as he could walk the nurse could take him there.

'I can walk now,' he said.

'No you can't.'

'Yes I can.' He sat up and swung his legs over the edge of the bed, but the blood rushing from his head made him dizzy. He lay back. The doctor nodded. 'I thought so,' he said.

'I have to see him.'

'You can try again tomorrow.'

'I feel fine.'

'By the time that couple brought you in you had lost a lot of blood. It's only thanks to their help you weren't dead already. You don't recover from that kind of injury in a week. You don't fully recover from that in *two* weeks. You can try again tomorrow,' he said. 'Now I suggest you get some rest.'

The doctor turned to leave. 'Who were they, by the way? That old man and his … daughter, was it? They were unusual.'

'Water,' said the raven. 'Please. Bring me water.' It nodded toward a corner of the room. Tucked into a niche behind the door stood a font chiseled from stone, tapered in the shape of an eye. Beside it, hanging from a nail driven into the masonry, an unremarkable tin cup.

The next morning, Samuel called the nurse and got himself out of bed. He said he was ready to see his friend now. The nurse checked his dressings and then called an orderly to accompany him.

Charleyboy was being stored in the basement. Under fluorescent lights Samuel and the orderly took an elevator down and entered a corridor. The same incessant buzz of fluorescence accompanied them down the long, grey hallway and through the swinging doors into the morgue. The orderly spoke to the mortician, a small man of no obvious humour, as pallid and clinical-looking as the atmosphere in which he worked and, it appeared, utterly indifferent to this interruption.

He led Samuel to the appropriate locker and unlatched the door. He slid out the table on which Samuel's best friend lay. He removed the sheet from the young man's face. Samuel looked down at Charleyboy for a moment, then glared at the mortician. Without a word the man left to go about his business.

Charleyboy had never looked so pale. He looked like the waxwork image of himself. It was cold in the morgue, and in his thin hospital gown, Samuel began to shiver. He looked around the room. There were two dozen other such lockers. Behind him the mortician was talking. He heard the orderly stifle a laugh. He considered Charleyboy again. Under the lights his lips looked blue. 'Brother, you were right about me,' he said quietly. 'You were right all along.' Samuel wept. Overhead the lights buzzed like flies. 'Am I a villain, or a fool?' Samuel said. 'What the hell am I going to say to your mom?'

Samuel drew the sheet back over Charleyboy's face. He turned and made his way to where the orderly was waiting, thumbing through a magazine inside the mortician's office. They both looked up when Samuel entered. 'So what now?' he said.

'Are you next of kin?' said the mortician.

'No.'

'Do you know how to find them?'

Samuel nodded.

'You can tell the police when they get here. Your friend,' the mortician added, 'he's an Indian?'

'Yeah.'

The mortician nodded. 'Then don't expect the police right away.'

When Samuel left the office the orderly followed him. He tried to look grave. He was a young man about the same age as Samuel. When Samuel looked into his eyes the orderly coughed and looked down. The orderly gestured at the swinging doors.

'Find me a mirror,' said Samuel.

'I'll let your doctor know you've asked for one,' said the orderly.

'Find me a goddamned mirror.'

The orderly led him back along the hallway to the men's washroom. Samuel pushed open the door. He stepped inside and stood before the mirror for a long time. He shivered with cold but took off his gown anyway and unwrapped the dressing from his chest. The scars were raw-looking still and very swollen. He counted fifty-seven stitches in his chest, another thirty or so in his face. His forearms were sewn together also but those stitches he didn't bother to tally. 'You look like one mean son of a bitch,' he said.

The orderly pushed open the door. 'You okay?'

'Sure.'

'I'd better take you back now.'

The nurse fitted him with a fresh dressing when he got back to his ward. He planned to leave that evening whether they let him or not. But first there was the problem of his clothes. He mentioned to the nurse, as casually as he could, that he wanted to get dressed and she told him there were some clothes set aside. He asked to see them. She brought him a new shirt and a pair of woollen pants, even new boots. In the pocket of the pants he found a five-dollar bill and a handwritten note that said 'Remainder: wages'.

That evening the doctor removed the stitches from his face, and once he left the ward Samuel threw back the bed sheets and reached for his clothes. The doctor had said he'd need three or four more days at least, before they could remove the stitches from his chest, but Samuel stole away as soon as darkness fell. He left Charleyboy's address on the pillow.

Half an hour later, he was wandering the streets of Portland. His feet had blistered in the new boots and he felt weak and very hungry. The people he passed gave him a wide berth, and when he asked one or two where to find the nearest bus station, they seemed unable, or unwilling, to look at him for long.

The clerk at the bus depot told him that five dollars would get him only as far as Spokane. Samuel decided to save his money. He caught a ride north with a man who would not stop talking, and before they'd made it halfway to the border Samuel asked to be let out. The driver took it for the insult that it was. When the man pulled over somewhere south of Ellensburg, Washington, Samuel climbed out without saying a word and the driver hit the gas before Samuel had even shut the door.

The next driver to offer him a ride was an Indian as taciturn as he. The Indian asked how far he was going and when Samuel said Canada the Indian nodded once and said, 'Is that home?'

Samuel stared at the dash. The radio was missing, and wedged into the letterbox-sized gap made by its absence, a pair of antique Kachina dolls returned his stare through eyes rendered melancholy by their patina. Their once wardrobed torsos had passed through so many hands that the cottonwood roots from which they had been whittled were smooth as polished stone. A saint of some description dangled from the rearview mirror on a tarnished silver chain. Samuel turned and looked out the window at the endless line of posts and fence wire rising and falling in a blur beside the highway, and behind those enclosures, reaching to the foothills of mountains to whose peaks clung still a few last rags of snow, the ranchlands of men whose lives therein were circumscribed and knowable and fixed. 'Home,' he said, after a while, with an irony the driver seemed to know something about. They did not speak again until well north of Wenatchee.

The driver dropped him off at a knacker's yard, where Samuel offered the owner five dollars for a length of sisal and a horse destined for slaughter. The owner of the abattoir looked skeptical, but shrugged and pocketed the money when Samuel persisted.

Samuel crossed the border on horseback and followed an old logging road north. Where the road petered out along the eastern reach of the Cascades, the abandoned logging camp rose, spectral and dishevelled, out of a clearing the forest had done much to erase. Thickets of alder grew thirty feet tall. Fireweed thrived in the available sunlight, its scarlet flowers humming with honeybees. Nootka rose covered the cistern's scaffolding and briars all but smothered the bunkhouse; the blistered roof seemed to hover in the forest without wall or foundation like a sorcerer's bothy. He thought to spend the night under the bunkhouse roof, but when he kicked aside the tangle of thorns before the door, he found the carcass of a coyote sprawled across the threshold, its eyeless head grinning through a swarm of flies.

In the days to come, he rode higher into the mountains with only the vaguest notions of where he might go, or what might become of him. He saw no one and ate little. Horse and rider grew thin. He made camp wherever he could—in the windbreak of small atolls of krummholz, or beneath obelisks of granite collapsed into natural caves—and in darkness sat listening to the air flute through those stunted trunks or stone openings until he believed that in the sound of the wind he heard melodies as old as the mountains that framed them, snatches of song acknowledged by others before him, by wayfarers of a different race and creed, and he came to an inchoate understanding that his life was but a single note in a ballad as old as the planet and that every living thing—every cricket, every river, every bristling stalk of grass—was inseparable from the song.

He found nothing to eat for the next three days and feared he was not in his right mind. Riding bareback into a valley through stands of fir so thick the sunlight never hit the ground, it occurred to him that he might not be in his mind at all, for early one afternoon he saw another Samuel Hewitt on the same horse riding bareback beside him.

Sitting beside the fire that night, flinching at the memory of Charleyboy's pale, bloodless face in the morgue, he heard a pack of wolves howl in unison like a choir. Their ballad was both mournful and intimate, and he felt a tingle up his spine that was not fear, exactly—not fear, but a shiver as if there were fur on his back also and it was hackling.

The stitches in his chest itched and would need to be removed soon. Above all he needed to eat, but without a knife with which to hunt or whittle a bow, he ate only what he gathered from the ground: salal berries, mountain sorrel, a little watercress. It had rained a few nights ago, and the forest floor was thick with moss and mushrooms. When Samuel was a child, Eloise had identified for him a handful of edible fungi, but had warned him away from most. If in doubt, she had stressed, leave them be, but hunger got the better of his judgment. The next day Samuel picked and ate a small clutch of mushrooms that looked familiar, but within minutes his stomach cramped. He tried to vomit them back up but failed. He sat down heavily with his back to a tree, holding himself around the belly, rocking backwards and forwards and yawning, yawning.

He feared that if he fell asleep he might die, so to stay awake he sang. Nothing in the forest appeared still. The whole mountainside was breathing like one enormous lung. Colours shone brighter than before—the fir trees a deeper, more lucid green, the moss an impossible neon. *Don't fall asleep, don't sleep.* He crawled on his hands and knees toward a shock of moss so dense and thick it was an ecosystem unto itself, a whole forest in miniature dripping with water and supporting all manner of insects he'd never seen, so fecund it was too much to behold, obscene in its teeming busyness and all of it indifferent to his witness. He tried to escape his senses by closing his eyes, but that allowed him no respite; geometrical patterns kaleidoscoped through his mind's eye like imploding mandalas, and when he opened his eyes again, collapsing backwards onto the moss, he felt imprisoned by the canopy above as if trapped inside the belly of an animal. *Don't fall asleep, don't sleep.* He gritted his teeth and breathed deeply. The treetops tossed like dark antlers, and beyond, clouds rushed before the sun with such alacrity they seemed animated by a common panic.

In time, his deep breathing relaxed him. He examined the back of his hands. He could see the blood pulse in his veins, see the texture of his skin as a supple mosaic, and he realized that he was not a solid thing at all, but a membrane opening and closing, drinking and leaking like a plant. It was suddenly very funny to Samuel that, after surviving Sheldrake, Coltrane and a knife fight with Lynch, he had killed himself with a mushroom. He yielded to the laughter, to the *moment* in which he was laughing, and he surrendered to suicide on that mountainside because he knew that while his body might succumb to the poison and his flesh rot into the earth, his self-awareness would not end.

Many months later, trying to rationalize what happened next, he reckoned that he had dreamed, though he did not fall asleep. He journeyed willfully into his vision as both actor *and* observer.

He climbed to the top of the stone stairwell and leaned against the wooden door. 'Water,' said the raven. 'Please.'

The chamber was lit by a single arched window that reached floor to ceiling. Tucked into a niche behind the door stood a font chiseled from stone, tapered in the shape of an eye. The raven strained against the nails, its blood splashed the floorboards, and for its suffering Samuel felt only pity. He seized the tin cup and dipped it into the pupil of the font's eye. He carried the brimming cup across the room. The raven strained at the nails. Samuel lifted the cup to the raven's beak. The raven drank greedily, and when it was satisfied, it rested its head against the wall. Samuel shouldered the raven's weight and drew the iron spikes out of its talons. They clanged together as Samuel dropped them to the floor. He reached and drew a bloody spike out of one wing, adjusted his grip on the raven's hips and removed the other. The raven groaned. Unburdened at last, the raven collapsed into Samuel's arms and wrapped its wings around him. The raven shuddered and convulsed. Its wings seemed to shrink, and by the time the raven had found its footing and stepped back it was no raven at all, but his father.

'We are such stuff as dreams are made on, and our little life is rounded with a sleep.'

When Samuel returned to his senses, he found the sun much advanced. He sat up and looked at the forest with fresh eyes. Evening sunlight slanted in between the trunks of Douglas fir, and where rock erupted through the moss, the lichens glowed in warming tones of ochre and oxidized copper. He heard a crack like the snapping of a branch and turned to find the horse watching him. There was fear in her eyes, and when he laid a hand along her neck he could feel her body shaking.

Another crack, followed by a pop like a bone dislocating, and Samuel knew instantly why the horse was afraid. He took off his jacket and hooded her eyes. He stroked her neck and spoke softly to her. He led the mare a quarter mile down the mountain where a swift, sunlit river carved its way through shallow canyon walls hung with moss and fern and cedar sapling. He tied her by the sisal catch rope to a tree, took his jacket and walked back up to the clearing.

The wolves were feeding on the far side of a bluff. Samuel descended through a shallow ravine, quietly climbed the other side, and when he reached the top of the rock and lifted his head, he saw a pack of four grey timber wolves fighting over the carcass of a doe. Beneath their silvery, bloodstained muzzles and black gums their teeth shone ivory-white.

Samuel ducked behind the bluff and tried to steady his breathing. His heart was pounding. He had lost his mind on mushrooms not a few hundred feet from where the wolves had felled their prey. When he reared up again one of the wolves stopped eating. It stood with one forefoot raised, ears forward.

Its almond-shaped eyes blazed like Baltic amber. The wolf spotted him and let out a low woof. The other three wolves followed its gaze. They circled and bunched together until all four were facing him. Samuel didn't try to hide. He looked into the eyes of the wolves, the wolves into his. They stared at one another for maybe seven or eight seconds and then, without any signal or sound, the wolves turned as one and trotted single file into the forest, fluid and silent as quicksilver.

Samuel ventured over the bluff and entered the clearing. The doe's entrails lay coiled over the moss like wet rope. Her eyes were wide open. The wolves had eaten most of her organs, almost all of her flesh. Scanning the clearing, Samuel spied an arrow stone jutting from the moss. He unearthed the stone and cracked it on the back of a granite outcrop, and with this improvised knife, quickly hacked a pound or more of muscle from inside the doe's thigh and walked back to the river to eat his windfall raw. It was the first meat he'd eaten in so long he was drunk with it. He stumbled to the water's edge and drank. He didn't use his hands. He just lowered his jaw to the river and drank like an animal.

He led the horse another mile downriver before making camp. He built a fire to smoke the remaining meat, and in the morning mounted up and rode out much fortified for having eaten. He didn't know it, but he was two days' ride from Emery Creek and the Ashnola road that wound down to Keremeos. From there it was no more than a day's ride beside the Similkameen River to Osoyoos. He knew only that he had to travel northeast, and guided by the sun, he began to climb again into that wild high country. The spruce and fir gave way to larch and it grew very cold. Then the trees ceased altogether. The little mare showed herself to be a mountain horse at heart for she handled the talus without flinching. They reached a high ridge where pockets of snow still lingered in hollows and in cirques and below overhanging cairns of scree, and from there Samuel had an unobstructed view north and south, and down the tree-lined slopes east to the dry grassland of the great Sonoran Desert.

Samuel rode on, and later that afternoon, still riding the alpine ridges, he came upon a meadow of such exquisite beauty he simply had to stop. He dismounted, walked out to the end of a promontory and stood overlooking a slope of white valerian and red paintbrush, lupine and yellow arnica, avens and ragwort, purple daisies and asters. A prairie falcon wheeled beneath the ridge on the rising air, and far below, in the Ashnola basin, the long lake shone turquoise. He sat down on the edge of that overhang to impress the scene upon his memory, and he was still sitting there at sundown when the hummingbirds dispersed and the flowers closed their throats. It began to grow terribly cold.

He found shelter and lit a fire. Sitting there staring at the coals, he believed he had come to understand the attraction of a life lived alone. His father used to speak of mountains like this with reverence, as if their solitary reaches were animate, like gods of an older world grown remote and laconic. Before he'd married, his father had been posted to a weather station by the Crow's Nest Pass, and it may have been there that he first discovered the silence which would come to define him later in life. Samuel thought his father had been searching for the sacred all his days, believing, it seemed, that grace made itself manifest in the humblest of objects, in things broken or bereft. Things overlooked or discarded. Seeking to make every gesture a blessing, he had grown remote himself.

One night, not long after Samuel's mother first left, Robert did not come home. Samuel had feared the worst. But in the morning when he walked outside, onto the front porch at sunrise, he saw his father standing just beyond the fence where a patch of milkweed grew thickly in a run-off ditch. It was August and the monarch butterflies had hatched. Samuel had called out to him, and as his father turned, Samuel watched monarchs lift off his dad's neck and shoulders in a flutter of sunlit orange and gold before settling back again, their new, recently translucent wings gently pulsing. For the first, and last, time since she'd left, Samuel saw his father smile. That was three years ago. And what three years ago had seemed to him a fearful image—his silent, bereft father bedevilled by insects—appeared to him now, through the lens of memory, as an image of astonishing beauty.

He was about to lie down and sleep when the image of his mother resolved on his mind's eye like a snapshot in a stop bath. He'd shunned her for so long the clarity of his recollection levelled him. He recalled a time before everything went wrong, when he was still a child, when his mother and father were in love, and he asked the stars how the weave of a life like his—one that began with such integrity—could ever manage to bury its thread.

But he was not alone, of course. Caroline had been a child herself once, an innocent with a lifetime of choices before her, and he had to concede that of her own private struggle, her hopes and dreams, and her sacrifices he knew nothing, and was not qualified to judge.

Early the next morning he rode down off the mountain back into the commerce of the world. The landscape changed, became more familiar. The fir gave way to bunchgrass and scattered ponderosa pine, and by noon the next day he rode clear of the trees altogether and followed the Similkameen River east, entering the south end of the Okanagan Valley as the sun began to set. It was hot and the air was redolent with the smell of sagebrush. The last time he had passed this way, he'd travelled in a convoy of circus trucks. He remembered the desert scattered with a few weathered-looking ranch houses down by the river where the grass grew long, and he intended to offer his labour at one of these homesteads in exchange for food and shelter until he felt ready to move on.

He joined the Oroville Road at Osoyoos and rode north through the heat of the day sipping sparely from his rough canteen. Toward sundown the horse smelled water and loped to the shores of the lake. She drank deeply and Samuel crouched and drank beside her. When he was done and had filled his canteen he sat back on the sand and watched the sunlight vanish from those folded slopes like the turn of a girl's shoulder, abandoning the valley to shadow. He closed his eyes and listened to the mournful, rasping call of burrowing owls passing overhead, and to the click of spotted bats hunting insects over the still, blue water.

The little meat he'd smoked was nearly finished and he knew he'd need food again soon. Summerland was a day's ride away and there he would find nourishment for certain, if not work on the orchards. There, too, he would find the company of other men, and all the vicissitudes of an existence predicated on common goals: divided labour, days apportioned into hours, and all of it, unto the smallest ceremony—the mere shaking of a man's hand—carefully designed to avert the violence to which he believed all men were born.

He slept that night beside the lake and there was dew on his blanket when he woke. He guessed it was somewhere near the end of August, and he realized that he had forgotten his own birthday.

He caught his horse and mounted up and rode on. He ate lunch with a passing caravan of migrant workers—Mexicans who would work for two bits a day and who were much resented by the unemployed. He shared his food with them, such as it was, and in turn they plied him with beans and fresh tortillas until he could eat no more. They did not speak. Samuel did not speak. When all had finished and their tin cups and their frying pan had been packed away, they rose and told him to go with God. Then they moved on.

He rode into the town of Penticton early that evening and stood his horse before the doors of a church. Attached to the little wooden structure leaned a series of outbuildings, and before one of the doors, he saw a line-up of men, hats in hand, patiently waiting their turn at a charity kitchen. The smell of freshly baked bread wafted out the open doors. Samuel tied the horse to a rail and joined the line. The men eyed him with misgiving.

When it came his turn to enter, the women fell silent. He stood just inside the doors waiting for some kind of instruction. After a while, one of them came and took him by the hand and led him to a table. She didn't ask him what had happened to his face. She sat him down and brought him a bowl of vegetable soup with barley, and a piece of bread. She broke the bread into his soup and watched him eat. He didn't feel he warranted her pity and he was thankful when she went away. A man he took for the pastor was the next one to join him, and this man simply sat and waited for Samuel to finish. He had sandy blond hair and blue eyes exaggerated greatly by the curvature of his bifocals. He introduced himself as Justin Swift. 'What happened to you, lad?' he said.

Samuel pushed the empty bowl forward. He composed his hands in his lap and looked up. There were two dozen others settled in that soup kitchen, all of them hungry, out of work, broken to a man. To and fro the women came in their long white aprons like silent, ministering angels.

'I tried to save a damsel in distress,' Samuel said. 'Turns out she wasn't in distress after all.'

There was a sparrow trapped under the rafters. He watched it swing in a perfect arc from crossbeam to crossbeam as if attached to a wire, settling at last on the edge of a table to peck at a crust of bread.

'Come with me,' said Swift.

He led Samuel through the dining hall and into the kitchen. The women stopped working to watch. 'Ladies,' said Swift. They nodded and started up again. Through a door at the back of the kitchen he ushered Samuel into a small walled garden formed by the L-shaped refectory, the church itself and a third building at the south end that looked like it housed offices, or lodgings, perhaps a hospital. Strung from one of the second-storey windows to a corner gable of the church was a laundry line hung with cotton sheets that snapped and billowed in the wind like sails.

The garden path had been paved in the shape of a Celtic cross and arranged around an ancient cottonwood. One of the lower branches was near collapse, and a two-by-four support had been erected to carry its weight. The four corners of the garden grew various herbs and perennials, even tomatoes and melons tucked into a south-facing niche. A circular bench had been nailed to the trunk of the cottonwood and it was there that they sat, in the shade, watching the play of light and shadow on the stone as the tree swayed above them.

'In the cosmogony of cultures less ... accelerated than our own,' said Swift, 'a tree forms the axis of the universe.' He gestured upwards at the branches, then down at the ground. 'The heavens swaying high up in the crown, the underworld clutched by roots. And here, in between, is the world as our five senses bind it. A world of both light and dark, of good and evil. There are many who see, in the iconography of the cross, the survival of these longstanding convictions: the cross as the tree, and Christ's suffering upon it a result of his divine origins, his being torn, if you will, between heaven and earth, between God and our ground of being. Our *ground* of being,' he repeated. He looked up through the branches of the cottonwood. 'Don't get me wrong, son,' he said. 'I'm not delivering a sermon. I'm not trying to persuade you to join the congregation of this humble parish. I'm telling you a tale. Merely. Without somebody to listen to it, a story can say nothing; it is as dumb as a stone.'

He reached into the pocket of his shirt and took out a pouch of tobacco. Inside was tucked a sheaf of rolling papers. Samuel watched the man roll a cigarette, tuck the papers back into the pouch and place the packet back into his pocket. He stopped and looked at Samuel, the unlit cigarette hanging from the corner of his mouth. 'Do you smoke?' he said, removing the cigarette from his lips.

'No, sir.'

The man nodded. He lit the cigarette with a Treibacher flint lighter and leaned back against the cottonwood. 'Two years after the Great War broke out,' he began, 'in 1916, there were two pastors assigned to the King's Third Infantry. One was a Catholic—a broad-shouldered Irishman, a boxer in his youth, and a pugilist at heart until the very end. The other was a Methodist, and a Protestant in every sense of the word. He protested the very war his country had been called to fight and yet answered that same call believing, in the end, that it was the will of God. The Irishman was by far the more popular of the two. He counted Catholic and Protestant alike among his congregation.' Swift drew deeply on his cigarette. Behind them the white sheets snapped, and the pulley that attached them creaked with a sound almost like birdsong.

'But that priest met his end at the point of a bayonet—he fought alongside his flock, you see, at the battle of the Somme, against the orders of his Commanding Officer—and so it fell to the Methodist to assume the Irishman's congregation. Before he died the priest offered his final confession to the young, reluctant Protestant, who absolved his colleague as requested. Death has a way of rendering certain distinctions irrelevant. Catholic, Protestant. Absolution, or simply holding a man's hand as he passes. Both were men of the cloth and called upon to comfort. So.' Swift looked at the end of his cigarette. The wind had extinguished it and he reached once again for his lighter. He cupped his hands around the cigarette and lit it anew. 'The priest's last words on earth were "Tell my wife I should never have left her."'

Swift shook his head. 'Which is itself a story, wouldn't you say? One left unfinished.' This seemed to give him pause for he sat with the cigarette half-way to his lips as he looked off over the roof of the refectory. He knitted his brows as if troubled by his thoughts and then continued to smoke. 'Then again,' he said, 'knowing the Irishman, he might only have been joking. Men who fight and lose often turn comedian.' Swift smiled. 'Epicurus once said that philosophy is useless if it doesn't teach a man how to die. Until a man learns how to die he can't begin to know how to live. The priest knew how to live, I'll give him that.' He smoked his cigarette to the nub and leaned to extinguish it on a patio stone. 'But our young Methodist? Well, he considered himself a man of philosophical temperament, but in his heart he was afraid. He lacked the contentment of Epicurus, that quietness of soul. In his defence there was violence all around him, and suffering—suffering on a scale that made him question the benevolence of his creator. Men cut to ribbons by machine-gun fire, men choking on mustard gas and vomit, grasping his hands on their deathbeds not for comfort now, nor in resignation, but out of terror, as if the pastor alone might have the strength to extract them from death's indifferent embrace, as if the pastor were the omnipotent God about whom he preached. But of course he was not. Men died terrified, looking him in the eye. His words of solace began to sound hollow to him, his blessings futile. His prayers simply ignored.'

A cat had entered the garden, and Samuel and Swift watched as it found a sunny spot among the stones and turned around twice before settling down.

'Epicurus again,' Swift continued, 'posited the following logical contradiction: If a perfectly good God existed, there would be no evil, no suffering.' He shrugged. 'Evil exists, therefore a perfectly good God cannot. To which the theologian will respond'—he raised one finger in the air to emphasize his point—'"God allows evil to exist in order to achieve a greater good." So that men will enjoy free will and come to Him of their own volition.' Swift shook his head. He leaned forward to rest his elbows on his knees, hands clasped.

'This did not sit comfortably with our Methodist then,' he said, 'nor does it now. For what greater good could God possibly have in mind that he should let so many young men die? Could he not have achieved his ends at the expense of fewer souls? What "greater good" could possibly be achieved by allowing children to be murdered, young girls to be tortured and raped—for make no mistake these luxuries are the spoils of war. Atrocities were committed as troops on both sides advanced and retreated. Our Methodist witnessed them with his own eyes. So. Perhaps you will not be surprised. With his philosophical turn of mind, such as it was, he deduced that if God could not prevent such suffering, or would not, then he was either indifferent to it, or he was no God at all. That he did not exist.' He shrugged. 'Such a crisis of faith cannot be resolved by philosophy. It requires pastoral care. But who plays pastor to the pastor in the middle of a war?'

The cat made its way over to where they sat and looked up at Swift. Swift sat back and the cat leapt into his lap. He stroked it for some time. 'You are a good listener,' he said. Samuel thought at first that he was talking to the cat but Swift glanced at him. He smiled.

'Our scars remind us that our past is real. Without them we become ... insubstantial. Unreal to ourselves. And by forgetting, we feel as if we have not lived at all. Our young Methodist, when the war was over, did not go back home. How could he? To what would he return? A sheltered life? The pastoral anomaly of an English village? Such unbearable innocence. He now drew his strength from his argument with God. He walked among the ruins of that theatre of war as a clown upon a derelict stage. He lived off the charity of others like the anchorites of old. At last he crossed the Pyrenees—on foot, on horseback, by any means of locomotion he could find—and made a pilgrimage to those places where God is reckoned to be most evident. He took the Way of St. James: Burgos, Carrion de los Condes, Santiago de Compostela. But he went not to praise, nor to bear witness to miracles. He went not to gaze upon the bones of an apostle or genuflect before a weeping saint. He went to engage God on his own ground, berate him, to shake his fist and call him to account. Make no mistake,' said Swift, 'he was out of his mind. For who but a madman would dare seek such a thing? And yet he had his followers, here and there, from whom he promptly fled. The ethos of a pilgrimage is itself a little mad, and a seeker can be easily misled by the ecstatic, the zealous—even against his own conscience. Many were impressed by his conviction. His ... *passion* even the orthodox could not fault. An audience always knows when the speaker has suffered for his story. Without the salt of authenticity his story will fall short. So.'

The cat jumped off Swift's lap, stretched its legs and commenced to clean itself.

'It was there our poor Methodist found his pastoral care. He was taken under more than one wing.' Swift smiled. 'Perhaps you have figured out by now who this pastor was. I was sent here, to this hospital,' he said, 'where I am instructed to forget. They tell me a man cannot become whole if he cannot let go of what ails him.'

Swift rolled and lit his second cigarette and sat smoking. Behind them the white sheets snapped. Finally, he said: 'To my mind, a man who lets go of his own past has no ground upon which to stand. The history of the world itself is written in its scars. The very mountains we live beneath are the product of a rupture. Would you fold them back into the ocean if you could? Erase their agony? Every grain of sand has a story. The healing takes place in the telling.'

Samuel leaned back and looked up at the topmost branches of the tree, tossing in a wind that would not let up.

'Anywhere can be the centre of the universe,' said Swift. 'As I've said. Things have their being in the witness. Trees. Stories.'

Samuel turned to him. 'Why me?'

Swift pressed down the corners of his mouth. 'You have that look about you.'

'What look is that?'

'The look of someone who's been born more than once. Who knows the banners under which death travels. Is it true?'

'I don't know.'

Swift nodded. He flicked ash from the tip of his cigarette. 'You don't know,' he repeated, emphasizing each word. Then he smiled. 'If I were Diogenes, I would lower my lantern,' he said. 'For here sits an honest man.'

CHAPTER FOURTEEN

Temecula, California

Helena took one look at Dimitry's face and left her tarot spread, unread, on the table. Halfway to the doors she stopped and returned to her bureau, yanked opened the drawer in which she kept the pistol and, as she suspected, found only the chamois leather wrap. She leaned on the baize with both hands, eyes closed, preparing for what she knew she was about to see. She hoped he'd wandered far enough away that the children, at least, would not have to witness it.

She was wrong. The circus had camped on the outskirts of Temecula, California, where groves of almond trees gave way to land cleared for development. Her father had walked no more than forty yards into an orchard, sat down with his back to an almond tree and shot himself in the heart. Half the circus had now gathered around—hired hands and performers, men, women and children, all waiting for Helena to arrive. Some of the women wept. Children too young to know what they were looking at played in the dirt or clung, disinterested, to their mothers' skirts.

Helena knelt beside her father, removed the pistol from his lap and closed the lids over his eyes. He was dressed in his ringmaster's livery, minus the hat, and the crimson jacket minimized the evidence of his gesture. His jacket looked merely wet, as if he'd been caught in the rain; his face showed no trace of pain, and it was only the powder burns clustered round the hole in his left lapel like a sinister boutonniere that betrayed him for dead and not simply sleeping beneath a tree, as he was sometimes wont to do.

Helena stood. She found Dimitry in the crowd and nodded once. Those of Catholic persuasion crossed themselves, as if only then, at Helena's definitive gesture, were they certain the ringmaster was deceased. Holding the pistol by its ivory handle, Helena made her way, expressionless and silent, back through the parting congregation.

On the morning of the ringmaster's funeral, Helena made the rounds of the local parishes, but not one of them wanted to bury a circus man, ringmaster or no. In the end, a young seminary student attached to the Catholic diocese drew Helena aside and told her of an old, abandoned cemetery in the hills southeast of town. It had serviced one of the first established missions in Temecula, he said, but the little church and barracks, the vineyard and vegetable gardens and the graveyard, were now derelict and overgrown with grass.

Dimitry steered the vardo up the last stretch of sandy road that led into those brown, treeless hills. When they came to the crest he cut the engine and Helena climbed out of the cab. She stood looking at the busted iron gates of the graveyard. It was eleven o'clock in the morning and already very hot. She wiped the sweat from her upper lip with the sleeve of her shirt and turned to survey the lot.

The mission buildings had been looted of everything but their foundations, and she reckoned the plateau they had sat on, like the flat spot of a dented sphere, would provide ample parking. The cemetery itself covered a quarter of an acre, the bones interred within surrounded by a crumbling stone wall that had once been whitewashed. Grass obscured most of the gravestones, and those that were still visible—mostly weathered wooden crosses toppled sideways—had been bleached of their lettering, rendering anonymous the remains they were intended to commemorate.

Helena entered the cemetery and toed aside some of the grass. Crickets scattered and a garter snake slithered deeper into the weeds. The chiseled inscriptions were mostly in Spanish and very old—the most recent she could read was dated 1898—but the plots were not crowded. There was no evidence of coyotes. It would serve.

It was well into the evening of that same day when the entire company—every man, woman and child, white and black—descended upon that tiny, ruined cemetery. Helena had sent four men ahead to dig the grave and mow the grass, and these men, as the first of the circus vehicles rolled up, hopped off the honey-coloured walls where they'd been waiting and stood holding their shovels and scythes before the entrance to the cemetery like figures in an ancient passion play.

Helena's vardo carried the ringmaster's coffin, and arrived last. Dimitry parked the vardo down the slope behind the last vehicle, chocked the wheels and threw open the doors. Helena had offered no instruction as to how the funeral should proceed, but her wishes would have been redundant anyway. The windjammers had decided on a funeral to music, New Orleans style. They gathered with their standing drums and brass at the vardo's painted doors, and as they launched into a dirge, eleven clowns in full character hauled the coffin from the back and held it aloft.

The bandleader began the march one slow step at a time; a pause and small bounce on the ball of the foot, then another shuffle and bounce to the beat of the music. The band followed his lead, then some of the hammergang. Draped with feather boas the costumed showgirls second-lined behind them, twirling parasols and dancing. The procession carried on up the hill, somber and slow. The treeless road was lined with circus folk on both sides, and as they all pressed forward to see better, and to pay their respects, the hierarchy dissolved. Performers stood shoulder to shoulder with labourers, white stood next to black. The sideshow were scattered throughout and those of smaller stature, or without legs, like Ethel Banks, were hauled onto the shoulders of the more able-bodied.

The windjammers stepped slowly, repeating their dirge for the length of the avenue until they reached the graveyard. The clowns carried the coffin through the gates and knelt, placing it beside the open grave. The music stopped. The congregation sifted through the narrow opening like sand through an hourglass and filled up the inside of the cemetery. Some stood on the walls. The midget settled himself onto the giant's right shoulder. And then out of the crowd stepped Moses, the old, grey-haired man who had preached that night beside the fire of Jesus and of Legba the Deceiver. Silence descended.

'Let the children come,' he said. He made a beckoning gesture with his hands. 'Let them see.' Parents pushed their children forward. They stood beside the coffin holding hands. 'Let them be the first to hear that death is not the end of life, that we bury this good man's bones only. His tired flesh alone shall rest because already his soul has found a new home. Can you hear me?' The old man turned around.

'We can hear you,' someone said.

'Can you hear me on the walls?'

'We can hear you,' said those standing along the walls.

'Mr Ballantyne is standing right now,' said the old man, 'right now, on one side of a stream, and his new life awaits him. So I ask you. Did he live a good life? Did he do right by us? For if he did, he will ford that stream with ease. Did he do right by us? What say you?'

'He did right,' came the loud replies. 'He was a good man.'

'Then let him cross that stream. Let him go. Let him take up residence in his new abode, in his new life. He did right by us,' said the old man. 'Let the music play.'

And so the band began another jazz, a ragtime with a hotter beat, and the bandleader, though still stern of face, began to skip and dance. The horn section swayed. Then the children joined in the dancing, and souls along the walls. Josephine danced with her brother by her side. Clowns lowered the ringmaster's coffin into the ground to a round of applause, and any who felt inclined filed by to take up a handful of earth and cast it down onto the casket.

Helena stood looking at the sky. The sun was down and the blue was deepening. The music played on. The circus folk danced around her as if she were the hub of a spinning wheel. Through the crowd she caught Moses's eye and smiled and nodded. He put his hand over his heart and nodded back.

It was only when Josephine embraced Helena from behind and kissed her once upon the cheek that Helena allowed herself to weep.

CHAPTER FIFTEEN

Penticton, British Columbia

Before Samuel left the soup kitchen, one of the women pressed a bun to his chest. When he flinched, she pulled aside his collar and noticed the stitches. She called out to the sister in charge.

Half an hour later, with his stitches removed, Samuel walked the old swaybacked mare through the streets of Penticton. Three boys pursued him down the street, laughing and talking in hushed tones. He turned around at one point and good-naturedly made as if to chase them. They squealed and ran, but after a short while they returned.

At the end of the street, before the road narrowed and wound up into the benchlands above the lake, he came upon the post office. Nailed to the outside wall was a bulletin board. He stopped and watched a young woman not much older than himself, with child in tow, reach up and pin a notice to the board. She glanced at him before she walked away, but the sun was low in the sky behind him and he thought—indeed hoped—she could not have seen enough to form much of an opinion. He watched her turn and walk back the way she'd come, leading her child by the hand. The boys who had been trailing him had lost interest and had drifted back into town, hands in pockets, kicking stones.

Samuel led the horse up to the bulletin board to read the notice. The young woman was advertising for help to bring in her harvest, in exchange for room and board. There was an address and that was all. Not even a name. Samuel unpinned the notice from the board. The young woman and child had rounded the corner by the time he climbed his horse, and he set off at an easy pace, anxious not to startle them.

The benchlands rose up the side of Anarchist Mountain like a giant's stepladder. Along the lower slopes, beside the lake, he rode among orderly grids of apple and cherry orchards, as well as open pastureland and land as yet untended, still littered with black sage and rabbitbrush that in seventy years' time would be parcelled out and planted edge to edge with grapevine. When he caught up with them the sun was down. She would be able to see him now, and all his scars. He rode up beside them and was silent. The woman looked up and kept walking. She was fair. Her child was dark, like a Gypsy. Like a circus child.

'I'd like to apply for the job, ma'am,' said Samuel.

The woman stopped. She turned and looked at him for a long time. There was nothing perfunctory in her study, only something remote. 'I can't pay you,' she said eventually.

'I don't need money. I'm just on my way home.'

The woman studied him some more. 'You'll sleep in the barn.'

He nodded. 'That's all I need.'

The child was silent. He was maybe four years old. He fixed his big dark eyes on Samuel and said nothing.

'It's been quite a while since my head's seen a pillow,' Samuel said.

The woman nodded once—just a slight incline of the head, almost unnoticeable. 'Okay,' she said. Then she turned and walked on.

Samuel followed. 'How far?'

The woman answered without looking up. 'Naramata. Five miles.'

'Then you should ride.' Samuel swung down off the horse. 'Please.'

The woman stopped. 'It's all right.'

'The child then. What's his name?'

The woman looked down at the boy. He was still watching Samuel. 'Liam,' she said.

'You and Liam should both ride,' Samuel said. 'Here.' He handed her the reins.

Before she took them, the woman bent to pick up her child and lift him onto the horse's back. Judging by the way Liam tightly gripped the pommel, it looked like the first time he'd sat on a horse. Samuel made a stirrup of his hands in which the woman placed her foot. He lifted her into the saddle. She squared herself and positioned the boy carefully before her, holding him firmly round the waist. Samuel held the horse by its hackamore and talked to it until the two riders were settled. Then the woman reached down for the reins.

The road began to wind up into the benchlands, and from their advantage, maybe three hundred feet above the lake, they could see a long way north and south—the granite bluffs of Okanagan Falls behind them, the widening valley up ahead. They walked for half an hour through the darkening evening before anyone said a word.

The woman was the first to speak. She told him to bear left at a fork in the road. The track to the right led to higher ground, the left down over the benchlands to the lake.

'You can ride with us,' the woman said.

'It's all right.'

'You can.' She looked down at him.

He walked the horse on a ways and then changed his mind. He stopped beside a rocky outcrop. She made room between herself and Liam. 'You'll have to hold him,' she said.

'Tell him to hold the reins,' said Samuel, 'just for a minute.'

The woman passed the reins over Liam's head and leaned in and told him to be brave. The boy was frightened but he did as he was told.

Samuel slid his left leg into the gap between mother and child and shimmied off his rock onto the horse's back. The horse stepped sideways and shook its head. He pulled Liam in close to him and reached for the reins and settled the horse and clucked her slowly forwards.

They rode on. The woman was sitting stiffly behind him looking over his shoulder. He could feel her breath against his neck. After a while she put her arms around his waist and he felt her body soften.

The track they had taken ran parallel to a rift in the benchland that was a watercourse for a day or so only in springtime, and otherwise a scar of pale grey clay and sage. It took them through to more level ground beside the lake, past other farms and orchards, one forlorn-looking homestead with a dozen or so slat-ribbed goats scraping their hooves in the dust.

The woman lived in a small wooden house surrounded by three acres of apple trees and an acre of cherries left unpicked and now littering the ground. Weeds choked a vegetable garden in which birds fed freely on the bent heads of sunflowers, unintimidated by the broken, desultory-looking scarecrow.

The woman swung down off the horse. She reached for her child. 'There is plenty of food,' she said. 'As you can see.' She would not look at him, ashamed perhaps at the evident neglect. 'I just need help bringing it in.'

Samuel passed her the child. She put Liam down and held him by the hand. 'The barn is over there,' she said. She pointed to a small, rough-planked structure with a hayloft in the peak. 'The tack room has a bed.'

'Thank you.'

'I'll bring you a blanket.'

'I have my own.'

The woman nodded. 'I'll bring you food then.'

'All right.'

'We'll begin in the morning.'

Samuel dismounted.

'You'll find hay for the horse,' the woman said. She nodded once, then turned.

When she was almost at the door to her house Samuel called after her. 'What do I call you?'

'Catharine,' the woman said. She looked over her shoulder. 'My name is Catharine.'

'Samuel.'

Catharine nodded. She entered the house.

In the morning Samuel and Catharine worked side by side picking apples from atop rickety wooden ladders. Catharine kept one eye on Liam, calling after him if he wandered too far. She was obliged, on occasion, to climb down and fetch him, but not once did she admonish him. She simply took him by the hand and turned him gently around so he could wander back. Liam did as directed, as if indifferent to which way he was aimed. Not once did Samuel hear him speak, and he began to suspect the boy couldn't. Or wouldn't.

There were signs of a man about the place: a worn saddle in the tack room, a pair of boots beside the door. The father of her child was either dead or disappeared and the intensity of his absence was as tactile as ever his presence had been.

Samuel watched mother and son from his ladder. He'd seen it before, this haunting. His father occupied the same rarified place, and depending on how long ago her husband had died, or abandoned her, the woman was either insulated still by the shock or her soul was in peril. He watched her bend down on one knee and look her child in the eye. She spoke to him but he couldn't hear what she was saying.

Catharine and Samuel filled six crates of apples before stopping for lunch.

'What do you intend to do with them?' said Samuel. 'The apples.'

'They're good apples,' said Catharine. 'I shall sell them.'

'In Penticton?'

'And the vegetables, too, if we have any.' She unwrapped a small brick of cheese and handed him bread.

'Have your neighbours been no help to you?'

Catharine did not answer. She broke bread and handed some to the child. She laid slices of cheese on the wax paper wrapping. In a pitcher that she held between her feet there was water mixed with wine. 'The man who makes this cheese,' she said, eventually. 'He has been kind to us.'

Samuel held out his cup and Catharine poured wine from the pitcher.

'How old is Liam?'

'Four.'

'Will you send him to school next year?'

Catharine stopped pouring. His cup was still half empty. She sat holding the pitcher over the lip of his glass, looking into the bowl of it. Then she continued to pour. When his cup was full she returned the pitcher to the cradle she had made with the soles of her feet. 'Next year,' she said absently, and did not elaborate.

Samuel asked no more questions. He watched the wind bend the reedy, unmown grass. He watched the child. September light the colour of honey enveloped the trees. There were many more apples left to pick and he guessed it would take them the week. Some would have fallen by then, but she would let the pig have his fill. She was right. There was plenty of food, but all of it useless if left much longer. He wondered how long her husband had been gone. He wondered why nobody had helped.

They worked through the afternoon and well into the evening, and by sundown they had picked sixteen crates. They continued the next day, and the next. On the fourth morning, a Saturday, they hitched Samuel's horse to a buggy, loaded the crates, and rode into Penticton to market. Catharine seemed to know nothing of the market but where it was located. She didn't know the going rate for apples. As she was setting up, Samuel visited other stalls to compare prices.

On account of his scars, the townsfolk gave him a wide berth. His scars and the fact that he was a stranger. They seemed to pass by Catharine's booth as well, shunning her, he suspected, because of her widowhood and because of her dark and silent child. Every community needed its scapegoat. It was unjust, to be sure, and un-Christian, but as inevitable as church on Sunday morning.

If she did not register much else, Catharine certainly registered their scorn. She stood helpless beside her crates of fine, ripe apples, watching the townspeople pass her by.

Samuel went to stand beside her. 'What's wrong with my apples?' she said.

Samuel took his knife and quartered one of the apples. He took up another and did the same. 'The apples are fine, but they see only what they fear,' he answered. 'They don't see you at all.' He climbed the box of the buggy and addressed the crowd. 'Ladies and gentlemen,' he bellowed, a passable ringmaster, 'nowhere in this market will you find better apples than right here. Nowhere in Naramata, ladies, nor at a better price. This good woman is offering two pounds of apples for the price of one. Call it a fire sale, call it craziness, call it, ladies and gentlemen, whatever you will, but I urge you to come here and taste for yourselves. Here'—he held aloft the quartered apples—'samples for everyone.'

A small crowd began to gather at the stall. Samuel leaped down and began handing out apples. He clowned with the children. He winked at the women and grinned. 'Today only, ladies,' he said. 'Any grocers here? Restaurateurs, step right this way for the best wholesale in the Okanagan Valley.'

Finally, Catharine began to sell some of her crop. Liam gathered the money in a leather satchel. By late that afternoon, twelve of the sixteen crates had sold. One grocer alone had bought four. He asked Samuel what else they might have.

Samuel gathered the empty crates and stacked them on the back of the buggy. When Catharine came over to help lift the unsold crates she was smiling. It was the first time in four days she had done so.

'One thing I learned,' said Samuel, 'is that if people are going to treat you like a freak you might as well give them a show. Put on a circus. It grants them the license to stare,' he said.

They made their way back to Catharine's orchard through the cool of the evening. Man, woman and child rode on the bench seat of the buggy, admiring the country with fresh eyes. Already the sun's rays lay long across the grass, and from the shallow swales and deeper gullies where the land dipped in pockets of darkness, small flocks of birds rose and flared away over the grass tops. Samuel spied a mountain bluebird hovering above a meadow, hunting dragonflies. He pointed it out to Liam, but the boy had already seen it, turning around and kneeling on the seat to keep watching.

In the days to come, Catharine and Samuel worked to salvage what remained in the vegetable garden. They went to market with garlic and onions, courgettes and summer squash, and Samuel re-enacted his pantomime. This time he rolled his jeans up to the knees, untucked his shirt and wore a hat he'd decorated with feathers. Shoeless, like some raggedy scarecrow, he clowned the marketgoers over to their stall.

That night, Samuel knew his contract with Catharine was coming to an end. There was little work left for him now the harvest was in, the garden in order, and he knew that he had to move on. He lay awake in his cot trying to frame what he would say to Charleyboy's mother but every explanation or condolence, every apology he composed fell short of what he truly felt: It should have been him lying dead on that mortuary slab.

He thought about Swift, about his need to keep telling his story, and he wondered if his story altered with each telling or if words could truly fix the past. Catharine also had a story to tell, but if she was not forthcoming was it his place to ask? Was it possible to save someone who wasn't asking to be saved? He had made that mistake already, by misreading Josephine, and in deceiving himself, he had killed his best friend.

At breakfast he thanked Catharine for the food and shelter and she nodded without looking up. She seemed to have anticipated his decision to leave. Watching her across the kitchen table, he believed he saw a change. It was not something in her eyes, or her smile. Certainly not anything in the few, necessary words she spoke. There was a new ease in her manner, as if a weight had been lifted, and he saw her as if for the first time, for the woman she once was, and maybe would become again. Graceful. Patient. Warm-hearted. The kind of woman any man would be a fool to abandon.

She tried to give him money but he wouldn't take it. In the end he agreed to sell her the horse, and she pressed ten dollars on him and packed as much food as he could carry. He bade a sad farewell to the horse. He had grown fond of the animal these past few weeks.

When he was finished with his goodbye he returned to the house. He stood on the threshold and smiled down at Liam. He glanced at Catharine. He saw the faint trace of a smile form in the corners of her mouth.

'You're going to be all right,' he said.

She nodded.

He knelt before the child. He held out his hand and the boy took it. They shook hands. Then Samuel stood. He walked a few paces away but then stopped and turned. 'What was his name?' he called. 'Your husband?'

Catharine hesitated and looked down, as if summoning his name from somewhere deep inside. 'Hector,' she said. She looked Samuel in the eye. 'His name was Hector.'

CHAPTER SIXTEEN

Samuel hiked the five miles into Penticton carrying food and his blanket in the canvas rucksack Catharine had given him. He made his way through town and stood on the side of the highway trying to hitch a ride north. It was one o'clock in the afternoon and very hot and no cars passed. After a while, he shouldered his bag and walked some more. Glancing back at the highway he could see thunderheads stacked over Osoyoos. It was an arresting sight, and he stopped to watch the sheet-lightning. He waited for thunder to follow but none did.

Soon the first car he'd seen in over an hour turned onto the highway and headed his way. He stuck out his thumb. A pickup piled high with empty bushels pulled over in a cloud of dust. Samuel caught up and opened the passenger door and climbed in. 'Good Lord,' said the driver. 'What happened to the other guy?'

The driver dropped him off in Kelowna and Samuel found his way to the train station. The platform was crawling with railroad bulls, but with the money Catharine had given him, he could afford to buy a ticket to Kamloops. From there he would figure out how to get home. The stationmaster sold him a third-class ticket and told him a passenger train would leave in two hours. Samuel thanked him, dropped his rucksack on one of the two benches bolted to the concrete and walked to the edge of the platform. He looked east. He heard the whistle of a westbound freight a mile out and watched the distant boiler smoke billow and disband above the chimney-stack like bolls of cotton in a gale. He stood his ground when the freight approached the station and watched it pass, car after car, ladder after ladder, until the whole caravan clattered away in a cloud of dust. Then it was quiet.

Across the tracks the flat, silvery leaves of an aspen clapped in the wind. Samuel decided to retreat into its shade instead of waiting on the platform. When he turned to retrieve his rucksack, he saw another passenger. The man walked down the platform with a heavy limp. The bulls appeared to recognize him and stared him down as he hobbled by. The man passed Samuel without saying a word and settled onto the empty bench. He reached inside his blue suit jacket, pulled out a package of tobacco and began rolling a cigarette.

Samuel carried his rucksack over and stood before him. The man looked up, the unlit cigarette dangling from the corner of his mouth.

'You don't remember me, do you?' said Samuel.

Bartlett looked him over. He turned from the wind and lit the cigarette inside the cover of his jacket.

'We hopped the freight with you from Kamloops to Kelowna.'

Bartlett nodded and drew deeply on the cigarette. 'You've changed some,' he said, and exhaled a plume of blue smoke.

Samuel traced the scar on his cheek with his fingertips. It felt like the join of two edges of leather.

'I don't mean that,' said Bartlett. 'Anyone can lose a fight.' He took another long drag of his cigarette. ''Tis not every boy comes of age. Samuel, isn't it?' It evidently pained him to get to his feet, but he stood and held out his hand.

'Bartlett,' said Samuel.

They sat.

'Where's your friend, then? The Indian lad?'

'He's dead.'

Bartlett paused with his cigarette halfway to his lips. 'I'm very sorry to hear it. What happened?'

'We got into a fight.'

'With each other?'

'No. With some circus folk. It's a long story.'

'What'd you do?'

Samuel shrugged. 'There was a girl.'

Bartlett drew on his cigarette and nodded. 'Ah. There's always a girl,' he said.

'It was my fault.'

Bartlett's cigarette flared in the wind.

'What happened to you?' said Samuel.

Bartlett nodded down the platform. 'Bulls,' he said with a shrug.

'Is it bad?'

'Doctor tells me I won't be doing a hard day's work for a while,' answered Bartlett, 'even if I did want to.' He smiled. 'You going home?'

'If it's still there,' said Samuel. 'I have a few things to answer for first.'

'Don't we all.'

Bartlett flicked ash from the end of his cigarette. They watched the aspen for a while. 'What happened to Pocock?' said Samuel.

'Who?'

'Pocock. He rode the rails with us. He lost his shoes.'

'Ah, yes.'

'Did he find his girl?'

'I believe he did.'

'And did she marry him?'

'Aye.'

Samuel nodded. 'There's one happy ending, then, in all of this.'

Bartlett looked at him askance. 'You think marriage makes you happy?' he said. He shook his head gravely. 'For a man like Pocock, maybe. But for us? We're men of the road, you and I. Peripatetic,' he said, with a certain chagrin. 'There's a word I learned. Fancy word for tinker.' He smoked his cigarette down to the nub and flicked it onto the rail tracks.

Bartlett reached again inside his jacket and this time took out a photograph. He gazed at it for a spell and then handed it to Samuel. In the photograph he was standing in front of a whitewashed farmhouse with his wife and two children—a boy and a little girl with curly blond hair like her mother. Bartlett offered nothing in the way of explanation, nor did Samuel ask. Samuel

— 183 —

handed back the photograph. Bartlett sat, expressionless and silent. At length he tucked the photograph back into his pocket.

Samuel studied Bartlett more closely, noted the lines about the corners of his eyes, the yellowing fingers that held his cigarette. He was about the same age as Samuel's father, more or less, and for the first time since leaving Ashcroft, Samuel pictured his father waking up to find his son had disappeared. Bartlett sensed this shift in Samuel's attention and turned. Samuel couldn't look him in the eye. He was overcome with emotion and did not want to betray himself.

'If you've got people who love you, son,' said Bartlett, 'for God's sake go home.'

The men with whom they rode back west proved to be good company. Many of them were the last trekkers to leave Saskatchewan after the Regina Riot and they had a lot to say about their clash with the RCMP and the calumny of Prime Minister Bennett. They'd been part of a convoy of unemployed that had hopped freights all the way to Regina and been beaten back by the police. They said two thousand unemployed men had descended on Saskatchewan's capital intending to take their grievance all the way to Ottawa, but Bennett had served them up twice. He'd separated the leaders from the group and paid for their fare east knowing that they couldn't refuse an invitation to a meeting they had so long demanded. By the time he sent them back empty-handed, he had amassed hundreds of RCMP in Regina and directed them to stop the protest from proceeding. On the night of July 1st, Dominion Day, the Mounties had charged a demonstration in Market Square and begun breaking heads. To their credit, the men had fought back, but their protest had been quashed. By the time the smoke cleared, a Mountie and three other souls were dead.

The protestors had been rounded up and processed at a way station outside the city that had proved little better than a jail. Many of them had abandoned Bennett's relief camps to make the trek and all of them swore they would never go back. If their protest had proven one thing, it had exposed the relief camps as a failure. Men would rather go hungry and free than waste their souls on make-work projects for an insulting ten cents a day.

One man said in Vancouver the longshoremen were mobilizing, and another tried to enlist Samuel in the Communist Party of Canada, by which time the train was pulling into Kamloops station. Samuel took his leave of them and of Bartlett, who shook his hand firmly. 'Gentlemen,' Samuel heard Bartlett say as he climbed down on to the platform, 'have you yet heard the Ballad of Samuel Hewitt….'

Samuel left the station and walked up Victoria Avenue for the second time that summer, and the first thing he saw was Padraig Coltrane riding Beckinsale's stallion. Coltrane commanded a lot of attention, but he did little more than glance at Samuel as he passed by.

Samuel stopped under the awning of a hardware store. His heart pounded. He watched Coltrane dismount and tie the stallion to a rail. Coltrane walked up a flight of stone steps and let himself into the nearby bank. In less than three minutes, he returned, sliding a packet into one of the panniers. He untied the reins and walked the horse in Samuel's direction. Samuel quickly turned his back, knelt, and pretended to tie his bootlace. He could see Coltrane by his reflection in the hardware store window. Coltrane was looking for somewhere to tether his horse. 'Hey, lad,' he said.

Samuel turned halfway. He was still lacing up his boot.

'Hold on to my horse for a minute,' he said, 'and I'll make it worth your while.'

'All right,' said Samuel. He stood. Coltrane arrogantly handed him the reins. The door of the hardware store was attached to a bell that rang when he opened it. He ducked inside and the door swung shut behind him.

Samuel told the horse exactly what he was going to do. He passed the reins over Phaeton's head and put his left foot in the stirrup. Coltrane was so tall that when Samuel swung up into the saddle his boots dangled loose, so he simply dug his heels into the horse's ribs and rode out on to the avenue at a gallop with the stirrups swinging up and down. He glanced behind only once as he spurred the horse forward and saw Coltrane burst out of the hardware store brandishing a handgun. Samuel lay flat along the horse's neck. He heard the crack of Coltrane's pistol, and above the clatter of the horse's hooves he heard the whiz of the bullet as it passed within inches of his ears. Coltrane fired again, and this time the bullet passed clean through one of the saddlebags and grazed the outside of Samuel's thigh. He reined the horse to the right down a side street and through the traffic, heading for the hobo jungle down by the river flats.

Samuel guessed what he would find in the saddlebags and he was right. As he halted in a cloud of dust among the shanties and called out for the doctor, he unbuckled the satchel and pulled up a handful of bills. Some of them were shot clean through. The men gathered round and held out their hands while Samuel passed out the bank notes.

'Where's the doctor?' shouted Samuel.

Men began running from all four corners of the shantytown, and finally, among them, he saw the doctor hobble forwards.

'Doc,' said Samuel, 'I owe you this.' He handed him a fistful of Coltrane's money.

The doctor looked puzzled. 'Do I know you, lad?'

Samuel looked over his shoulder at the road. No sign of Coltrane. 'You once patched me up and my friend Charleyboy.'

The doctor still looked bewildered.

'Charleyboy was an Indian.'

'I remember,' said the doctor, tucking the money into his trousers. 'You've been in the wars again, I see.'

'I need to hide this horse.'

The doctor shook his head. 'You can't hide a horse like that,' he said. 'Especially not from Padraig Coltrane.'

'You know him?'

'Everybody knows him and that … preposterous horse. Keep riding, lad, while you can. I'll try and detain him when he comes.'

Samuel handed the last of the money to the doctor. 'See this gets around, then,' he said.

'I will. Hang on, lad.' The doctor disappeared into one of the huts. He came back checking the cylinder of a Webley service revolver. He snapped it shut and handed it over. 'You've only got three bullets,' he said. 'Should Padraig Coltrane find you, you save at least one of them for him.'

'Thank you.'

'Now go.'

Samuel dug his heels into the horse's ribs. Phaeton tossed his head and snorted. He seemed to approve of this change in his fortunes.

He headed west with a mind to outrun Coltrane all the way to Ashcroft. It was a long shot, but he reckoned if he could return the stallion to Beckinsale, then Coltrane would have to fight Beckinsale over it, and Beckinsale still owned the papers, after all. Samuel rode hard past the rail yards and quit the road to head up into the hills. He looked behind. No sign of pursuit yet. His path took him among alkali lakes, chalk-white at the edges where they'd dried out, then red and sulphurous yellow in their centres where nothing would grow. There were numerous tracks along that higher ground, and he rode toward the setting sun without the cover of the trees until his path began to dip into a valley forested with ponderosa on the upper slopes, then fir as the valley swung north and opened out onto the shores of Kamloops Lake.

It was dark by the time he struck the steep Kamloops Road. He reckoned Coltrane's men had likely come after him in a motor vehicle, and he gambled that he could go unnoticed on the road for a few miles before cutting up into the hills and hiding for the night. It was too dark to ride any farther. At first light he could ride south over the mountain to the Thompson, but from there he would have to take his chances over open ground.

He crested the hill and left the road as it began to wind down the other side to Savona, but he'd not ridden more than two hundred feet before he could see, among the few spare trees down the leeward side of the mountain, the shape of four horses and beyond them, the glow of a campfire. One of the horses was Ignatius. He halted the stallion. He could have hit the horses with a stone. He'd gotten a half hour head start on Coltrane and his men and they'd still caught him up.

He dismounted so as not to be sighted in the moonlight and turned the stallion around. He led Phaeton back downhill to the road and tied him to a tree, but the stallion was not happy about it. Samuel swore softly and took off his coat to cover the horse's eyes. When Phaeton had calmed down, Samuel crept back up the hill and quietly approached the hobbled horses.

Ignatius woke and nickered softly as Samuel neared. Samuel raised his hands in a placating gesture and kept his knife in his belt lest he spook the other horses. Ignatius was coming home with him. The rest he would cut loose. By the time the men realized their mounts were gone, the horses would be scattered over the slope.

Samuel knelt and cut the hobbles of all four horses, but as they began to separate, one of them stumbled into a tree and let out a high whinny. Samuel quickly hid behind a fir. He took the pistol from his belt.

The man who ran over was so busy cursing he didn't see Samuel right away. By the time he caught the panicked horse and saw the severed hobbles, Samuel had stepped out from behind his tree and levelled the pistol. The man put his hands up slowly. The horse drifted away.

'If you're carrying a weapon, drop it,' said Samuel.

The man did not answer right away. He tilted his head inquisitively to one side. 'I don't remember cutting you,' he said.

'Turn around,' said Samuel.

The tattooed man turned and walked back toward the fire. As they drew closer, Samuel recognized the other two men beside Coltrane. One of them was Coltrane's right-hand man, the other was one of the thugs who had beaten him and Charleyboy in the alley. The two men stood up. Coltrane didn't. He didn't even look over. He sat watching the fire as if hypnotized.

'Just shoot him,' said the tattooed man.

'Throw your weapons in the fire,' said Samuel.

The men hesitated.

'A loaded pistol in a fire might explode, boy,' said Coltrane.

Samuel pressed the barrel to the back of the tattooed man's head. 'That's a chance we'll all have to take,' said Samuel.

Coltrane turned his head wearily, as if no more than annoyed at this sudden inconvenience. 'You know we're going to get you in the end,' said Coltrane. He directed the men to throw their weapons down. They reached for their pistols and dropped them at the edge of the fire.

'Kick them into the fire,' said Samuel.

The men glanced at Coltrane. He jutted his chin. 'Even if Beckinsale gets that horse back, it's you we'll be coming for. It's just a matter of time. Nobody steals from me.'

'I know three men who did,' answered Samuel. 'Made a real fool of you.'

The two men standing glanced sideways. 'Ask your men here what they did with your money, after they robbed us in Kamloops.'

Coltrane studied the men. The men would not look at him. They kept their eyes fixed on Samuel.

'Did you get it back?'

'He's lying,' said the tattooed man.

'How much more do you think they've stolen?' said Samuel.

'You little shit,' said the tattooed man.

'And if their loyalty is in question, then it's only a matter of time for you, isn't it? Like you did to O'Neill, they'll do to you.'

'Is that gun even loaded?' said Coltrane.

'You bet,' said Samuel. *Three bullets, four men.*

Coltrane stared at him, unblinking. His blue eyes flickered in the fire-light. 'What did you do with the money you stole from me today?' he said.

'I gave it away.'

Coltrane nodded. He pursed his lips. 'To those bums in the hobo jungle, then. A regular Robin Hood you are,' he said. 'What do you want?'

'Just the horses,' said Samuel. 'The stallion and my father's horse. The gelding.'

'And if I say no?'

'Then I shoot you.'

'All four of us?'

'All four of you,' said Samuel. 'And you wouldn't be the first.'

'You never killed anybody,' said the tattooed man.

'Two days out of Ashcroft,' Samuel said, 'Riding that stolen horse I killed the man who tried to take it. Crushed his temple with a rock. An Englishman. Sheldrake was his name.'

Coltrane and his men had heard of Sheldrake's murder, without knowing who had committed it. Sheldrake had enemies all over the province.

'What about the man he was with?' said Coltrane.

'Sheldrake shot him in the head,' said Samuel.

'What did he look like?'

'Heavy-set. Black hair. Long beard.'

Coltrane nodded. 'His name was Lepp,' he said. 'A good soldier.'

'He's bluffing,' said the tattooed man. 'He won't shoot us.'

'You shut up,' snapped Coltrane. He turned back to Samuel.

Samuel's arm was beginning to shake from levelling the pistol.

Coltrane squinted at Samuel. 'I know your name,' he said. 'I know your mother is fucking Daniel Beckinsale. I know your father's done nothing about it.'

'The kid's lying to you, boss,' said his right-hand man.

'Tell you what,' said Coltrane. 'I'll let you take that stallion. You do what you have to do and then you disappear, you understand? I ever see you again I'll kill you. And your cuckold of a father as well,' he added. 'If your mother's with Beckinsale she's already suffering a fate worse than death. Go on then.' Coltrane nodded. 'Couldn't find a buyer anyway.' He shrugged. 'Horse breeders these days need proof of the pedigree. It's criminal,' he added, with a half smile.

'So we're even?' said Samuel.

'We're even.'

Samuel nodded. He slowly backed away, keeping the pistol levelled at Coltrane and his men. Ignatius stood waiting where he'd been hobbled and Samuel backed square into the horse's flank. Ignatius nickered and turned his neck. With his free hand Samuel fumbled for the bridle and just turned and made a run for it. He heard three gunshots in quick succession and flinched. When he made it back over the rise, out of sight, he heard three more shots, more evenly spaced, and methodical.

CHAPTER SEVENTEEN

Dawn found Samuel sitting Ignatius in Kamloops Lake watching the desert country form itself out of the grey light. He had looped Phaeton's catch rope round the pommel of his saddle and the reunited horses stood together, belly deep, drinking the cool, clear water. Soon the first bars of sunlight broke over the Monashees and fell fifty miles across the surface of the lake. A gaggle of geese honked overhead in V formation. Horses and rider raised their eyes to the sky, and when the geese had passed, the horses lowered their heads to the lake and drank again.

When Samuel turned both horses around to ride out of the lake, he saw two children standing on the shore. The little girl was wearing a canary-yellow dress. He reached the shore and got down off his horse. 'Hello,' he said.

They did not answer. He guessed the girl was about seven or eight. The boy was older, eleven maybe. He watched Samuel warily.

'What are your names?' said Samuel.

'What's yours?' said the boy.

'Samuel Hewitt.'

The boy gave him a look like he was wise to adults and their tall tales. 'You ain't Sam Hewitt,' he said.

'No?'

'Nah. Sam Hewitt's a modern-day Robin Hood. Steals from the rich to give to the poor.'

Samuel nodded gravely. 'Is that right? Well, what does he look like, this Sam Hewitt?'

'He's not much older than us,' said the boy. 'Rides a white horse.'

The little girl looked up at Samuel. She put her hands on her hips. 'Everybody knows Sam Hewitt,' she said.

Samuel nodded. 'Everybody but me, I guess.'

'Is that your horse?' said the boy.

'No,' said Samuel. 'He belongs to a man in Ashcroft. I'm taking him home.'

'That's a nice horse,' said the boy. He had yet to smile. He bent and picked up a twig off the sand and snapped it.

'Sure is,' said Samuel. 'But the gentle one, the gelding, that's the one I'd choose.'

The little girl was watching him closely. 'What happened to your face?' she said.

'Mabel,' the boy admonished.

Samuel crouched down to look her right in the eyes. 'I got in a fight. A man cut me.' He watched the girl look at his face. She reached and traced the line of the scar with her fingers. Her brother grew visibly uneasy.

'What were you fighting over?'

'A girl,' said Samuel.

'A girl? Did you win?'

'No,' said Samuel.

'He did.'

'No.'

The girl looked confused.

'I'm going to get Dad,' said the boy.

'Was she pretty?'

'Yes,' Samuel said. 'She was beautiful.'

The girl nodded. Then she frowned again. 'Where is she now?'

'I'm not sure.'

The girl looked away. She let out a long sigh. 'She was stolen away, wasn't she?'

Samuel sat down in the sand. 'No,' he said. 'It wasn't quite like that.'

'So what happened?'

Samuel thought about how best to reply. 'I don't know,' he said, eventually. 'Maybe she got scared.'

'Why?'

'Well. You live around here, right?'

The girl nodded.

'Have you ever been somewhere you've never been before?'

'We went to Kelowna once, last summer.'

'Then imagine yourself there all alone. Where you don't know anybody. And everything's different.'

'But she'd never be alone,' said the girl. 'She'd have you.'

Samuel looked at her. Then he looked off along the shoreline. He saw the boy and his father approaching down the beach. 'Well, then,' he said. 'I guess it just wasn't me she was waiting for.'

The boy and his father were nearly upon them.

Samuel stood up. The man balked at the sight of him, the scars on his face. He held out his hand to Mabel. 'Come here, honey,' he said.

'Good day, sir,' said Samuel.

The man nodded. He looked at the stallion, then he looked back at Samuel. 'Where are you headed?' he said.

'Ashcroft,' said the boy. 'It's not his horse.'

'Well. Godspeed,' said the man. He turned and led the two of them away. The man leaned in to talk to his son. 'You never leave your sister alone like that again, you hear,' he heard the man say.

Samuel rode west toward the Deadman River and by noon had reached the petroglyphs. He turned the horses out to graze and ate some of what Catharine had packed for him—mostly dried meat and rye bread, a little fruit. He sat studying the ancient rock paintings. Some of them had faded beyond recognition but many were still clearly defined, though what they were supposed to be was still obscure. The birds looked like no birds he had ever seen. They seemed half-bird, half-man, and dancing. Like dreams of birds.

Samuel fell asleep. He dreamed that his hands were burning and he could not put them out. He sank them in the river but the river began to burn. He buried them in the sand but the sand caught fire. He ran and the air itself burst into flame.

When he woke he smelled woodsmoke. Somewhere to the north a real forest fire was burning, and when he caught the horses and set out once more the sky had become thick with smoke, making ghosts of the low mountains either side of the Thompson. Evening sunlight, diffused by the haze, had turned the sky orange. Against all odds, a rain cloud settled over the valley, and the rain, when it came, fell so heavy it bounced off the surface of the blacktop and turned the road into a river of molten copper.

By sundown Samuel had ridden through the storm and into the ruins of Walhachin. He built a fire from the fallen roof timbers within the ruined church, hung his clothes out to dry and ate what remained of his food.

Ignatius and the stallion stood at the edge of the firelight, heads bowed. Their shadows occupied the entire wall of the chancel. Wrapped in his blanket, Samuel watched the firelight flicker on the stallion's glossy black flank. He recalled the first time he'd seen Josephine, wet from bathing in the lake, and the sadness in her smile, which he'd presumed to understand. He wondered if the ringmaster, left unattended, had yet walked to his death into the sea. He thought about what Helena had said—*that his life was none of his business*—and, indeed, while it seemed to Samuel that his story was but one thread folded head to tail into a far larger pantomime, at what point, he wondered, is an actor called to account? A gangster's blood on his hands he could live with, but Charleyboy's?

In the morning he left without building a fire. The rain had swelled the river and the water ran brown. Spawning chinook rested at the river's muddy edges, waiting for the level to subside. He rode beside the river until midmorning when he left the valley altogether, avoiding the gorge into which he and Charleyboy had fled a lifetime ago. He climbed the valley side to rejoin the highway, riding the blacktop for a mile and a half and then cutting across country once again to avoid the town of Cache Creek. When he came at last to the cliffs above the Bonaparte, he found a trail of sorts that led down the sandstone slopes. He followed it to the valley floor, forded the river, and approached the abandoned cabin from the east.

Smoke rose from the riverbank, and when he rode closer to the source of the fire he saw sides of raw sockeye dangling from greenwood poles above the flames, swaying gently in the updraft, and a man hunched before the coals, wreathed in smoke.

Robert Hewitt turned at the sound of Samuel's approach. He stood up. Ignatius recognized Robert and whinnied. He trotted over to Robert and nuzzled him. Robert smiled and rubbed Ignatius's neck.

His father had cut his hair and trimmed his beard, and though he still wore his hair long he looked grounded. He looked clean.

'I've been worried about you, son,' he said, without looking up.

'What are you doing down here?'

'Well'—he glanced up—'I've got a lot to tell you.'

'So do I,' said Samuel.

'Is that—'

'Yeah. Phaeton. Beckinsale's stallion.'

His father let out a short laugh. He looked at his son and shook his head with a mixture of admiration and parental disapproval.

When Samuel climbed down and stood eye to eye with his father, Robert's face became grave. 'It's all right,' said Samuel.

'What happened?'

'I got into some trouble.'

Robert gently seized his son's jaw, turning his face sideways. Then he saw the scar under his collar. He pulled his shirt aside. 'Your mother's gonna have your guts for garters when she sees you,' he said. 'Her beautiful boy. How many stitches?'

'I lost count.'

'We've heard so many things.'

'We?'

'Sit down, son.'

They sat beside the fire on upended logs, and at his father's urging Samuel told his story. He described how he'd narrowly escaped getting shot stealing Beckinsale's stallion, how he'd passed this very spot beside the river, this paradise, and felt like Adam expelled from Eden. He said he'd seen a man shot through the head a mile or so beyond Walhachin, watched his brains arc out the side of his skull and fall like bloody rain upon the river. He said that later that same day he'd taken aim with a rock and, without thinking, felled the killer with a blow to the temple.

Samuel's father listened intently, nodding occasionally and saying nothing. Samuel told him about Coltrane, about getting robbed and knocked out in an alley. He showed his father his missing tooth. He said he'd joined the circus and there he'd met a villain, a witch, and a wounded king. He said that he'd tried to save a damsel in distress who didn't ask to be saved, and learned that love could never be stolen—only offered. He said that he and the villain had more in common than he'd wanted to admit. In the end, Samuel said, all he'd succeeded in doing was getting his best friend killed.

After that he'd wandered, lost and aimless, into the mountains, and, overcome with hunger, eaten a mushroom that had made him lose his mind, then find it again. He said that when his mind was lost he'd had a waking dream, the same dream that always haunted him, of the raven crucified upon the wall. He said that since he thought he had poisoned himself, and had nothing left to lose, he confronted, at last, the fearsome raven, and to his surprise felt only pity. He said that when he gave the raven what it begged for—what it had always begged for—the raven had turned into him, into his father.

Samuel's last words hung in the air between them for some time, suspended for each of them to confront.

After a while, Samuel said that when he'd come to his senses he'd seen a family of wolves feeding on a deer, and that the feast had seemed to him a sacrament, a fact of life both terrible and holy—base, bloody, yet beatific all at once. In the mountains he'd watched the wind, like an unseen hand, smooth the surface of a meadow so full of flowers, so beautiful, that he'd thought to remain there forever. But in the end, he said, he'd come down from that mountain because he believed that living on one's own entailed an exile that, while blissfully without enmity, was also devoid of compassion, and therefore without grace.

As he composed his thoughts, Samuel stared intently at the coals. He did not see the tears well in his father's eyes; he simply poked the embers with a stick until the smoke rose anew. Robert stayed silent, watchful.

Finally, Samuel said that on his journey back to Ashcroft he'd met two broken men with the blues. One sought to heal himself by remembering. The other did his best to forget. One would not leave his lodgings, the other would not stay put. Neither one, Samuel said, had succeeded in again becoming whole.

'I heard about Charleyboy,' said Robert. 'His father went to Oregon—Portland, was it? Got a call from the sheriff there.'

'I have to go see his mom,' said Samuel.

'You'll have to see your own as well. Face the music. She's been beside herself. I'm living down here now,' his father said, after a while, 'because the house burned down. With me in it,' he added. 'Which was quite the rude awakening—literally and figuratively.'

Robert poked the fire with a greenwood stick and piled on more branches. Sunlight began to slant through the smoke where it billowed up around the pinking salmon.

'What's Beckinsale going to do to me for stealing his horse?'

'I'd be more worried about Padraig Coltrane,' his father said. 'You stole that horse back, I gather?'

'I did.' Samuel smiled. 'But we cut a deal. I've got to get out of town, is all.'

A short distance away, beyond the cottonwoods, the sockeye massed in the river shallows like a marching band.

'What are you going to do?'

Samuel shrugged. 'I don't know. Join the army.'

'You're in the killing business, now, Samuel Hewitt?'

'Everybody's good at something.'

'You don't know what you're talking about,' warned his father. 'Look at me.'

Samuel looked into his father's eyes. He'd not seen him so fired up in years.

'You stay away from war,' his father admonished. 'You hear me? Getting killed is the least of it.'

'I'm not a child anymore.'

'Promise me,' his father urged.

'What happened in France, Dad?'

But his father would not answer. He sat back. He watched Samuel intently. After a while he turned back to the fire and shook his head gravely. 'And don't fall in love either,' his father said. 'It'll break your heart.'

Samuel spent the night on a cot in his father's cabin wrapped in a Hudson's Bay blanket. In the morning he rose and washed at the river's edge. He cleaned the sweat and dust out of his clothes. The salmon scattered as he bent to his ablutions, and when he finished, they drifted back to fill the gap in their ranks. He carried his clothes back to the porch and laid them over the rails to dry and sat down on the steps in just his shorts. The sun was not long up and warm for all it was October. He sat there with his eyes closed listening to the river, to a late dragonfly, to the snap of a twig and soft thud of an apple striking the earth.

After a while, Robert joined him on the porch. He sat down and handed Samuel a steaming mug of coffee. They sat there for a while in silence.

'What day is it anyway?' said Samuel.

'October 20th,' said his father. 'If you'd asked me three weeks ago I wouldn't have been able to tell you.' He picked up a package he'd brought with him and handed it to Samuel—a small box about six inches square, wrapped in brown paper and tied up with twine. 'Caroline Hewitt' was written across the front in his father's small, neat handwriting. 'When you see your mother,' Robert said, 'will you give her that?'

'What is it?'

'Just something I saved from the fire. If Beckinsale sees *Hewitt* he'll likely toss it. Make sure you put it in her hands.'

'You don't think Beckinsale will shoot me?'

His father pursed his lips and shook his head. 'I think your mother quelled his vengeance after you ran off with that horse. She'll do the same again now.'

Samuel reached into his boots and retrieved the revolver. 'Then I'm leaving this with you,' he said. He handed the revolver to his father, handle first.

His father recoiled. He looked at the gun like it might be alive and have a mind of its own.

'I didn't use it.'

After a while, his father reached for the revolver. He quickly cracked the cylinder and emptied the rounds into his hand, before snapping the cylinder shut and sliding the pistol along the porch boards, out of arm's reach. He dropped the bullets into the top pocket of his shirt.

Robert drained his coffee and got up. 'You'll want to go to Charleyboy's soon,' he said. 'While his father's still in Oregon.'

Samuel untied the reins from the porch rail, mounted Phaeton for the second last time and climbed the same trail he and Charleyboy had descended not four months ago. On the main road he met two men on horseback who studied the horse he was riding and nodded warily. They turned their horses in the road to watch him go. One of them called out his name like a question, but Samuel pretended he didn't hear. When he reached the bottom of the switchbacks and the bridgehead he left the paved road and followed the north side of the river onto the reservation. Charleyboy's house displayed the same neglect and disrepair it had the day they'd left. The screen door hung off its hinges. The porch steps slanted sideways, and a busted front window was boarded up. A mean-looking dog on a chain barked at him as he climbed unsteadily off the stallion and approached the house.

Charleyboy's mother sat in what passed for her kitchen, staring spellbound at the door as if she'd dropped whatever she'd been doing upon hearing the news and was waiting for proof—this pale angel of death, this disfigured boy—and it was not until Samuel stood there in the flesh, without Charleyboy, that she could believe her son was dead. Samuel took off his hat.

He'd not so much as crossed the threshold before Charleyboy's mother collapsed. The words he'd tried so hard to piece together proved unnecessary, and of no use. Her grief was soundless, and profound. With a grimace she gripped the edges of her kitchen chair and rocked backwards and forwards. The chair legs creaked beneath her like a metronome. After a time she struggled to her feet, seized the closest thing at hand and threw it. The drinking glass missed Samuel by a hair's breadth and smashed against the doorjamb. She groped for something else—a glass ashtray—and threw that too. This time it struck Samuel in the chest and he stumbled backwards out the door onto the porch. The dog lunged at him, barking fit to burst. Charleyboy's mother sprang off her seat. She slammed the screen door shut and it fell off its last hinge. Only then did her voice find its range. She screamed at the door and she screamed at Samuel with a rage decades old.

Samuel didn't speak, or turn away, until her face became expressionless. Charleyboy's mother would not look at him. After a while she knelt, swept her long black hair over her shoulders and began picking up the shards of broken glass. Samuel tried to help her but she warned him away.

Samuel descended the slanted steps and made his way toward the waiting stallion. The dog stopped barking. It lay down with its head on its front paws. Samuel was shaking so badly he could hardly fit his foot into the stirrup, but he managed at last to climb onto the stallion and rein him around. He looked one last time at the house. Charleyboy's mother knelt beside the front door, collecting the last shards of glass with bleeding hands.

With a grim and determined expression, Samuel rode over the bridge into Ashcroft, past the fire hall and up Railway Avenue into town. He was in no mood to trade small talk, and not a single citizen ventured to engage him. They simply stopped whatever they were doing and watched him go. He pushed the stallion to a trot, and without so much as glancing at the fork that led up to his father's house, he rode the stallion up to Beckinsale's estate, between the cherry trees that lined the driveway, around the back of the house and up to the stable gate. A groom filling the water trough saw him waiting there and went to fetch Silas. Silas ducked out of the side door halfway along the barn, crossed the yard and swung open the gate without saying a word. Samuel rode the stallion into the yard and dismounted. He handed the reins to the groom and Silas inspected every inch of the horse before he told the groom to put him up.

Silas turned and confronted Samuel. 'If it were left to me,' he said, 'I'd string you up.'

'If it were left to me,' answered Samuel, calmly, 'I'd let you.'

A young woman interrupted by opening a back door to the house. She gestured at the entrance and stood aside, holding the door open with her back.

Samuel crossed the yard and preceded the young woman through the door. She was pretty and had a scar of her own across one cheek. He left his hat on a low bench just inside the door and with his father's package in hand, followed her down a corridor into the kitchen. She sat him at a long refectory table reserved for the stable hands and poured him water from a pitcher, unwilling to look him in the eye. When he thanked her she blushed before hurrying off. He heard her footsteps retreat down the hallway and up a flight of stairs.

Samuel glanced about the kitchen as he drank. The servants were busy preparing what appeared to be a banquet. The room was so large that women cooking at the massive cast-iron range were forced to shout their orders to the scullery maids beside the pantry at the opposite end, away from the windows and the heat of the ovens. The kitchen was bigger than his father's whole house. Nobody paid him any mind.

When he had finished his glass of water, another, better-dressed girl arrived and led him from the kitchen and down a long corridor that opened onto a vestibule the full height of the house. The parquet floor gave way to a carpeted staircase that swept up to a landing and split in two directions to wrap around and meet again in a minstrel's gallery. The walls above the wainscoting on the stairwell were hung with portraits of Beckinsale's forebears—grim-looking patriarchs dressed in regalia either real or pretended—and painted landscapes that did not look Canadian. On the landing, in a glass bell jar, a taxidermied peacock perched on a branch. Behind it hung a tapestry in imitation of the Bayeux. The girl asked him to wait a few moments, then entered a door across the way. He heard voices from inside the room, one of them a man's.

A short while later, Daniel Beckinsale burst through the door. The man was smaller than Samuel remembered. He stopped dead when he saw Samuel. He slammed the door shut and began to stalk back and forth over the black and white flagstones, his plump, well-fed face scarlet, his dark eyes drilling into Samuel's until, at length, he roared like an animal in a cage and stormed up the stairs, taking the treads two at a time. Samuel heard another door slam. Beckinsale yelled something. Then it was silent.

The young maid emerged discreetly from the tall, panelled doors that led into the drawing room. She gestured for Samuel to enter. Samuel crossed the vestibule, stepped into the room and the maid quietly closed the doors behind him.

Samuel's mother stood before a large picture window, looking out into the garden with her fists pressed into the window ledge. She turned to him as he entered. She looked furious, defiant, and she had clearly been crying. 'Samuel,' she said. Relief drained the violence from her eyes. She quickly crossed the room, her silks rustling, and when she saw the scar upon his face she stopped short. 'Dear God.' She wept. 'What did you do?'

'I brought your horse back,' Samuel said.

Caroline tried to compose herself. She embraced him. Samuel had forgotten the smell of her hair. It smelled like yellow roses.

Caroline released him. She took him by the hand and led him farther into the room. By the light of the enormous window, she looked more closely at his face. 'I know why you took it,' she said, tracing the seam on his face with her fingertips.

Samuel turned to the window and took in the view. Beckinsale had spent a fortune irrigating the benchland, excavating the rabbitbrush and bunchgrass to plant fescue he'd landscaped into a sloping lawn. Close beneath the window, before a ha-ha dropped the lawn to another level, he spied a rectangular knot garden of begonias and small ornamental roses laid out in orderly rows, the borders trimmed perfectly, the low topiary immaculate. It seemed to him a thing so utterly foreign, so fragile and temporary in that otherwise wild and inhospitable land that he was moved beyond his distaste of its artifice toward something approaching pity.

'Are you ever coming home?' he said.

His mother turned to the window and wiped her eyes. She smoothed her dress across her thighs. 'Did you not read the letter I left you?'

'No.'

'Well,' she said. 'That explains a lot. We have lost so much time.'

Samuel remembered the package his father had given him. He handed the brown-paper-wrapped box to his mother.

'What's this?'

'Dad asked me to give it to you.'

His mother took the package and placed it on the window ledge. 'Come and sit down,' she said.

She gestured to a settee arranged before the fireplace. Above the mantel hung the Gainsborough-like portrait—the one Charleyboy had told him about—of his mother riding sidesaddle wearing an ostrich feather hat. In the picture she carried a golden apple in her left hand.

'Do you know why we came here?' Caroline began, more composed now. 'To Ashcroft?'

'For a job.'

'There were jobs in Vancouver,' said his mother. She looked into his eyes. 'Four years into our marriage, your father left me. You were a year old. He went off with'—she paused—'another woman.'

Caroline looked down at her hands. She fidgeted with a ring Samuel had never seen before. 'Your father eventually came back and things improved for a while, but they were never the same. I didn't trust him. We moved here and he became close with Eloise—an old woman, but even she made me jealous.'

'So this is revenge,' Samuel said. He gestured at the massive room, at her portrait on the wall.

'No,' said Caroline. 'This is … growing up.' She shrugged. 'I was a girl when I met your father. He had already been to war.'

Samuel studied her portrait. He tried to interpret her gaze, her Mona Lisa smile. 'Tell me about the golden apple,' he said.

Caroline reached for her teacup. Her hands were shaking and the cup rattled on its saucer. 'A fairy tale,' she said dismissively.

'Tell me,' said Samuel. He looked his mother square in the eye.

Caroline sipped her tea, then placed the cup and saucer back on the table. 'Do you know the story of Atalanta? Our Classics professor told us one day during a lecture—the very class in which I met your father. There was once a king in Arcadia who wanted a son to succeed him, but his wife gave him only daughters. When she gave birth to a third daughter, the idiot king, in his rage, cast the babe out onto a hillside to die.' An habitual actress, Caroline convincingly mimed tossing a hat, or a rag. Suddenly self-conscious, she adjusted the hem of her dress.

'A hunter found the crying baby and took her home. He raised her as his own. She grew to be a proud girl, a fast runner, and accurate as any man with a bow and arrow. She also found no lack of suitors among the men of the region. But even as word of her beauty spread and men came from far and wide, she refused to marry any man who could not beat her in a footrace. If he won, she would marry. If he lost, he lost his head as well.'

They heard a knock on the door. 'Come in,' said Caroline.

Samuel half expected Beckinsale, but it was the young maid who had escorted him through the vestibule. 'May I take the tray now, ma'am?' she said.

'Thank you, Miranda,' said Caroline.

They waited for Miranda to depart.

'Many men tried,' Caroline went on, more self-assured now, more at home with her role. 'All of them failed. Until a certain fellow came along by the name of Milanion. He was handsome, and his heart was kind. But still, Atalanta would not relent. Milanion would have to defeat her in a footrace or suffer the same fate as his predecessors. Milanion accepted the challenge, but got some unexpected help. You see, Atalanta had angered Venus, the goddess of love, by murdering so many potential lovers. So Venus devised a plan. She plucked three golden apples from her orchard on the island of Cyprus and told Milanion to toss them out in front of Atalanta as she raced. Atalanta would not be able to resist picking them up and, weighed down with gold, would lose the race, and her heart, to Milanion.

The race began. The crowd cheered. Atalanta and Milanion ran neck and neck for a while until Atalanta began to pull ahead. Milanion rolled the first apple in her path. It tumbled into a ravine. Atalanta, attracted by the glint of gold, abandoned the race to pursue it. You can guess how it goes from here,' said Caroline. 'She caught up to Milanion, he tossed another apple. She caught him again, he tossed the third. In the end he crossed the finish line first to the ovation of all the spectators.'

Samuel waited but his mother did not continue.

'Like I said, fairy tales,' said Caroline. 'However,' she went on, 'when I woke up the next morning after that class, imagine my surprise when I found a golden apple outside my dormitory door. Though surprised is not an adequate description. Stabbed would be more accurate. Wounded, more germane. He must have persuaded Matron,' said Caroline. 'I always suspected her hustle and bustle was a cover for something more … venal.' Caroline glanced at Samuel. 'Your father was a hopeless romantic,' she said, 'and very charming.' She smiled weakly and adjusted her new diamond ring. 'You're a good listener, Samuel.'

Samuel glanced again at her portrait. 'Who commissioned that?' he said.

'Danny, of course.'

'Does he know that story?'

'Of course not.'

'Then why are you holding an apple?'

Caroline didn't have a ready answer. She fidgeted again with the hem of her dress.

'Do I owe Beckinsale anything?'

Caroline shook her head. She did not look up.

'When I was crossing back into Canada through the mountains,' Samuel said, 'I realized I don't know your story. Not as you might tell it, anyway. Everyone's the hero of his—or her—own story. But it really doesn't matter, in the end, what we think. Our stories tell *us*, not the other way round.'

His mother pursed her lips and nodded. 'When did you become so wise?' she said.

'When I lost my best friend.'

'Charleyboy. We heard. I'm sorry.'

'I don't like Daniel Beckinsale,' said Samuel. He looked up one last time at her portrait, and either side at the severed heads and glass eyes of mounted game animals that ran the length of the wall. 'But it's none of my business, is it?'

Caroline looked relieved. Tears returned to her eyes. Samuel stood and made to leave. 'Thank you for the tea,' he said.

'You didn't drink any,' his mother replied.

After Samuel left, Caroline went to the window and looked for him on the driveway. She watched him walk down the aisle of cherry trees, through the gates and onto the road until she couldn't see him anymore. For a moment, she fooled herself that he might come around, in time, then sadly dismissed the notion. He had always been his father's boy. Just as unyielding, just as … remote. She looked down at the package she had left upon the windowsill, her name printed across the surface in Robert's neat hand. She untied the string and slid her fingers beneath the fold of brown paper. She removed the wrapping and opened the lid, then dropped the box as if it were on fire when she beheld what it contained.

At the same time, Daniel Beckinsale opened the drawing room door, knowing that Samuel had departed. With a furrowed brow, he stopped with the toe of one boot the wooden apple, painted gold, that rolled toward him across the floor.

When Samuel stepped onto the track that led up the benchlands to his house a mile distant, he could already see the grassland turned black. The wind had blown the fire to the very edges of the acreage, burned the fence and gate and blackened the mailbox on its post. The flap on the mailbox hung wide open. When he reached it, he groped inside and found a yellowed envelope with a postmark from Toronto and inside it a cheque for two dollars made out to his father.

But that was all he found. Rummaging around in the wreckage, he tried to find something worth saving. Anything. A keepsake maybe, or a photograph that had survived the flames. But there was nothing. When he toed aside the fallen roof timbers, his boots raised only small clouds of dust that settled in the cuffs of his jeans and that a few days later, washing his clothes once again in the river, he would find as a silent reminder that nothing endures.

Samuel stuffed the cheque into his shirt pocket, filled the envelope with ashes, sat down in what had once been his bedroom and wept.

It was late afternoon before he rose, stiff from sitting for so long. His face and hands were smeared with tears and soot. He walked the four miles through Ashcroft, spoke to no one, crossed the bridge and laboured up the long switchbacks to the top of the hill. When he'd caught his breath he quit the road and made his way through the rabbitbrush to the edge of the cliff. Tired and footsore, he sat for a while and studied the canyon. In the early evening light the river ran like gold through a sluice. Even from a distance he could see the sockeye massed in the shallows like a gathering army, and he blessed them for their struggle, for their return after years at sea to the same gravel fan or shallow eddy where they were conceived, only to burn in their birth water, their skin torn to shreds, their strength utterly spent.

At length he rose and made his way down into the canyon. He looked for his father in the garden, in the orchard, and then inside the cabin, but Robert was not there. Samuel could hear the river clearly now, catch the splash and surge of fish thrashing upstream, and when he made his way among the cottonwoods and their long, protracted shadows to the water's edge, he saw his father standing midstream, naked to the waist, encircled by sockeye as if he'd called them to communion. Robert bent and splashed water over his face and neck, then again, then a third time, and only after these ablutions did he look up and notice his son. He raised one thin arm in greeting, his face grave. Samuel waved back. 'Look how they fight,' his father called out.

At length he waded out of the river and sat beside his son. He wrung the water from his hair and put his shirt back on. As he began to snap the buttons, Samuel asked, without anger, 'Why didn't you fight for her?'

His father paused for an instant, then continued to button his shirt in his slow, contemplative way. 'Because I didn't blame her,' he said, rolling up his shirtsleeves. 'I was too far gone.'

'She told me you cheated.'

'I did,' said his father, 'which is itself unforgivable. But by the time I was your age, or thereabouts, I had already seen and done things no one should ever have to do.'

'What happened, Dad? She always said you'd never speak of it.'

'Which I see now was wrong. I didn't give your mother enough credit. And I was scared. But listen, a man does what he can to shield the ones he loves from certain … dire truths. And reckonings. The terrible irony, of course, is that by shielding your loved ones you also wall yourself in. And that's when the voices … well, they amplify.'

'What voices?' said Samuel, but his father only shook his head and would not answer.

'And why Beckinsale?' said Samuel, shaking his head.

'Not important.'

'He's such an ass.'

'Think of him like an overgrown schoolboy,' said his father, 'showing off his shiny toys. Still staking his claim in the sandbox.'

'That makes it worse.'

'He never went to France, Sam. They wouldn't let him. He has an irregular heartbeat. The man might die tonight, in his sleep. You see? Every man has his own cross to bear.'

In his mind's eye, Samuel saw Charleyboy lying dead in the morgue, his face like grey wax.

'How did it go with Charleyboy's mom?' said his father, as if he'd read his son's mind.

'Not well.'

'That's two she's lost,' his father said. 'I can't even imagine.'

Robert watched the river and the salmon. The sunlight was leaving the surface of the water, crawling up the canyon walls. The bright crimson backs of the spawning sockeye darkened to a wet brick red.

'Did you get that package to your mother?'

'I did.'

'What did she say?'

'She didn't open it.'

His father nodded. 'I owe you an explanation,' he said.

Samuel thought his father was about to explain the package. Instead, he took a deep breath, gazed out at the river and began: 'I was sent to a stalag on the front lines,' his father said. 'The worst of the worst. I was strong, in those days anyway.' He smiled thinly. 'If you were an officer and a POW you stayed in a hotel. Literally. You read the morning paper, you played cards. But if you were an enlisted man like me? Well. It was different. It was my job to retrieve the German dead,' his father continued, 'from the field of Mars. My partner was a Greek lad—Adonis Kazantzakis. Raised in England. Both of us nineteen, turning twenty. Still kids, really, gathered up as cannon fodder for that ridiculous war. Adonis?' his father remembered, shaking his head, 'he came by his name honestly. He was a specimen of a fellow. Heavily muscled. Really handsome.

'They would send us out beside a horse and cart and we'd stop at the bodies, and Adonis and I, we'd pick them up by the hands and feet and swing them up into that wagon like so many sacks of wheat. Fifty, sometimes eighty in an afternoon, two or three trips, and each time the bodies piled so high there was nowhere for us to sit. We'd slog back to camp through the mud. Unarmed, of course. Praying our own troops wouldn't shoot us.'

His father bent and picked up a smooth river stone. He worried it between his thumb and forefinger. 'There's a certain shame that comes with being a prisoner of war,' he went on. 'No one ever spoke of it, but each of us wore it like a badge. Like a tattoo.' He looked at his son. 'You're not fighting, you see. You're not … contributing. It's a dishonour. And so the only honourable thing to do is try and escape.'

He turned back to the river. He worried the stone. 'There were two men in charge of us. Neither one fit for active service but conscripted, nonetheless. Both of them fools, in their own way. The first an old soldier and a terrible drunk. Riddled with gout, missing an arm. He'd already shot and killed three men before us who'd tried to escape. His name was Bernhard, and we hated him. He took pleasure in our pain. If we stumbled in the mud, or collapsed with exhaustion he would kick us back onto our feet.'

His father gripped the stone in one fist now. He leaned forward and dropped his elbows to his knees. He looked down at the ground.

'The driver of that wagon, on the other hand, was a fool of an entirely different order. He was a natural, a *dumbkopf*, and no more … innocent a human being had I ever met before, or since. His name was Hans. He stood about four and half feet tall, and about as wide. Like Humpty Dumpty. Had this tight, curly blond hair that every morning he'd try to plaster flat against his skull. By the end of the day, it'd be standing straight up.'

Robert smiled. 'For the first few days he would only peek at us from between his fingers. Then after a while he just smiled at us, openly, no matter what we were doing. This great, giant grin,' his father said, shaking his head. 'He drove that cart with a songbird in a cage on the seat beside him and whenever that songbird sang he would break into song himself. Always the same. The libretto from Beethoven's 9th symphony—the Ode to Joy. Can you believe it?'

His father sat up and placed his hands on his knees, the rock still buried in his fist. He was trying to compose himself, force himself to go on. He began to rock gently back and forth. 'Adonis and I would be covered in the blood of dead Germans,' he continued, 'sometimes throwing only *pieces* of men onto the cart, and Hans would be up there on the bench seat just singing his heart out in this high-pitched soprano: '*Freude, schöner Götterfunken, Tochter aus Elysium, wir betreten feuertrunken, Himmlische, dein heiligtum!*' his father sang. He let out a short laugh.

'The fool was oblivious to what he was doing, of course. Immune to the death he saw everywhere. Because every day, without fail, whenever he saw us, he would climb down out of the wagon like he'd not seen us in months and embrace us, one at a time, like brothers. We came to depend on that embrace, you know, upon *him*, like a talisman to get us through the day. He used to smuggle food for us under his overcoat. We truly loved him. If the horse wouldn't go he never whipped it. He'd climb down out of the seat and hug the horse around the neck and talk to him and this would go on sometimes for … twenty minutes, half an hour. Horses' hearts can break as well, I believe. Anyway, the horse always started moving in the end, the bird would start to sing: '*Deine Zauber binden wieder, was die Mode streng geteilt*', we'd join in, and when the dead were all collected, we'd lurch back over those rutted fields to the camp. It was crazy, Sam.' His father looked at him, but he couldn't hold his gaze for long. He bent forwards again, worrying the stone. 'It was like being stuck in some … evil German fairy tale. We depended on Hans—upon his innocence—for our sanity. And I realize now that we depended on that labour, too, in a way, because the conditions in the camp were worse. The mud we had to sleep on. The barbed wire. Mouldy bread and thin turnip soup. Adonis wasted away. The guards sought to humiliate us. Sodomize us.'

He looked sideways at his son. 'Am I telling you too much?'

'You've never told me anything.'

His father nodded.

'But you escaped.'

'Yes,' his father said eventually. 'We escaped. But at a terrible cost.' His father looked at the stone in his hand. He closed his fist around it one more time then threw the stone clean across the river. Samuel waited for him to continue. He watched his father catch his breath, watched him will himself into remembering. 'We were very close to Allied lines one day,' his father continued. 'Bernhard, the coward, hung back for fear of getting shot so it was just us, and Hans. Adonis and I had discussed at length our plans to escape and decided that when the moment was right, at just such a moment, we would make a run for it. We started walking, at first, away from the cart as if we'd seen more dead to collect, but Hans, from his perch atop the wagon could see the fields were clear. He started calling out to us. We had to walk back. Adonis embraced him, as a way of signalling our intent—even had my German been adequate, there was no guarantee he would have understood—but when Adonis let him go Hans looked hurt. Confused. I pulled Hans toward me and hugged him the same way, in farewell, but Hans wouldn't let me go. He held on. His expression became that of an indignant child. He started yelling out Bernhard's name.

Samuel's father clutched his head. He grimaced as if a bird of prey were tearing at his skull.

'I put my hand over his mouth,' he managed, 'to keep him quiet, but Hans wouldn't let up.' His father breathed very heavily now, trying to rein in his emotion. 'He started beating me about the head and neck, thrashing like a cornered animal and all I could think of to do was hug him closer, my hand over his mouth.' His father threw his head back and gasped. 'I smothered him,' his father said. He wept. 'I literally … hugged him to death.' He wiped his eyes with the back of his hand. 'I was crying while I did it, and when I laid Hans down on the ground, like a … like a sleeping child, I just stood there, knowing that nothing would ever be the same again. That I had committed a crime so heinous that I would pay for it. I would pay. I had murdered an innocent. It was biblical. And for what? So I could survive, get married? Become a teacher in Ashcroft and cheat on my wife?' His father shook his head with chagrin. 'You promise me, Samuel Hewitt, you promise me you won't ever go to war.'

'Okay, Dad.'

'Promise me.'

'I promise,' said Samuel.

Robert nodded and continued quietly. 'We ran. By now Bernhard had figured something was wrong. He hobbled our way brandishing his pistol. Shot Adonis through the head. I watched him just fall beside me, a dead weight. The movies never get that part right. I heard Bernhard's pistol fire again, and again, but I didn't feel anything. I made it.' His father shrugged. 'Like every other escapee I was interrogated, but I don't remember what I said. I don't even remember how I got home. Thinking about it now, that was the beginning of my great forgetting. I worked really hard to forget the things I'd seen, what I'd done. I forgot about Adonis. I forgot about Hans. Or I tried to. But I could still hear his voice singing the Ode to Joy.'

'Maybe his voice will stop now,' said Samuel.

'Maybe.'

'I don't dream that dream anymore. With the raven.'

His father nodded. 'We all become what we fear, in the end,' he said.

'Two farmers either side of a roadway plough their land as neighbours,' began Samuel, without quite knowing why, 'but secretly plan to steal each other's land. One day a funny-looking man walks down the road, a clown of sorts, wearing a hat painted black on one side, white on the other. The one farmer calls out, "Hey, did you see that fool with the back hat?" "You mean the white hat?" says the other farmer. "Black," says the one. "White," says the other, until the two come to blows. They kill each other in the road and the fool returns, laughing, stepping over their dead bodies as he goes.'

Samuel's father looked at him and smiled. Slowly, his smile turned into a grin. They both began to laugh, quietly at first, then with less and less restraint. After a while, they couldn't hold it in. Samuel's father cried and laughed at the same time, his face changing seamlessly from a grin to a grimace, like two sides of a mask. Samuel and his father laughed that way, beside the river, until the sun no longer lit the canyon walls.

In the morning, at first light, Samuel made his way down to the river with his envelope full of ashes. He surprised a pair of ravens pecking at a spent salmon carcass. The ravens bundled clumsily into the air at his approach, crying in protest. Samuel sat on a rock and took off his boots and socks. He took off his jeans and folded them and left them on the riverbank. Carrying the envelope, he waded out to stand among the salmon. The sockeye thrashed and divided either side of his knees, flaring electric red. He thrilled to the slick, icy feel of them muscling past his calves.

Standing there with the sun coppering his face, the wind lifting the collar of his shirt, it seemed to him that, despite the beauty he beheld, home was not a place of stones and trees, nor anywhere one was loved. It was a movable privilege, and one that belonged rightly to the soul. Only if the soul came to know itself could a man be at home, but he first had to die, then be reborn, in order to see it. The ashes in his hands were naught but that. Meaning was all of a piece with its maker. And so into the river did he commit the ashes of his childhood; the current swept them instantly away. When the envelope was empty, he dropped it and watched it bob and spin downstream.

Lastly, he removed the St. Jude from around his neck and held it out over the water. The wind set it spinning like a lure. He watched it spin one way and stop, then unwind and spin again the other way.

He smiled. Then after a while, he let it go.

END NOTES

The author acknowledges the assistance of the Ontario Arts Council in the preparation of this manuscript. He would also like to thank three early readers whose patience and encouragement were vital: Marilyn Bowering, Catherine Bush and Erica Lepp. Thank you to my editor at the Porcupine's Quill, Stephanie Small, for not pulling any punches, and finally, a big thank-you to my wife, Stephanie Tooke, who endured the many revisions this book required.

Nick Tooke was born in the UK, immigrated to Vancouver Island in 1982, and has since lived in Vancouver, Montreal, Tucson, Edmonton, Toronto and Niagara-on-the-Lake—in that order. He now lives in Cayuga, Ontario, with his wife and daughter. *The Ballad of Samuel Hewitt* is his first novel.